Borrowed

Tides

Tor Books by Paul Levinson

The Silk Code
Borrowed Tides

Borrowed

Tides

All best wishes?
Paul J...

Paul Levinson

 TOR® A Tom Doherty Associates Book / New York

This is a work of fiction. All the characters and events portrayed in this novel are either fictitious or are used fictitiously.

BORROWED TIDES

This book is printed on acid-free paper.

Edited by David G. Hartwell

Design by Heidi Eriksen

A Tor Book
Published by Tom Doherty Associates, LLC
175 Fifth Avenue
New York, NY 10010

www.tor.com

Tor® is a registered trademark of Tom Doherty Associates, LLC.

Library of Congress Cataloging-in-Publication Data

Levinson, Paul.
    Borrowed tides / Paul Levinson.—1st ed.
        p. cm.
    "A Tom Doherty Associates book."
    ISBN 0-312-84869-2
    1. Interplanetary voyages—Fiction. I. Title.

PS3562.E92165 B67 2001
813'.54—dc21   00-048809

First Edition: March 2001

Printed in the United States of America

0 9 8 7 6 5 4 3 2 1

To Tina, Simon, and Molly

Acknowledgments

I first and foremost thank David G. Hartwell and his associate Jim Minz for their excellent editing of this book, and my agent, Christopher Lotts, of the Ralph Vicinanza Agency. I also thank Rick Nestler—whom I've never met—but who wrote a captivating folk song called "River That Flows Both Ways." The title was metaphoric inspiration for the start of this novel (the song is about the Hudson River), and indeed was too good to pass up as a title for the first section. I should also thank Betty Radens and the Fieldston Outdoors day camp, where my children, Simon and Molly, spent many wonderful summers, and at whose singalongs they and then I first heard Rick's song. And speaking of family, I thank my wife, Tina, and Simon and Molly, who make so many of the good things in my life not only possible but better. They are the inspiration for good things you may find in this novel about life in the stars. . . .

Contents

Part 1

The River That Flows Both Ways

One

The white birches and slender oaks were the corner's last stand. They fell in the spring of 1964 to bulldozers and brusque men—a construction crew clearing the last of the lot on Bronx Park East for the highrise that Aaron Schoenfeld would soon be inhabiting.

Aaron surveyed the rubble with mixed emotions. His apartment would have a terrace that jutted way out over the park—"a view straight to the Hudson," his father had been telling everyone. There would be two bathrooms—no more waiting for his sister to stop staring at her face in the mirror. He liked all that. But he didn't like what happened to the trees.

"The people who used to live here said there were moon spirits in those pale trees," a quiet voice said to Aaron. He turned to see a kid with burnt-brown eyes.

"People?" Aaron didn't usually have conversations with kids this young. The kid looked to be about ten or eleven, three or so years younger than Aaron. The kid sounded much older.

"Yeah, Indians," the kid said. "Years of Indian history are being wiped out here."

"How do you know there were Indians right here? I don't see any teepees."

Aaron was instantly sorry he'd said that. He could see the kid struggling with whether to walk away from him or share his secrets. And something about the kid's intensity made Aaron want to hear more.

The kid reached into his shirt pocket and pulled out a few pieces of chipped, flinty stone. "Arrowheads," he said, "made by the people whose main lands were in Pelham Bay. I found them right here."

"How'd you know to look here?" Aaron asked. "I mean, even before this construction, it was just a—"

"I could see the signs," the kid said. "I live right down the block." He pointed to a small semidetached house, with a big off-white hibiscus in front that looked like it had been watered by every mutt in the neighborhood. "This place was my backyard. I spend a lot of time here."

"Did you tell anyone about the arrowheads?"

"Who'm I gonna tell?" The kid gestured to the construction crew, just about packed up and ready to leave for the day. "I tried to talk to the foreman once, but he laughed in my face. Why should anyone pay any attention to what I say?"

"Well, I am," Aaron said, surprising himself and extending his hand. "I'm Aaron Schoenfeld."

The kid shook it with a tight grip. "Jack Lumet." He smiled for the first time. Aaron could tell this was a rarity.

"The only reason you're even listening to me is that you're not much older than I am," Jack said.

"You're a smart kid," Aaron said.

"It's not that I'm against tall buildings or stuff like that," Jack said. "I just wish they could build these things where they don't hurt what's already here."

Aaron thought about the birches. He thought about a spring afternoon years earlier, when he was four or five, and saw a crew building part of the Bronx River Parkway. He'd cried when he saw them blast away a field of buttercups.

"Don't worry—they'll plant new ones," his father had said.

But new ones—deliberately planted ones—weren't the same. They lacked something of wildflowers.

Aaron understood that day what Jack Lumet was saying.

But he also knew that he was very much looking forward to seeing the Hudson from his terrace, looking forward to the clearer view of the stars that he imagined his new outpost would provide. And if his high-rise weren't built here, where else? Everywhere you looked, there was something that people wanted to keep, didn't want to build over.

In the spring of 1964, wildflowers were still in long supply in the Bronx.

Aaron ran into Jack maybe once or twice a year after that—usually on that corner of Bronx Park Towers where he lived. He never knew what to say on those occasions. Usually hi, how're you doing, OK, you? all right, I guess, and the wind's howling down the block and they're shivering and they'd better both be on their ways. But Aaron always knew that Jack had some sort of drama percolating in his head, some take on the universe that Aaron would have wanted to hear if only he could have figured out some common ground, some pretext for the two of them to talk. But he also knew he had too many other important things to do, too many life-and-death crises—impress that girl, finish this report, impress that girl, deal with his parents, impress that girl, respond to that insult, impress that girl—erupting on an almost daily basis as he was growing up in those years.

Aaron went on to City College. He started as a bio major, until the smell of fetal pigs at eight in the morning gagged him out of biology. Then on to psychology, and what made people, not pigs, tick. But Freud didn't satisfy, so Aaron drifted into sociology, where he hoped he could write some papers on the Beatles. He finally wound up with a Ph.D. in philosophy of science and an uncanny capacity to dazzle the crowd with quotes from Kant, Nietzsche, and Russell. An easy path to a safe professorship. But Aaron thought that maybe he'd picked up some important insights along the way.

Jack had turned up at City College too, though his emergence as a scholar followed no such meandering course. To everyone he met, Jack talked the same thing: Indians. He studied Indians in the anthropology department. He gave lectures on Indians to New York City schoolkids. He showed up naked at a departmental party one night, dressed like the people who originally lived there, he'd said. Aaron heard about this from a girl he'd talked into having dinner with him. He burst out laughing and said good for Jack; the girl said they both were perverts; that was the last he saw of her.

Jack came out with a small book a few years later—*Native American Legends in New York City*. Aaron saw a one-paragraph review of it in *The New York Times*. He'd intended to buy it. But he never saw it in the bookstores.

And that was the last Aaron heard of Jack for a long time. He was nowhere to be seen in the new millennium. Neither on-line nor at any of the scholarly conferences Aaron regularly attended.

Jack was certainly close to the last person on Earth Aaron ever expected to see at any of the desperate meetings he'd been chairing in the space station off Mars.

Aaron was an unlikely director for a less likely project. His article "Philosopher Speaks on Behalf of Space Exploration" had made a big impact in *Spired*—more than two million e-mails raged in reply and debate within twenty-four hours of its publication. The president of the United States had seen it. The president had a taste for philosophy. The president personally phoned Aaron and asked if he'd like to serve on a task force in preparation for a possible mission to Alpha Centauri.

Aaron didn't have to be asked twice.

But five years later, Aaron and his people were worried. The Connelly administration was on the verge of shelving the project. Two prior chairs of the task force had already quit. Now Aaron was in the hot seat.

"Joe's absolutely firm on this," Naomi Senzer, the president's liaison, told the assembled team. "He says he's stuck out his head far enough already."

Alexei Primakov grunted. "He sure ain't JFK."

"He's better," Aaron replied, though he shared every bit of the Russian's frustration. "JFK had the Soviets—your grandparents—to compete against. JFC has a peachy, cooperative world, on the surface. Everyone claims to be happy with it. Hard to wring support out of Congress in that kind of environment." The demons of the twenty-first century, Aaron knew, were inner, panhuman, far more difficult to oppose with science and funding than had been Communism.

"Indeed," Naomi said. "So if we do this at all, we'll have to make do with just what we have."

"Which gives us a one-way trip to Alpha," David Percival, Aaron's chief assistant, said. "Which means we do it either nonpersonned, or as a ticket to oblivion."

Aaron shuffled through his papers and his options that night. Neither contained anything new.

Most people knew that Alpha Centauri was the closest star system to Earth's own. Fewer knew that its distance from Sol was about 4.3 light-years. Even fewer knew that it was actually a triple star—and that Alpha Centauri A was a G2 V star, just like the sun.

Next to no one knew of the coincidence that had come about in 2016.

Alpha Centauri C—the faint M5 star aptly named Proxima because it for some time had been the closest of the three to Earth—suddenly seemed to switch positions with Centauri A and B, bringing the Sol-type star closer to Earth than before. And lo and behold, when the Hubble II stared at this star in its new position, it saw what could have been an Earthlike planet or two circling around it. This was a surprise—Tau Ceti had previously been deemed the closest star likely to have worlds, and the evidence for its planets was still very inconclusive. But seeing via the Hubble was believing, even if what was seen was little more than a trace on a screen, a smudge of suggestion.

Meanwhile, almost to the day that the Hubble began looking at Alpha Centauri A in a new light, Lawrence Livermore/Microsoft Labs announced to the president's secret committee that they had developed a hybrid chemical/fusion drive that could move a spaceship faster than any heretofore known, at a cumulative velocity of .48 speed of light in deep space.

The upshot: Alpha Centauri A, a star with as good a chance as any at cooking up Earth-type life, was suddenly just a little more than eight years' travel away from humanity. A pittance in time, for species and solar systems.

The catch: The LL/M drive required enormous amounts of fuel to achieve its initial speed, make the trip to Centauri with any necessary adjustments along the way, and decelerate once there. It presumably would need at least an equal amount of fuel to make the trip back home. Not only was that amount of fuel beyond any budget that Congress or even a global consortium was likely to approve, it was also quite beyond the capacity of any conceivable holding tanks to hold—especially traveling at half-light speed.

The result: By the year 2021, it was becoming clear to even the most starry-eyed enthusiasts that humankind had perhaps been dealt a maddeningly frustrating hand in the matter of Alpha Centauri. Humanity apparently now had the capacity to travel to this nearly unblinking star.

Period.

One way.

Aaron finally put down his papers and rubbed his eyes and thought what he always did before drifting off to sleep these days: He had no intention of letting this get in his way.

"Tea brewed at .78g is a true delight," Aaron said, and passed a cup to Naomi the next morning. Devotees of the beverage on Mars Vestibule space station had been quick to discover this. "Water under pressure permeates the tea leaves more thoroughly at our lower gravity," Aaron added.

"Ah, yes, pressure as friend, pressure as foe," Naomi said. "A double-edged sword." She held up the glass cup of tea to the sunlight that poured through the real-view window in Aaron's office, as if she were measuring the refraction of its rays. "What's the point of pressuring the president when we already know that even if we had the money, we couldn't do the trip?" she asked, her tone suddenly changing from philosophic to prosecutorial. She placed the tea on the table without drinking, and looked straight at Aaron.

"It gives our group something to focus on," he answered. "And we need the time to come up with a solution to the fuel problem."

"You have any ideas?"

"Plenty," Aaron said. "But what we need are solutions. Here." He pushed a printout of a paper across the table to her. "What do you think of this?"

Naomi leafed through the paper, eyebrows arched. "This guy's a specialist on Native Americans," she said. "Why the hell should we pay any attention to his theory about the stars?"

"Because his theory addresses the nub of our problem," Aaron replied.

"So the Iroquois had a notion that the currents between our sun and the star cluster we call Alpha Centauri—whatever they may have meant by 'currents'—were the same as the currents in the Hudson River, the river they said flowed both ways. You really want me to tell this to the president?"

"A search of more than two hundred years of logged publications on Combinets came up with nothing better," Aaron said. "In fact, it came up with nothing that really could be useful to our problem at all, other than the possibilities presented in this paper."

"It's likely nonsense," Naomi said. "What good is that?"

"What if it's not?"

Naomi shrugged. "The paper's more than fifteen years old. Is this guy still around? Can we talk to him?"

Aaron smiled. "He's due here in about an hour."

Mars Vestibule shimmered like a spider's web in a moonlit field. A hundred little compartments hummed with information and life—the fragile cutting edge of enduring human penetration of the cosmos, a result of the brief powerful fluorescence of space urge in the twenty-first century. Its inhabitants yearned with an inspiration surpassing that of any insect population to expand this human web ever farther. But the task was enormous. Webs don't fly. Even when humanly spun in synchronous orbit around Mars.

Jack Lumet walked with a scowl on his face into one of the glittering rooms. He moved as if he were tiptoeing on oil-slicked ice back in the Bronx—a common reaction of those who were new to low g.

"You look good, Jack." Aaron stood up and shook his hand. "In fact, you look great for, what are you now, sixty-eight?" Jack also looked as intense as ever, only now the face was topped with singed gray rather than ink black, more than six decades in the smoldering.

Jack nodded. "A long way from Bronx Park East to Mars Vest, isn't it?"

"What were the odds that the two of us would have made it," Aaron said and motioned Jack to a seat. "This is Naomi Senzer"—the two exchanged hellos—"and you already know why we're here. Basically, we'd like you to tell us about your Hudson River theory."

"It's not a theory as far as the Hudson River is concerned," Jack said. "It's a fact that the Atlantic Ocean current is so strong that it flows well past Tarrytown. And of course the Hudson River, like all rivers, flows back to the ocean. So it's a river that flows both ways. And the people who originally lived along its shores noticed this."

"Right," Naomi said. "But what can you tell us about the Iroquois theories of star currents? I assume those were indeed theories, not facts."

Jack ignored the sarcasm. He had spent a lifetime preaching the wisdom of Indians to skeptical audiences. Likely it was the only time he was really happy, Aaron thought.

"You know, Native Americans had notions of the stars that were not all that different from the star stories of other peoples," Jack said. "The Algonquins, who lived near the river with the Iroquois, saw a bear chased by hunters in the same place the Greeks saw the Great Bear and we see the Big Dipper. And the Greek explanation of the Centaur—which contains your Alpha Centauri star—has lots of resemblances both to subcontinent Indian myths and to the stories of the Iroquois. Though, as I pointed out in my paper, the Iroquois stories go a bit further."

"When in their history did the Iroquois come up with their cosmology about Alpha Centauri?" Naomi asked.

"Legend is pretty specific about that—an oddity, since Native American mythology was obviously oral, and so not easily traceable. But according to my research, an Iroquois sachem by the name of Wise Oak first said that the currents flow both ways not only in the Big River—the Hudson—but in the Big River to the star cluster that we call Alpha Centauri. That would be about fifteen hundred A.D."

"And how exactly did Wise Oak come to know this?" Naomi pressed.

Jack looked at her—his frown replaced now by a full smile, an event Aaron still had the feeling was as infrequent in appearance as Halley's comet. "He claimed to have traveled there," Jack replied.

"Ah. I see. Pity you didn't mention that in your ridiculous paper, Dr. Lumet. Would have saved all of us a bit of time." Naomi tossed her copy of the paper in Jack's direction and stalked out of the room. It made a graceful, air-glider arc in the low g, and landed on Jack's lap with a pirouette.

"So here's my problem," Aaron said to Naomi after catching up with her—after he had directed Jack to some constellations visible from the far side of the station. "I've known this man since we were kids. He's a fanatic—pretty much humorless about everything except his beloved Indians, but that he would lie in any way about them is inconceivable, precisely because of his obsession."

"Demented people often think they're telling the truth when they lie," she said. "That's part of their illness."

"True," Aaron said. "But given our situation, doesn't it make sense to see what's right with his game rather than what's wrong with it?"

"Weren't you the one who wrote that Wittgenstein was one of the worst philosophers of the twentieth century? Now you're paraphrasing him?"

"Point well taken." Aaron bowed. That politicians actually read his philosophy still floored him.

Naomi relented a little. "OK, putting your friend's overactive imagination in the best possible light: Suppose his sachem, Wise Oak, had a vision about traveling to Alpha Centauri and back. Visions are the source of most Indian knowledge, right?"

"Presumably," Aaron said.

"OK. So where do we go from that?" she asked.

"Well, first, we recognize its possible relevance to our difficulties. After all, Wise Oak had this vision—if that's what it was—about the very star we want to travel to."

"Not as significant as you're saying," Naomi said. "After all, the Centauri cluster is third brightest in Earth's skies—not surprising that the Iroquois would spin legends about it."

"True again about its brightness," Aaron said. "But it's not visible in northeastern skies—the regular Iroquois haunts. So the fact that their wise man had a vision about it may be significant after all."

"Why? Maybe the Iroquois just heard about it from some Seminoles in Florida. Maybe they were talking about another star entirely. That's my point—this whole Indian thing is just mystical nonsense."

"Jack's not some irrational mystic. His paper offers a legitimate scientific principle to back this up."

"The boomerang effect?" Naomi scoffed. "Come on. That worked for *Apollo 13* around the moon. It worked around Venus. I'd be willing to risk, maybe, a trip to Saturn with one-way fuel, on the hope that the ship would swing around and get a free ride back to Earth. But all the way to Alpha Centauri? Traveling at .48 speed of light? That's crazy."

"All right," Aaron said. "Let's play it your way—it's crazy. What then? We just forget about this project? And you tell the president, what—he pissed away billions of the taxpayers' hard-earned money on this? You're comfortable with that?"

She shifted in her seat. "I gave up being comfortable the day I got involved in this goddamned project." She glared at Aaron. "Too much time in low g must've deformed my brain. Otherwise I would have put a stop to this a long time ago."

Aaron stared back at her. "I'm saying there's no need to do that. Look, all we need here is a decent cover story and everyone's ass is saved. The earliest our LL/M ship can return from Alpha Centauri, if we can make the round-trip with one-way fuel, is sixteen years. By that time JFC will be long out of office, and God knows, with your smarts, you'll likely be president yourself. And if for some reason the ship doesn't return—if Jack's or whoever's theory we use turns out to be wrong—well, you'll be too well situated then to be really hurt by that. The public's memory spans maybe a year or two at most in these kinds of things. Certainly not a decade."

Naomi exhaled slowly. "Tell me more about this boomerang theory. I'm not going to go to the president with just some goddamn Indian fantasy in my hand."

"Well, as Jack explains in his paper," Aaron replied, "the configuration of the projectile and the environment allows the initiating power to in effect contain within it the power for the return trip—no additional fuel is needed. This is obviously well known in smaller arenas. It brought *Apollo 13* back from the moon, like you said. The first *Galileo* probes to Jupiter also spun around the sun to get there—a variant of the boomerang. And it worked around Venus in 2009. But, yes, it's totally untested at the interstellar distances and speeds we're talking about here—though Freeman Dyson and others were theorizing about it as long ago as the early 1960s. Unfortunately, the money it would cost to test it with an uncrewed ship big enough to hold people is the same money it would cost to send a ship with people there—the big cost is the fuel, which would be the same. So there's no payoff in testing."

"Other than no one gets killed in a nonpersonned test," Naomi said. "No cheaper, but at least we get to sleep at night."

"Nonpersonned won't do it," Aaron said. "You yourself said robots are like masturbation—remember your SmithSONYan speech?—when it comes to space exploration. They can miss the really important things. They don't cry when they see the Earth trembling in the void. And reports from automated systems don't have much effect on the public anyway—they'd just as soon see a movie altogether. They want real people bringing home eyewitness accounts for the bucks they're paying." And there were reasons more profound for humans to be on this first outing to another star and its possible planets—reasons of the soul, philosophic and scientific, reasons having to do with humanity's place and purpose in the universe—but Aaron knew that these were of less concern to the president's special assistant.

"So your plan is that we chance sending a shipful of people out to the star on a suicide trip, that it?" she asked derisively. "And I'm supposed to let that happen because it'll help my career any way it pans out?"

"I wouldn't put it quite so starkly," Aaron said. "My guess is we'd have no difficulty fielding the volunteers we'd need for such a mission. And there's a big difference between risk and suicide."

"Yeah? Maybe, if the risk is informed," Naomi said. "We'd field volunteers on the basis of what? The Iroquois' Hudson River in deep space? Or the Aborigine-cum-*Apollo* boomerang?"

"Whatever does the job," Aaron said. "At the distances and speeds we're dealing with, I can't say for sure that one is better than the other."

"My point exactly," Naomi said.

Aaron said nothing.

Naomi shook her head in disgust. "Well, at least the boomerang has some scientific plausibility."

"Yes."

"How will the starship have any time to even see anything near Alpha Centauri, whipping around it at half speed of light?"

"That's the beauty of the boomerang," Aaron replied. "According to Ulam and Dyson and others who worked out hypothetical equations for gravity-assisted propulsion—that's what they called the boomerang back then—the star imparts enormous velocity to the starship as it makes the turn. So the ship decelerates on approach, has time to look around, and then whips back out to Sol at half speed of light with no additional fuel."

"The trajectory would have to be just right," Naomi considered. "Incredible precision at incredible speeds and distance."

"True," Aaron allowed.

"Too many incredibles for my liking."

"As you said, we don't have the luxury now of looking for a solution we like or feel comfortable with," Aaron replied. "We're down to going with anything that has a chance of working."

"You know, I think the only reason you even trotted out that Indian thing was to make the boomerang look possible in comparison," Naomi said.

Aaron smiled. "Jack's paper made the connection."

"You're one damned piece of work for a professor," Naomi said. She stood up. "You'll have my decision next month. But I'll tell you this: The most I'll agree to—the *most*—is a ship filled with shit-can robots. I may be a political cutthroat. But I'm no murderer."

The launch was ready two years later. The LL/M drive had performed just as expected in two round-trip probes, one without people, the other with, to the Oort Cloud beyond Pluto—a startling, sparkling place that was farther than any human had ever been before by a long shot. The data from those two trips alone would change some basic conceptions about Earth's place in the solar system.

Unfortunately, the Oort didn't have enough of its own concentrated pull to test the boomerang. But an LL/M jaunt to Neptune had returned via boomerang, providing a confirmation that the whip-around worked at least on very short half-speed-of-light voyages.

Aaron had prevailed upon Naomi to build the starship—recently christened the *Light Through*—as if it would be carrying a crew of nine humans. A central purpose of the expedition, after all, was to determine not only if a ship with the LL/M drive could travel to and from Alpha Centauri, but if it could make the trip with people. The only real difference in design for the people-ship was a self-contained biosphere system that could generate oxygen and food and medication, and process waste back into production. Such biospheres had already been in extensive use in various outposts from Mars to Jupiter for nearly a decade, and posed no great expense.

But the crew was all robotic.

With one last-minute exception.

"He's going to his death if he's wrong," Naomi said as she looked over the final preparations with Aaron. "And we have no real proof that he's right."

"Columbus had no real proof either—just theories," Aaron replied. "Proof isn't all it's cracked up to be."

Naomi rolled her eyes in exasperation. "The only reason I'm allowing Jack to go is he has no close family to contest his signing of the forms," she said. "The last thing I and whatever administration is in office eight or even sixteen years from now need is a wrongful-risk suit."

That, and you don't mind the possibility of sacrificing Jack to test out the biosystem that you weren't too thrilled about putting in the ship just for robots, even despite its minimal cost, Aaron thought.

"I could think of a worse place to have a yam sandwich." Jack smacked his lips and looked at the *Light Through,* suspended in docking just off Mars Vestibule outside the real-view window.

"You mean looking at the ship like this, or inside that ship?" Aaron asked.

"I guess both," Jack said, almost with a smile.

The prospect of flying in a starship to Alpha Centauri was making Jack a happier man—even if that prospect was uncertain in its ultimate outcome, to say the least. But Aaron understood.

The ship itself looked like an opal or a pearl, a basic form that had been pleasing to humanity for at least as far back as people had been making records of what pleased them. Plato had imagined his world of ideal forms, from which all imperfect human concepts of beauty emerged, to be inhabited with the likes of this. His pupil Aristotle, more enamored of the physical here and now, had claimed such spherical perfection for the planets themselves.

The *Light Through* had no front or back—no bow or stern. The physics of the LL/M drive required thrust from a myriad of sides in carefully computed multiple sequence to achieve speed at half-C. Form followed function, and the result was a sight to behold.

That was the outside.

The inside? Well, who gave a damn what robots thought of it.

That's why, in addition to many other reasons, Aaron was glad that Jack would be aboard. For the inside was beautiful too. And Jack, more than any other person Aaron had known, was a keen appreciator of such beauty.

"So, have you made your decision yet?" Jack asked.

"Oh, I guess I made it a long time ago," Aaron replied.

Now Jack did smile.

"We're going to the end of the line." Aaron extended his hand. "Just like we used to say about that spur of the old New York Central that ran up to Chatham."

Jack took Aaron's hand, shook it. "The end of the line," he said. "Like that Bob Dylan song."

"Travelling Wilburys," Aaron said.

"Were they a real group?" Jack asked.

"About as real as the two of us as astronauts."

"No!" Naomi cried out. "Even *I* won't allow *that*! We've been friends for too long." She put her hand on Aaron's arm.

"I appreciate the sentiment," Aaron said, "believe me, I do. But my wife has been gone five years now, our kids are all well established—they haven't given me any grandchildren; misguided population control!—and I've already served my purpose here. No one's going to let me lead another space task force until the world sees that this one pays off."

"OK, I'll have to be blunt with you then, Aaron. You're too old to go on this trip. Jack is too, but he's not my friend. Look at you: You were seventy-three last month. The round-trip—if it works at all—will be at least sixteen years for you. Latest theories agree that no significant relativity effects should set in at half speed of light, as you know. So you'll be aging normally on the trip—seventy-three years plus sixteen. Doesn't add up at your age."

"No? Your math is a bit out of date. We're in the age of miracles and wonders, remember? Average life span was up to ninety-seven for those in their seventies, last time I checked, assuming you don't have IMMies. Besides, I tested positive for the Russell-Shaw factor; so did Jack."

Naomi shook her head. "Russell-Shaw hasn't been completely proven yet. There's no definitive evidence that—"

"We back to absolute proof again? Let's shoot for something more reasonable. How about, Bertrand Russell and George Bernard Shaw both lived into their late nineties, fully functional mentally, in a world with none of the gene therapy that Jack and I have been undergoing for the past two years?" Aaron involuntarily shivered with the recollection—life-extending gene therapy wasn't the most pleasant experience in the world, or off it. "It's a fact," he said more softly, "that there's a genetic factor correlated with longevity and mental agility to age one hundred, and that people who have this factor also seem to pursue the philosophic life in one way or another. Thomas Jefferson and John Adams also likely had it, though in their day the best they could do without medication was make it to their eighties, early nineties."

Naomi's eyes narrowed. "So you've been planning this the whole time?"

"Right. All my life, in a way."

"But that's no reason to squander what's left of it on this," Naomi said.

"Feelings of uselessness can be far more deadly than most diseases," Aaron replied. "And that *is* a medically documented fact."

"So what do you expect me to do?" Naomi asked. "You and I know just what feet of clay this leap to the stars has. That's why I— the president—okayed the trip for robots, not people. I made the exception for Jack—"

"Right, because he's no big deal, just some nut with a fixation on Indians. But I'm different, right? I suppose I should be flattered."

She smiled. "You *are* different, Aaron. You want me just to say good-bye to you next month—say, have a good trip, see you in sixteen years, when I think there's a fair chance I'll never see you again?"

But Aaron could see she was not completely immune to the appeal of such a possibility; otherwise, the discussion would have been over already. Her first instinct had been to say no to his going. She said she was motivated by friendship, but she needed to protect her own reputation, her own conscience, from a charge that she had sent not one but two old men to die of old age or worse on this mission. But if Aaron was right about this supremely political woman, she was now entertaining the thought that if the mission as a whole didn't make it, never returned, then Aaron lost somewhere in space would leave one less person behind who could bear witness to her complicity in the dead-end star run. Of course, other members of his task force who wouldn't be on the ship had a pretty good idea of what was going on—he'd included Percival in particular on every facet of his thinking—but Aaron knew that his own absence would be a great boon to Naomi in dealing with any recriminations that might follow the *Light Through*'s failure to return, certainly in responding to any congressional witch-hunt that might ensue. Despite what he'd said about the public's highly perishable attention span, congressional committees had a way of raking up old coals and blowing them into nasty new flames. Aaron as a witness would likely provide more fuel, however he testified.

"Let's say you take ill on the ship," Naomi said. "Neither you or Jack is an M.D."

"That's what medisim is for, isn't it? Hell, AI-MD modules are hardwired into the computer systems of every simple planet-going vessel—the *Light Through* has them packed into the system with quadruple redundancy. They should have us covered for any illnesses known to our species. And for those that aren't . . ." Aaron shrugged. "Well, I doubt that a flesh-and-blood human doctor would be of much help to us then anyway."

Naomi made a sarcastic sound. "You don't believe that, Aaron—you're a master of arguing whatever side of an issue suits your needs, aren't you? We both know humans are far and away the best hedge—the only hedge—against the truly unknown." She looked away for a few long seconds, then sighed. "I'll let you know next week. But if I do agree that you can go, you'll need not only a human doctor on board, but some kind of a proper, minimal crew." She shook her head in self-reproach. "What a mess."

Aaron nodded.

Politicians acting in their own best interests were a feature of the universe far better proven than boomerangs.

———

But the next week passed. And so did eleven others. And there still was no decision from Naomi.

Aaron began to suspect the worst: The entire mission might be canceled. . . .

He got the call from Naomi three weeks later. "I'll see you in your office on Mars Vest tomorrow," she said.

She showed up with a lilliputer in her hand. "Listen to this," she said.

Aaron listened. "It's all hash and ping to me," he said. "Same background radiation we always get from Alpha Centauri."

Naomi nodded. "I'm with you. But the SETI people think it's something different."

"A message?"

"No," Naomi replied. "Just something different from the usual hash." Her face looked pained. "I'm still not sure. It's likely just some random change. But it happened at the right time—it tipped the scales with the president. He'd like flesh and blood to check this out, if we can field a small crew."

Aaron didn't even try to suppress his smile.

The crowd that saw them off in the corridor was small. Even a big crowd would have been minuscule compared to the billions viewing the event on their screens.

Percival and Primakov were on hand, keeping their distance from Naomi, glaring their quiet, unforgiving fury at her for not being included on the mission. You're needed back here, Naomi had insisted. Aaron hugged each of the bon voyage party in turn, Naomi last.

Jack hugged no one. He just looked off into the distance, eyes focused nowhere, everywhere, as if he were viewing some story that no one else could see.

"You look like you've just seen a ghost, Jack." Aaron clapped him on the back as they started walking down the corridor, toward the portal of the starship. "So how does it feel to be among the first humans to travel to another star?"

Jack disengaged his contemplation of the infinite to take in the immediate. "Who says we're the first?"

———

The rest of the crew—seven others—were already on the ship, which was soon under way.

Sarah Chichester was thirty-seven. She had high cheekbones and brilliant white hair. She was also brilliant in all matters virtual, telematic, and computional. In fact, Aaron had known she was exceptional since he'd first spotted her at a philosophy and cyberspace conference nearly fifteen years earlier. And she'd just proven it again.

"It was actually pretty easy," Sarah said. "I call it my enhancement algorithm." She looked out the real-view window at the Oort Cloud, floating straight ahead. "I think of my algorithm as a computer enzyme, because it helps the analysis program digest the data, and points the conclusion in a certain direction."

"So there was something unusual in the readings from Alpha Centauri to begin with, and your . . . virtual enzyme just made it more apparent." Aaron hadn't allowed himself the luxury of discussing this at any length with Sarah prior to now, when the *Light Through* was beyond recall range for anything except a major technological failure or a life-threatening condition for the crew. He had needed something to get Naomi off the dime, so he'd sent out desperate feelers to several well-placed contacts, and he'd hit pay dirt with Sarah and the SETI people.

"Oh, yes," Sarah replied. "We get anomalies in readings from lots of stars, especially with the new listening equipment in the past decade. But there was something a little different about Alpha Centauri this time—that whole area's been in flux since ACA–ACB and Proxima made the shift. But the latest reading was different, and my enzyme made the most of it."

"You told Naomi that it felt like an invitation," Aaron said appreciatively.

"Well, it could be." Sarah's turquoise eyes crinkled and twinkled. "Invitations don't have to always come in fancy letters and envelopes."

Aaron looked at those eyes, then at the Oort.

He hoped the other six volunteers on the ship were in Sarah's league.

They would have their human M.D. after all, as well as a botanist to cultivate their gardens for food, and folks in the other essential positions for a starship carrying nine to Alpha Centauri—a starship composed of undoubtedly its most important elements. Human beings.

All had been briefed on the dangers nearly a year earlier, and had elected, for whatever reasons, to take the risk.

Their dossiers were impressive. They seemed to have all the requisite talent, and more.

Aaron sighed, and contemplated just how far absurd chance and unyielding passion had gotten them—and about the enormous role such factors played in great human ventures.

The only thing that really concerned Aaron about his new colleagues was that, on the personal level, he barely knew most of them. How could he? Training, however intensive, was not the real thing. Coming to work, even seven days a week, could not be the same as living together for sixteen years.

And he wondered, as the Oort and its desolate beauty filled the screen with a light so different from any he had ever known, how well he knew himself out here.

It didn't matter, as long as he was going.

Two

Sarah took ill a little after a year into the voyage.

Kathy Lotari, their young M.D. in residence with a Biosphere V credential, had no idea what was causing it. "She hadn't been sick a day in her adult life back home—at least according to the records. And now she gets fevers and sweats every other month." Kathy shook her head. "At least it doesn't seem too serious. Maybe deep space just doesn't agree with her."

"I'm beginning to wonder how well it agrees with any of us," Aaron said.

Kathy's eyebrow arched. "Is anyone else feeling sick? How about you? Are you OK?"

"Oh, I'm fine," Aaron replied. "I didn't mean the universe doesn't agree with us physically, though maybe that's part of it. I meant...I don't know, some of the crew seem to be on edge lately. Sometimes a lot of the crew. It's hard to pin down—it comes and goes."

"It's natural," Kathy said.

"To feel uncomfortable out here? I guess so. But sometimes I get the feeling that deep space is allergic to us, or maybe we're allergic to it."

"It's the first time we've ever been out here," Kathy said. "It makes sense that we'd feel ill at ease—we have no bearings, no standards to judge what's normal, no backlog of experience to gauge what we do."

"No sure way to get back home," Aaron added.

Kathy nodded. "That too. It's all new."

Aaron considered. "You think Sarah's problem is psychological? She seems so in control of herself."

"No, I don't think so," Kathy replied. "I don't think her ailment is psychosomatic. I can't say what it is, though. Just that, somehow, life out here doesn't seem to be working as it should for her."

Aaron sighed. "Well, we'll need to keep an eye on her, then. And the rest of the crew, too."

Sarah seemed to stabilize in the months ahead, though she continued to suffer periodic bouts of a variety of ailments—coughing, sneezing, dizziness—all without apparent cause, none life-threatening. Kathy took careful notes and kept them in a file called "Deep Space Syndrome."

The rest of the crew got worse.

As the voyage progressed, they grew increasingly restive. Some began wondering aloud if it didn't make sense to turn back while there was still enough fuel for a voyage home.

It came to a head about three and a half years into the trip, as the *Light Through* hurtled toward its point of no return.

"It's not good, sir."

Roger McLaren likely would have been a marine in the previous century. As it was, he was a dedicated Whole Earth ecocop and a decorated DNA discoverer—of necessity a multitasker, like everyone else on the ship. He had logged only five years in space prior to the voyage, but Aaron had quickly come to like his intelligence and his style. He had become Aaron's unofficial aide-de-camp. Aaron relied on him.

The stress lines near Roger's eyes were deeper than usual. Just about every face on the trip other than Jack's had them now. Acceptance of death as an abstract is one thing; actually moving at half speed of light through a black void to your possible demise is quite another.

"It's the shift we picked up again last month between Proxima and Alpha," McLaren continued. "There's concern that it might be enough to throw off our boomerang equations."

"How bad is it?"

"The shift's the same as last time—slight, but we're in no position to judge the consequences of what that means in this case. Obviously the stars aren't as stable as we'd assumed back in our solar system."

"Maybe those stars were always shifting slightly, but we were unable to see it before Hubble II, or before we got this close to them," Aaron said. "And the crew?"

"Kathy says the people who want to turn back have a near-majority now," McLaren said. "Even if they don't, it's getting hard to keep them in line—we can't watch them twenty-four hours a day."

Aaron sighed. Like McLaren, he had learned to trust Kathy's judgment. Also like McLaren, Aaron enjoyed playing a little patient and doctor with her—in his fantasies. But if Aaron's excuse was that he was too old, McLaren's was that Kathy had said she was off-limits for the trip—she didn't want the complications of an intracabin romance. She'd said her Biosphere experience had been enough, whatever, exactly, that meant. Unconfirmed rumors on the *Light Through* said that maybe she had left the Biosphereans because of some quietly settled sexual-enticement suit against her. If that was the case, more power to her, Aaron thought. He was old-fashioned when it came to seduction: He liked it.

"Any pattern in those who want to turn back and those who want to continue?" Aaron asked. He ran his hand through a shock of tousled white hair.

"Yeah," McLaren replied. "Those who want to end this are the most experienced in space. They see the rest of us as naive dreamers."

"Which we are," Aaron said. "And in your case, it seems like your lack of experience was your best qualification for this mission."

"Thank you, sir."

"But of course, that doesn't help us much now with our specific problem," Aaron said. He had given up on telling Roger not to call him sir. Perhaps because a part of him liked it.

"Precisely, sir."

Aaron sipped his Darjeeling tea and made a mental note to slightly change the blend. His tolerance for tea blends in the ennui of deep space had decreased to about two weeks. And he'd never fully adjusted to any blend brewed in the full 1g of their ship. His aching bones and far less than fully toned muscles also dearly preferred the lower g of Mars Vest—but traveling at nearly half speed of light gave the artificial gravity more bang than expected. Engineering had all it could do to keep the g at just 1, and no higher. Unforeseen consequences—the devil of this expedition was surely in the unforeseen.

And that included the behavior of people.

"Can Jack be any help with this?" Aaron asked. "He does project a kind of confidence."

McLaren scowled. "He's part of the problem. Every time he opens his mouth, he advertises the Indian legend leering over the voyage. All of us, of course, already knew this, but we prefer to focus on the boomerang as our ticket home."

"Yet you and Kathy aren't fazed."

McLaren smiled. "As you said, sir, I'm naive."

"Right," Aaron said.

"And I spent nearly a year and a half with several Amazon tribes," McLaren said, "and I learned to respect the wisdom in their mythology. As far as I'm concerned, it's a plus when ancient legend and modern physics coincide. There's a DNA in folklore as strong as the DNA in the forests."

"So there is," Aaron said. "You really ought to take up philosophy sometime."

"Thank you, sir. I already have."

"All right, then." Aaron stood up and clapped him on the shoulder. "We'll touch base again this evening."

They shook hands and McLaren left.

Aaron fiddled with the phone for a while.

"Jack, you free for lunch?"

The Connected Cafe served as both a little restaurant and personal com center for the ship; "Food, for Thought and Palate," said the Old English–lettered balsa-wood sign that someone had hung over its entrance. Like everyplace else on the ship, it was designed to give a highly convincing illusion of much more room than it physically afforded.

The seating area was comfortable—room for everyone, though the nine-person crew rarely ate together. Each table had a screen that could be used to access anything from the ship's huge internal net and ports that could send and receive messages to and from home.

A constant stream of data, largely automated, made its way back and forth. But this was of diminishing value to Aaron and the sanity of his crew. The farther the voyage proceeded, the longer the round-trip for even speed-of-light data between the ship and Earth—communication between the *Light Through* and home now took nearly two years to travel one way. Aaron sometimes wondered if the information they were sending back was actually getting back at all. No surprise that the crew was on edge. Absence of information was a fertile ground for paranoia: the mind always seems to fill in what it doesn't know with the worst.

Jack was at his usual table, poring over his screen, when Aaron arrived. "All of Antarctica's been declared a Whole Earth park." He picked up his head and gave what passed for him as a smile. "Looks like they're finally seeing the light back home."

"Don't get too excited," Aaron said. "By now they could have reversed themselves and turned the whole continent into a launching pad."

Jack resumed his more customary expression. "I gather you've come to talk to me about the impending mutiny."

"You don't seem too worried about it," Aaron said.

Jack shrugged. "Columbus faced a mutiny too, and talked it down."

"Somehow I don't find that comparison all too flattering, coming from you," Aaron said.

"I'm doing my best to make sure it doesn't hurt us," Jack said.

"Oh?"

"The best policy with this sort of thing is to bring it to a head before it gets too far—while there's still room to decisively put it down. Chief Joseph of the Nez Percé once faced a similar situation—"

Aaron waved the history lesson away. "I'm not in the mood, Jack."

"So why'd you want to talk to me?"

"Because I heard that you've been stirring people up with your talking," Aaron said. "You're far too intelligent not to realize the damage you could do to this trip by going into detail about your ideas."

"I think the detail is just what we need at this point—let's get our worst fears out in the open, where we can confront them. Besides, I thought you, at least, had a somewhat open mind about my ideas," Jack said.

"I'm not talking about *my* mind," Aaron said. "I'm talking about the minds of some of the other people on board. I'm talking about *your* mind, Jack."

For the first time in the conversation, Jack looked a little surprised. "You couldn't think for a second that I would do anything to undermine our chances on this trip, could you? Surely you know how much it would do for the honor and reputation of the people I revere—the people who are no longer really here, and for whom I must therefore speak—if we succeed in our return voyage, and prove the words of Wise Oak to be true."

Aaron regarded those dark brown eyes. "So what do you suggest we do," he asked, "to safeguard the continuation of this trip whose success we both so very much desire?"

"Not much we *can* do," Jack answered, "except try to crystallize the discontent so it can be more easily countered. As I said."

"Thanks," Aaron said sourly, and pulled back his chair to leave.

"Not at all," Jack said. "And one other thing. I'd keep a close eye on McLaren if I were you. He rubs people the wrong way with his military posing."

Aaron walked down the corridor to Kathy's office, aggravating himself with the distinct impression that everyone was angry at him. The lighting was designed to simulate sun coming through puffy white clouds, but the clouds Aaron saw on the horizon were much darker. Hiro Matsohito, the nutritionist, seemed to glower when Aaron said hello, and Bo Ivanoff, second in command of engineering under Sarah, didn't respond at all. Aaron was beginning to feel like Captain Queeg in *The Caine Mutiny*.

Kathy's office was small, but its plants and light gave the sense of being in a soft green clearing in the woods somewhere. As always, she had some music from the middle of the last century playing in the background, this time the Elegants' "Where Are You, Little Star?" appropriately enough. Most of the people on the ship only tolerated her peculiar taste in music, but Aaron loved it.

Kathy motioned him to a seat and smiled. The sheen of her jet-black hair and keen blue eyes were as distracting as ever. "McLaren filled me in," she said. "You want my take on what he told you?"

"Please. I also had a little talk with Jack about this."

Kathy frowned. "He's really not the cause of any of this. We'd be dealing with the same problem around now even if he never said a word. You know that—we've been talking about it for years."

Aaron nodded.

"One of the things I learned pretty quickly in the Biospheres is that closed environments inevitably magnify doubts about their viability, to those within," Kathy continued. "It's that way for everyone. But some people need unattainable assurance from outside their surroundings that everything's on track, and without that, they can go out of control. Any little thing can set them off. Doesn't matter if the concern is warranted—like maybe it is about the Proxima-ACA shift—or not. And after all, we are moving quickly to the halfway point. It's quite understandable that even the calmest among us would be evaluating our options one last time, while we still have fuel enough to get back home."

Aaron told her about Matsohito and Ivanoff.

Kathy laughed. "Hiro's depressed because he lost a whole cluster of high-protein algae yesterday. And Ivanoff's been a boor from day one. My guess—"

The chime for an incoming call interrupted her. The name "McLaren" came into being in rippling beige letters on the screen above her head. She pressed a key that put him on holaround, so that Aaron as well as she could see him, and McLaren could see both of them and everything in Kathy's office.

"Sir . . . Kathy," McLaren said. "Part of engineering's been seized. So far it's a stalemate. We've locked them out of most of the access, so they can't turn the ship around. But we need to make a crucial course adjustment in, uh," he looked at his watch, "twenty-three minutes. And they control that part of the access. And if we don't make that adjustment, God knows where we'll wind up—certainly nowhere near ACA."

"Who exactly is doing this?" Aaron asked.

"Boris Ivanoff seems to be in charge."

"Worse than a boor," Kathy muttered. "So much for my assessment."

The long-suffering Russian people, Aaron thought, as Kathy and he rushed over to engineering. How many times had he heard that damn phrase in the media in the past thirty years? There were two kinds of Russians afoot in the twenty-first century. One group, successors of Gorbachev and Khrushchev and the Soviets who had opened space that first tiny *Sputnik* crack to human penetration, had gone on to infuse the world and the space program with their sense of poetry and human destiny. Alexei Primakov was part of that group.

But the others were forever losers. They saw their forebears as victimized by a brutal form of government—which indeed they were— and thought the rest of the world owed them a living. Bo Ivanoff was revealing himself to be of the second stripe. Ironic, since Alexei had recommended Bo for this mission. But Aaron had witnessed that kind of irony before. How many times had he seen an excellent dean at a university handpick an atrocious successor?

Nikki Dee Webber, who doubled as head of communications when she wasn't working on programming, was standing next to McLaren when Aaron and Kathy arrived. Aaron could tell from McLaren's face that he was less than 100 percent sure about Webber's loyalty.

"Good to see you, sir," McLaren said.

"Aaron, I think you better talk to him." Webber gestured to Ivanoff, who looked like he was sweating over his console on the other side of a clear partition. McLaren gave Webber a look, as he did anyone who had the temerity to address Aaron by first name in an official encounter.

Aaron pressed the com button. "Bo, what are you up to?"

"You know very well." Ivanoff turned his head from the console and looked at Aaron without losing a beat. His hands were still deftly working the keys. "I'm coming to see reality after three years of illusion."

"And what reality is that?" Aaron asked, and directed Webber's attention to Ivanoff's hands on the keys.

"He can't do any more than he's already done," she said quietly. "His lockout from the main course program is secure. He can make sure we never arrive at ACA, but only we have the capacity to turn this ship around."

"Don't play games with me," Ivanoff was saying. "You ask your buddy Jack Lumet about fantasy and reality. He'll tell you some idiotic Native American legend. Hundred percent untested. Now that the boomerang's even more in doubt, no way I'm going to risk my life for some cigar-store Indian. Other people on the ship agree with me."

Aaron looked at Webber. She returned his gaze. Aaron wondered again about Hiro—and about Aviva Zerez, the bioprogrammer. He even wondered about Sarah, though he figured she was likely in her cabin with the odd fatigue that had begun plaguing her the past few weeks.

"Get Jack over here," Aaron whispered to McLaren, then turned back to Ivanoff. "Surely you never thought," Aaron continued to Ivanoff, "that this trip was based on an ironclad scientific certainty. After all, how, under the circumstances, could any theory about our voyage have been really tested at all?"

"I told you to stop with those philosophy games—I'm not one of your goddamn graduate students," Ivanoff said. "Any imbecile knows that even an untested scientific theory is better than an idea that comes to someone in a bullshit vision."

"The boomerang effect has been scientifically demonstrated, Bo; you know that's true. Nothing's happened so far to make us think it won't—"

"Right," Bo talked over Aaron. "It's scientific. I agree. It could possibly work. That's why I took a chance on this in the first place. But not with the stars themselves doing some sort of slow dance out there—"

"—and don't sell primitive visions short," Aaron continued. "They're not always complete bullshit. Maybe the Iroquois somehow grasped something about celestial mechanics and the boomerang effect from their vantage point on Earth. People used spiderwebs as an antibiotic years before science found penicillin; they thought the webs had magical powers."

"Very impressive," Jack said in Aaron's ear and sidled up to him. "I couldn't have said that better myself."

McLaren looked like he was at great effort controlling himself from hitting Jack.

"It's better we face this now," Jack said to Aaron and looked at Ivanoff, "when we can still control it."

"He's right," Kathy said, with a slight sideways look at Nikki Dee that only Aaron could see.

Ivanoff was shouting. "I don't give two turds about antibiotics. Just another fucking dangerous panacea that you Americans and English unleashed on the world. Ancient history now anyway."

Aaron could feel Nikki stiffen. Maybe this was an opportunity. Her parents had both died of antibiotic-resistant fever in the same year, when she was nine. She was a ghetto kid who had somehow pulled herself up and done good things with her life. She didn't talk much about her past. Ivanoff likely had no idea what buttons he was close to pushing.

"Antibiotics saved a lot of good lives in its day," Aaron began.

"Ancient history, like I said," Ivanoff interrupted. "Who cares now, anyway? Diseases breed in Africa. Everyone knows it. They live like pigs there. The rest of the world had to build up immunity. But that's not my problem now. My problem is this damned ship."

"Seven minutes till the course correction," McLaren said in Aaron's ear.

Aaron nodded and looked at Ivanoff. The man's bile ran deeper than he had realized. Had he drawn enough of it out for Nikki to see that Ivanoff was no one she wanted to team with?

Aaron confronted her. "You have the capacity to override Ivanoff."

All heads turned toward Nikki. She hesitated.

"You were top of your class at the Media Lab. Don't tell me you can't outprogram that slob in there," Aaron urged.

"All right, of course I can," Nikki said.

"So will you? We've got only six minutes left," Aaron said.

Ivanoff was saying something. "Cut him the fuck off," Aaron told McLaren.

"I don't want to die," Nikki said.

"But don't you see? Our proceeding to Alpha Centauri is the only chance we've got now of *not* dying. The boomerang effect may well work. We might find a habitable planet there if not. But if we don't set the course correction, we'll be certain to die. We'll be headed to nowhere. And our death will do Earth absolutely no good—it will have no meaning."

"You could turn the ship around," Nikki said. "We still have enough fuel for the trip back home. Some of us feel that makes sense. And then we could do this voyage again, when we work out how to carry enough fuel for the full trip out and return, or maybe take better account of the shifting stars."

Some of us, Aaron thought. He wondered again about Sarah. Hadn't she seen this coming? Had illness impaired her judgment? Aaron sighed, and wondered whose judgment was really the most off here. Any normal human being had to have more than a dollop of queasy terror sloshing around inside as he plunged farther from home with increasingly less fuel to return. And yet—

Jack mumbled something. McLaren and Kathy were silent.

"What you're saying is not unreasonable, Nikki, but I can't do that," Aaron finally said. "I won't turn this ship around. The history of our species is filled with lost chances that took hundreds of years to be recovered—sometimes never at all. Look what happened to our own space program, how we nearly squandered the great first leaps of the 1960s. Now we're on the road again. We're halfway to a new star for humanity. We may never get this far again—we may never figure out how to carry enough fuel for a guaranteed return voyage. But even if the boomerang doesn't work this time, for whatever reason, we may well learn enough to make it work for the next ship. We'll send the information back to Earth, whatever happens. We might well find a planet we can orbit, maybe set up shop on, until the next ship arrives. Surely those kinds of possibilities mean something to you, or you wouldn't be here now."

McLaren signaled that only four minutes remained.

"We're running out of time, Nikki," Aaron pleaded.

"You can't know for a fact that there'll be a next ship," she said.

"No, not fact, just possibilities. But that's what the leading edge of human life has always been, hasn't it? Possibilities make us human."

If Nikki was breathing, only she knew it. Aaron knew there was no point in saying anything more. And now time, which had been flitting inside him like a wild-hair electron along with the terror, turned suddenly cold and still. . . .

Nikki exhaled like a burst balloon. "OK," she said, only a decibel above audibility. "But this will take a few minutes."

"Thank you," Aaron said.

Two minutes left, McLaren signaled.

Nikki pulled a keypad out of her pocket and got to work. McLaren mouthed the time left in seconds.

Aaron stopped looking when McLaren mouthed "Fifteen. . . ."

"OK!" Nikki cried out. "I've got control of all systems back now. And I locked Bo out from everything. You sure you still want to keep going forward? It's all preprogrammed; all I have to do is press in the go code—last chance to say no—"

"Do it!"

She bent her head to the keypad and looked up a split second later. "Done."

Jack squeezed Aaron's arm. "You're better than Columbus."

Don't be so sure, Aaron thought. At least Columbus got some of his people back home.

Aaron's manipulation of people had so far gotten this mission launched, and had seen them through this crisis.

But he'd have to manipulate a lot more than people to get them home from Alpha Centauri.

Three

Nikki sat down in Aaron's office. She always looked older than he expected, but he always pictured her looking exactly as she had in the confrontation with Ivanoff four years earlier.

"You're looking good, Aaron," she said, "younger every time I see you."

"You too," Aaron lied. In fact, she not only looked older, but more worried than usual.

"We seem to be about three light-months now from the Centauri system." She pulled out her pad and focused on its glimmering calculations.

"Yes," Aaron said. "The orange of ACB turned really vivid yesterday. I asked Hiro if he could increase the output of citrus fruit—you know, in honor of the sister star."

No response from Nikki.

"That's good news, right?" Aaron asked. "I mean, our arriving in under half a year? We'll get there with a bit more of everything."

"Not necessarily." She looked up with a frown.

Here it comes, Aaron thought. "No? Why not?"

"Well," she said slowly, "according to my latest simulations from the data we've been receiving, it, ah, doesn't seem that Alpha Centauri A is the star we're actually approaching."

"What?"

"I know," Nikki said. "It doesn't make sense. Up until this morning all the data was looking exactly as it should for ACA. Then we started seeing subtle but significant differences. Which means that the star we're moving toward looks a lot like ACA, but apparently isn't. I came to you with this before checking any further, because I didn't want word getting out and alarming everyone before we knew what was happening."

"Your instincts were good," Aaron said. "But I'm not clear about what your new reports are showing. The star we're headed toward looks a lot like ACA but isn't? I assume you're not talking about Proxima, which is just a sixth of a light-year—ten thousand AU—from ACA? Or ACB, which is practically right next to ACA? I mean, we're just about fifteen AU away now, a little more than one and a half times the distance of Saturn to our sun, so a new course correction would be trivially easy if we're headed there—"

"Aaron, please! I know the difference between ACA, ACB, and Proxima—very different specs. This is something else entirely."

Aaron sighed. "What, then? A fourth star in the family that looks a lot like ACA?"

Nikki shook her head no. "It's a star that looks like ACA, but differs in some important respects—like there's no ACB and Proxima anywhere near it. And some of the other stats are off."

"Is it still showing planets?"

"Yeah, we seem to be OK on that score," Nikki said.

"And you're sure that we've been sticking to our preset course— no one's been putting in any unauthorized 'corrections'?"

Nikki's coffee-colored cheeks flushed to a full mocha. "Yes, I'm sure. We're right on course—no deviations, no errors . . . no sabotage that I can see."

The word *sabotage* still brought Ivanoff's face to mind. Bo apparently was enough of a realist not to try anything crazy after they'd passed the point of no return. He'd been working just fine, as far as Aaron could tell. The two had had some heart-to-heart talks over the years. But Aaron still couldn't trust him the way he did Roger, Kathy, Sarah—even Nikki.

"But we seem to be knocking on the wrong damn star," she added, "a G2 V, just like the Sun, just where it should be in terms of our course trajectory, but not Alpha Centauri A. Indeed, other than being G2 V, nothing like it, if these new data are right."

Aaron walked slowly down the corridor to Kathy's office. Who really knew where they were heading, where they were about to arrive? Only their instruments knew. And these in turn were confirmable only by other instruments. A fine kettle of instruments they were in ...

Kathy's sylvan office looked as inviting as always. In fact, more so, because of Noah, her beautiful three-year-old, who greeted Aaron with a big smile. The boy was sweet proof that Kathy had forsaken her policy of abstinence, at least once, though she as "a matter of integrity" never said who the father was. All Aaron knew for sure, and not entirely unregretfully, was that it wasn't him.

Noah's arrival had raised some eyebrows even among their generally liberated crew. Food and oxygen were not matters of concern—there would be more than enough to go around in the ship's self-generating biosphere. And one more body added no extra burden on the boomerang. But bringing a child into the world when that world was a ship in flux with no certain voyage of return did seem a touch irresponsible, if not insane. On the other hand, those who saw humanity's destiny in space usually viewed a bigger population as an important precondition for expansion to the stars. "Love productively in low g" was the modest graffito seen in many a crystalline warren of Mars Vest. Tea wasn't the only pleasure especially savored there.

After Aaron had recovered from the initial shock of Noah, he'd looked in the mirror and realized Kathy was entitled to her decision—who was he or anyone to insist that her right to motherhood be sacrificed to this trip, *especially* in view of the trip's uncertainty—and he appreciated the vote of confidence in their voyage that Noah's existence declared. Now, three years later, he exulted in the little boy, delighted in being the grandpa he'd never been back home.

Linda Scott's "I've Told Every Little Star," an early '60s remake of a 1950s hit, was playing in the background in Kathy's outdoor office. Aaron hummed a little harmony to it under his breath. Noah looked up at him from half across the light-managed clearing and sang some notes too.

"Here, take a look at this." Kathy pushed a sheerscreen over to his side of the picnic table. She had an identical image on hers. Aaron had already e-mailed her about Nikki's discovery.

"It's a workup I just did of the main possibilities," Kathy continued.

"Branch A assumes we are, notwithstanding Nikki's report, still on course and three months away from ACA. How to reconcile this with what she told you?

"One, Nikki's incoming data are wrong, and/or her simulation process is faulty; because the source of either or both of the above is sabotage; or, the source of either or both of the above is natural noise or error.

"Two, our stats on Alpha Centauri prior to now, until Nikki's sim today, have been wrong. Since this info goes back more than a century, sabotage can almost certainly be ruled out; persistent natural error would be the only reasonable source.

"Three, Nikki has uncovered a brand-new star, right next to Alpha Centauri A, which for whatever reason has been unknown to us until now, and whose properties now include cloaking the presence of ACA, ACB, and Proxima. Maybe the star came into being on little cat's feet, maybe it's been hidden from us by some superior alien intelligence; who knows? This in a way is a special case of Two, above, but I liked it so I gave it a separate number. Highly improbable. But I like it.

"Now Branch B. It accepts the most obvious upshot of Nikki's report: We are in fact quickly approaching a star that not only is not ACA, but nowhere near it. Assuming that number Two above is not the case, this in turn means that we've been traveling in a wrong direction for quite some time. The same dichotomy of sabotage/natural error as a source of this mistaken course applies, though why would Nikki or anyone deliberately do anything to misdirect the voyage in the past four years, since we passed what we thought was the halfway mark? What could they hope to gain? Having passed that halfway point, we have enough fuel only to reach the ACA family—all other stars, including Sol, are beyond range. This mistaken-direction hypothesis also carries an implausible burden of the coincidence that a course error brought us to another G2 V star.

"So there you have it."

Aaron exhaled slowly. "Fine analysis, as always. And I guess we'd do better starting with the assumption of everyone's trustworthiness at this point."

"What does *trustword* mean, Momma?" Noah piped up.

"It means someone's telling you the truth, and also wants to do good things for you," Aaron said. "Sort of both, mixed together."

"Oh," Noah said, satisfied for the moment.

But he wouldn't be satisfied for too long, Aaron thought. Noah was a prodigy—in his speech, his reading, but most of all his understanding. The only kid that Aaron had ever seen with a comparable mind was Jack, and that was when Jack was, what? Ten? More than three times Noah's age. Maybe the human brain developed faster, deeper, at half the speed of light in deep space. Maybe that's the way people were supposed to be; maybe something about growing up on a planet whirling around and around the same old sun somehow stunted cognitive growth. Centrifugal retardation that the whole species suffered . . .

"So what now?" Kathy asked.

"Well, we've got to expand your workup to consider how each of those possibilities will affect our chances for survival, the crew's attitudes, all the pertinent variables."

"Why is it I know the 'we' in that will boil down to 'me'?" Kathy smiled. "It's OK—Sarah's been all right the past few years; everyone else has been so healthy so far that I've plenty of time on my hands even with little Mr. Trustword over there." She threw a kiss to her son. "But we may not need an expanded workup anyway—does it really make a difference to the success of our mission if we get to one Sol-type star four light-years away or another?"

"You're beginning to sound like Jack already."

"Well, think about it," Kathy said. "A G2 V star has pretty much the same likelihood of habitable planets around it. The same chance—"

"If it's not a triple star, all bets about the boomerang effect are off," Aaron said. "Shifting stars is one thing. Two out of three missing is something quite else—it will shoot holes light-years wide in our projections."

Kathy shrugged. "There's no reason our ship's biosphere can't keep going for dozens of lifetimes, wherever we end up."

Aaron looked at her. "You want to spend the rest of your life on this ship? You want Noah . . ." He looked at the boy and was glad to see that he apparently wasn't listening. Aaron shook his head. There was a lot that he still did not fathom about Kathy, about everyone on this ship. He resumed talking, more quietly. "Even I with my bottomless confidence would like to know where in this universe we're going now. When we reach that star, whatever it is, we'll have a lot of life-and-death decisions to make, and it would be nice to know just a bit about where we actually are. Don't you agree?"

"Well, the only way we'll really know more about where we're going is to go there," Kathy replied. "In the meantime, the best source of answers is in here," she gestured to the little screens shadow-pulsating under her fingertips, "in digesting and redigesting every ounce of this data."

"Yeah," Aaron said, "the good old bovine, quadruple-stomach method of science. Keep me posted."

He tousled Noah's hair and left.

Two thousand three . . . two thousand four? Aaron couldn't remember the exact year, but he could picture the room precisely. Donna sitting in the front row, half his age, twice his bedmate, his sole indiscretion, crossing her legs seductively . . . The hot June air of Washington Square Park steaming the room because the air conditioners at NYU were always broken . . . Donna looked a lot like Kathy, didn't she? And he lectured on. . . .

". . . about one of the big paradoxes of computers and technology: They're most useful, you see, precisely in those areas where we don't already have means of gaining knowledge. But this very value makes us incapable of corroborating the accuracy of computers where we most need them—because our only reliable sources of knowledge in these new areas are the technologies whose very performance is what we'd like to verify. . . ."

Donna's eyes closed, her mouth opened. . . . Maybe she was fantasizing about him, her eyes in early, merry REM. . . .

Aaron saw the lecture all over again in his mind. He soaked in the impressed expressions of his students one more time. It was one of his best lectures, no doubt about it. But the last thing he wanted to do right now was play the lesson of his lecture out in this strange reality, where everyone's life was at stake, including little Noah's. Those who can, do. Those who can't, give lectures. . . .

McLaren joined Aaron and Sarah in the central data room. Aaron had McLaren bring along Aviva, who was not only a computer programming geneticist but also a computer artist in her spare time. Her work had received favorable notice at the Jerusalem World's Fair two years before they'd left—"She does impossible things with a light brush," "A new mistress of the palindromic image, aptly suited to her name," the reviews had said. Aaron agreed. He liked what he'd seen of her pixel dabbling on the trip. She was a quiet, even shy person— dark hair, dark lashes, dark eyes—the least known to Aaron of the crew. But she seemed to see with a clear inner light that burned to overcome impossibility. That's what the critics had seen. Maybe it came from her being half Israeli and half Palestinian.

Aaron asked Sarah to preside. He still worried about her, even though her symptoms had disappeared shortly after the *Light Through* had passed the halfway point to Alpha Centauri. Perhaps she, like everyone else on the ship, had deep fears about proceeding past the point of no return, and had turned those fears against herself, so they made her ill. Aaron scowled. He didn't really believe in that kind of psychology. What he did believe was that Sarah had helped make this trip possible.

She turned on the screens. They lit up with before-and-after shots of Alpha Centauri A, or whatever was really on them. Sarah's hair flared around the edges, computer light spilling over her ethereal, pre- maturely white filaments, as she leaned in and pointed out the differ- ences in the two star shots. Aaron could see them immediately—could see what had caught Sarah's attention—large amounts of free oxygen and hydrogen, likely in liquid form, suddenly circling the new star in today's images.

"Anything new in the readings other than the H and O?" Aaron asked.

"Difficult to say," Sarah said. "The new colors are so intense that they're essentially cloaking the star—so a large part of what is behind the colors is bleached out and inconclusive. We could recalibrate our equipment to get beyond the new glare, but that could take some doing, because the glare itself is continuously changing. And recalibrating would, of course, introduce a whole new set of problems."

"Right," Aaron said. "The one thing we don't want to do is mess around with our equipment and its settings now—we need to keep them as constant as possible to gauge what we're seeing out there."

"And we're sure that our equipment is working properly now?" Aviva asked. "Color errors are among the most common minor failures with sims and the like. Some of my best paintings take advantage of them."

"We have quintuplicate-trebled redundancy and then some in the central sim net—more redundancy than sperm in ejaculate—and all the systems show the same thing," Sarah said. "The source-data feed is of course ultimately singular—it comes from one origin, the star—but independent tests of the data entry points show that they're all functioning just as before."

"So as best as we can tell, what we're seeing out there is reality: an Alpha Centauri A–type star with large new amounts of hydrogen and oxygen, likely liquid, around it," Aaron said.

"That's it," Sarah said. "And in the same exact position as ACA itself has been for the entire extent of our voyage."

"So why would it change now?" Aaron wondered aloud.

Sarah held her arms up in an I-have-no-idea gesture.

"Any history at all of ACA having such, ah, eruptions?" Aaron asked McLaren, whom he'd asked to do some hurried research.

"None, sir."

"Any sign yet of Alpha Centauri B or Proxima out there?" Aaron asked. "If those two are still in the picture, then our boomerang calculations could well hold."

"Impossible to say with one hundred percent assurance," Sarah said. "The H and O color blooms would block out any lesser light in the area. We could recalibrate the equipment to give us finer readings in the peripheries, but—"

"Right, we've just been down that road," Aaron said. "OK, then, let's look at the other side of this coin. What are the dangers to us of proceeding to this new star, or this enhanced ACA, or whatever it is?"

"So we're accepting as fact, then, that we're not way off course—say, four light-years from Sol in some other direction—and that these new readings are in reality where Alpha Centauri used to be, always has been?" Aviva asked.

"We're not ruling out anything," Aaron said. "But the course logs are so clear and secure that, for the time being, yes, we'll assume that our course is correct—that what we're seeing is Alpha Centauri in some form or other."

"We don't have much of a time being, if you don't mind my saying so," Aviva said. "Just one hundred eighty odd days."

"No, I don't mind," Aaron said. "In fact, I appreciate your thoughts; that's why you're here." And he meant that—the last thing he needed in this sort of crisis was a bunch of yes-drones. That was one of the reasons he'd wanted people rather than robots as the crew in the first place.

McLaren cleared his throat. "The main danger is explosion—hydrogen and oxygen are obviously very combustible. But more likely, in the presence of a star, they'll turn into steam."

"Which should clear away and reveal to us what we're really heading to?" Aaron mused.

McLaren nodded. "The question is when."

"So our only option," Aaron said, "is what? We continue just as we've been, to a class G2 V star that may or may not be ACA, except with an ocean of hydrogen and oxygen around it, that may or may not turn to steam sooner or later, and show us where we're really going?"

"That's how I would put it," McLaren said. "But that option isn't so terrible. After all, Columbus thought he was on his way to the Orient, and discovered something else that was pretty good."

Great—now McLaren was starting to sound like Jack too. By the end of this trip, his whole crew would be Jacks.

"Aaron," Sarah called out excitedly from a far screen. "Come have a look at this."

Aaron hustled across the room. "Tell me what I'm looking at," he said. As fast as his mind processed words and ideas, that's how slow it usually was to make sense of new images.

"H_2O," Sarah answered. "Hot blessed steam."

Jack and Aaron took their dinner by the droplet lake in Hiro's garden the next evening. Aaron loved this little piece of water, dappled with the light of an artificial sun in various shades of ascension and setting, one of the real triumphs of biospheric engineering on the ship. He did some of his best thinking lying on his back in a half-submerged float, slapping the top of the water with his palms as if he were playing a conga....

He brought a tray to the table for Jack and him. "So you think the bigger significance of all this is we're being given a series of challenges by some greater force in the universe, and our best response is to calmly accept them, because that way we'll overcome them?" Aaron asked.

Jack put a slender, multicolored stalk in his mouth and smacked his lips. "Hiro outdid himself with this carrot hybrid this time. Marvelous."

Aaron sipped his soup slowly. It was also quite good—a sort of airy version of miso. Star soup, Hiro called it.

Jack closed his eyes as if further savoring the carrot stick, or consulting some inner oracle for a suitable response to Aaron's question. "What else can we do?" he said at last.

"Then we're pretty much wasting our time with all of our science—all of our expert, mathematically informed analyses," Aaron said ironically.

Jack shrugged. "You already know what they'll tell you. ACA for some reason released a large amount of free hydrogen and oxygen. It's either the first time, or for some reason it hasn't been visible to us before, or whatever. Who knows, maybe our very approach somehow triggered the release, like a cloaking defense mechanism. Maybe the star's like a big skunk. That's consistent with grand quantum mechanics, isn't it?"

"No, not really," Aaron said. "Grand QM operates on mesoscales—what you can hold in your hand—not star-size phenomena. And—"

"—And the heat of the star turned those elements into water: steam," Jack continued, apparently unconcerned with Aaron's GQM correction. "And the steam is clearing, and revealing Alpha Centauri A behind it, and ACB and Proxima just where they should be. That's a happy ending to this episode, isn't it?"

"No, not entirely," Aaron said.

The speed with which the next stalk was about to enter Jack's mouth slowed just a fraction. "Why not?"

"Because the free liquid hydrogen and oxygen could've been fuel for our trip home," Aaron said. "Our engine has that capability—just like the early Delta series."

That stopped Jack cold. "And the steam the hydrogen and oxygen produced is, I assume, no use as a fuel? No help for either the chemical or the fusion part of our star drive?"

"Right," Aaron said. "Steam power's no option here in deep space."

"Well, you know, steam power has surprised Western civilization before," Jack said. "The British admiralty in the 1830s confidently predicted that steam was too unreliable to ever be of any use in naval operations—"

Aaron shook his head. "We don't have time for general principles about unexpected uses of technology now."

"You're wrong, my friend—looking for unforeseen opportunities is all we have time for," Jack replied. "The moral of this hydrogen and oxygen thing is that we're heading into the unexpected. Radically, ultimately unexpected. Unexpected by an infinite margin more than anything we've ever unexpected before. You've got to be open to any and every thing the cosmos may see fit to offer you in such environments. That's the only path to survival. Who knows, maybe that star will fart out something else that we can use as a fuel. Maybe we'll fly into something useful from another star. That's the only way."

"And that was Wise Oak's way?" Aaron asked, not sarcastically at all.

Jack nodded. "You're going to see Kathy later, right? Here, give this to Noah—something I made for him."

It was a small wooden doll, done up in the Iroquois sachem style.

Four

Aaron was warming his hands by the cyberplace in his office when he got the news. The room temperature, of course, could have been set higher, but sometimes he purposely set it at chilly, just for the joy of the crackling heat of the cyberfire upon his body and face. The flames were simulated, but their pleasures were real.

"Come see!" Noah poked his head in the door and said with glee. "Our star looks like the sun!"

Aaron could have called the image up on the office screen, but instead he let Noah take him by the hand to the real-view window.

"See? Just like the sun! Maybe smaller." Noah, of course, had never seen Sol with naked eyes, but he had seen it plenty of times—and from plenty of inner- and outer-planet perspectives—on screen.

Aaron beamed at the golden handball shining through the window. He had looked at Alpha Centauri A just yesterday, but today it indeed seemed to have broken through some barrier, like a tomato ripening from white to color, and for the first time it looked decisively like a sun, not a star. It was better than the best sunrise he had ever seen on Earth.

Alpha Centauri B, more than four-fifths ACA's mass but just a third of its luminosity, looked like a big orange moon beside ACA. Proxima Centauri, just a tenth of ACA's mass, was a feeble, flickering throb, a ghost of pale diamond in the backdrop. "Here am I, with Noah in the Sky with Diamonds," Aaron said.

Noah laughed. "Momma's song says Lucy!"

Aaron smiled. "But you're here with me now." He pointed beyond the window. "The sun'll be growing every day now, more and more."

Noah looked dubious. "You mean like a flower? Momma has flowers that grow every day."

"Yes," Aaron said. "Especially like the face of a flower, with petals that get bigger every day."

Noah's face scrunched up. "But flowers have stems. Momma says that's how they get their food to grow. There's no stem out there."

Aaron thought for a few seconds. "We're the stem, Noah. This ship, all of us. We feed it with our dreams come true."

"Oh," Noah said. "Like a fairy tale?"

"Yeah, a fairy tale." And the little boy in Aaron hugged the little boy in front of him.

Imminent arrival at Alpha Centauri A tripped off a thousand tasks, which, like a swarm of seven-year cicadas slightly overdue, had been patiently waiting since the start of the voyage to come forth and clack for attention. Rerun all of the boomerang simulations; check them against the newly calibrated real data of the three stars; make sure the shuttles were all operational, ready to go with telemetry; triple test the robots, most of which hadn't done a thing during the journey; eyeball a sample of the multiple incoming recordings to make sure the error-free certification itself wasn't by some quirk corrupted; rerun the boomerang simulations yet again, just for good measure . . .

Aaron was in the thick of addressing these things, dispensing instructions for this job and that, happier than he'd been at any time on the trip, when Kathy called.

"Sarah's sick again. I'm not sure what's wrong with her. I'm in her room."

Aaron knew immediately from Kathy's tone that Sarah was worse than just sick again. He rushed down the corridor.

Kathy's face confirmed the worst. One look at Sarah, half under blankets in bed, face afloat in soft white hair, confirmed it even more.

Kathy pounded on Sarah's chest and rolled back her eyelids and syringed her with every stimulant on board, but she was dead. She was only forty-four. How on Earth could that be? She had been OK these past few years. . . .

They weren't on Earth anymore—was that somehow the answer? For some reason, the universe had called her out here, via that anomalous signal from ACA, and then rejected her, like tissue from an alien body. Why hadn't it rejected the rest of them?

Aaron looked at Sarah's face, at her breasts dead white, still pert— one of them blotched rouge where Kathy had pounded, petitioned in vain for life—and he thought of his own mortality. For all his talk about Russell-Shaw, he knew that Naomi hadn't been wrong years earlier when she'd said there was no hard evidence of its effect. There was a connection, sure, a finding that those who lived very long and had a contemplative existence had a 77 percent chance of having a DNA thread slightly out of place in a remote, minuscule area of the X chromosome. But genetic correlations were notoriously tricky. Russell-Shaw had also been found in a few people who died young. Not every philosopher lived to be a hundred. Blaise Pascal, no less imbued with a sense of awe at the human disequation to the cosmos than Jack and Aaron, had died before his fortieth birthday. Younger even than Sarah.

"Any idea what the hell happened here?" Aaron asked, barely able to speak.

Kathy performed all the many tests at her disposal. "No foul play, no penetration by needles, knives, poisons, projectiles of any kind. No sign of semen. No sign of suicide. She just . . . died."

It was likely a stroke, the still-fashionable placeholder for deaths of unknown causes. A stroke—OK, a stroke—but what actually caused it? Small numbers of people still died for no apparent reason in their thirties, forties, and fifties—far too young to die of anything in the twenty-first century except the odd untreated case of pneumonia and IMMs, the weird immuno-offshoot that fortunately afflicted only those with a rare genotype. The dark side of genes in action.

"She opened her eyes a moment before she died," Kathy said.

"Did she . . . say anything?"

Kathy nodded. "She said, 'I came here to die. It's OK.' " Kathy took a shaky breath. "It was heartbreaking."

Aaron and Kathy gently dressed Sarah and notified the rest of the crew. They were in shock. They discussed what to do and decided on a funeral. Jack said a few words about the first space angel ambassador. Then they released her, white hair gleaming in the yellow-orange light, to drift near Alpha Centauri . . . a new bit of matter, only this one had been sensate and intelligent just this morning.

Sarah was the first person ever to die in deep space. Part of the first group of fleshly intelligence from Earth, of DNA sprouted into brain and tissue, to venture out this far from home. She hadn't had an easy time of it. And now her flesh would likely last forever—far longer than a digital photo or holograph, surely immune to bacterial decay or oxidation—though her brain was already devoid of any thought or feeling.

"We've got to make sure this is the first and only time this happens," Aaron said. And everyone nodded. Everyone agreed. And everyone knew just how little that meant.

Aaron was sure he felt worse than anyone else, for his was the sweet voice of possibility that had lured Sarah aboard the *Light Through*.

Bo Ivanoff had tears in his eyes. Well, he'd be in charge of engineering now, and Nikki Dee in charge of programming. Aaron was glad he'd pursued the high road with Bo in the past years—no recriminations, no punishment, passive or aggressive. He'd have to rely on Bo now. Everyone would.

They would need all the help they could get entering the Alpha Centauri system. And even more if they were to leave it.

Aaron called an all-hands meeting for the very next day. Aviva, Hiro, Nikki, and Bo joined Jack, Roger, Kathy, and Aaron in the cafe, with Noah napping on the mom-screen. His sleeping image hung like a cybergraphic angel above. Kathy didn't feel comfortable about leaving him alone, and if she did, she at least wanted to stay in virtual touch with her son.

"Sarah would've wanted us to focus on the demands ahead," Aaron began. "We've got lots of things to do, but here's what I see as our three most important jobs now: one, inspection of this star system and its planets for possible life; two, relaying as much data as we can back to Earth; three, keeping focused on how *we* get back home."

Ivanoff grunted at the mention of this last task.

"Bo," Aaron said, "you're our best expert now on propulsion and the boomerang effect. How about your going over again exactly what we should be looking for to see if it's happening."

"OK. We've already reduced our approach speed, as you know," Bo replied. "We need to break about ten percent more to avoid being sucked into the star. If we steer this just right, we'll be whipped around the back of ACA, and come around the other side with an added kick from ACB and Proxima to give us an acceleration high enough to send us back on our way to Earth at half speed of light."

"The river that flows both ways," Nikki said. Her tone was neither sarcastic nor especially confident.

"Yeah, but it's a tricky river," Bo said. "Slight errors in the speed or approach angle could lose us in the star, send us off in a wrong direction, or leave us here as permanent guests of Alpha Centauri. And the position of Proxima relative to ACA and ACB is less stable than we thought from back on Earth—the shift that launched this whole project in the first place was probably just the first expression of some trend toward instability over here. I tried to tell all of you that four years ago."

"I know, Bo," Aaron said, and tried to look conciliatory. To himself he thought: So if I'm wrong, I'll leave a note of apology to you and all on my personal screen for all the stars in the universe to see. At least I tried.

But then Aaron looked up at Noah—he hadn't volunteered to be here. He deserved more.

"So if the boomerang works," Kathy said, looking at Aaron, "we won't be able to actually spend any time on any of the planets, even if we find them thriving with life." Her dream, Aaron knew, her likely mother's magic faith that kept her going in the face of doubt, was that they would find a planet to live on out here. And if not, she was willing to settle for life in the *Light Through*'s biosphere.

"That's right," Bo said. "We'll of course be able to close-scan them, and leave some unpersonned probes behind, but that'll be it. The original trip, remember, was planned with robots in mind."

"Pity," McLaren said.

"Not to any life forms that may already be there," Jack said quietly. Kathy gave him an exasperated look.

"Good thing they have you around to look after their interests, then," Bo said.

For a second, Aaron wondered again exactly why Jack was even here on this voyage, given his heartfelt misgivings about molesting the natural scheme of things. But Aaron already knew. Jack was here to help prove the validity of Wise Oak's wisdom, to demonstrate that star currents indeed flow both ways—and having done that, to leave the stars as untouched as possible. As perhaps some part of Jack really believed Wise Oak had done already?

"So when can we expect the first confirmed reports on the planets?" Aviva asked.

"As soon as two to three days, maybe," Nikki said. "Depends on just where in the system the planets are, how big they actually are, that kind of thing."

"And how long after that before we verify that the boomerang is working?" Aaron asked.

"Same factors," Bo said. "Could be days, could be weeks, maybe even months—depends upon how close the planets are to the star, precise relationships between the three stars, whether there are any planets around the other two stars—whole bunch of stuff. We have contingencies for most of those configurations. How they'll work, of course, depends upon our exact escape speed as we round the star. But we don't know that yet, and we can't make course corrections on a course that doesn't yet exist."

"In the interim, we'll look for sources of fuel, signs that any of the planets might be able to support us—anything that we can latch on to," McLaren said.

Bo took that as a comment responsive to his concerns, and nodded vigorously in agreement.

Aaron noticed that Nikki was engrossed in her earpiece, her head bobbing slowly, nostrils flaring out and in as she followed some sort of blow-by-blow report from one of the ship's autocoms. Had to be something major to pull her away from this conversation.

"OK," she finally said to herself, sucked in a breath, and looked at Aaron. By then she had everyone's attention.

"Scan's spotted something on the screen," she said with awe, and controlled jubilation.

"Our first planet?" Kathy shouted.

"No," Nikki said, lips trembling. "Too small for a planet, and it just seems to be drifting out there."

"Well, what then?" Aaron said, almost shouting himself.

"It looks artificial. Maybe a ship."

What is it about cosmic space, Aaron wondered, that invites certain people to leave their comfortable planet, pulls nine of them into a ship, now ten, now nine again, in pursuit of starlight four light-years from home?

Making contact with alien intelligence actually wasn't high on Aaron's list. He'd always been a pragmatist about intelligence in the universe other than the human kind on Earth—like Fermi, Aaron would have expected it to have already arrived in some scientifically confirmable way on Earth, had it existed out there, out here. After all, considering how apparently unique the biological process of intelligence was around old Sol, and how likely humans would be in the future to search as hard as they could for any trace of it other than their own, Aaron figured that alien intelligence would want to do the same.

Yeah, he knew the argument that alien intelligence could be so different from ours that we might never be able even to recognize it as intelligence. But if that were the case, if human and all other alien intelligence were indeed two blind ships passing in the night, fundamentally incapable of exerting any influence on each other, what was the point of even talking about an alien mind? Why bother with it, as Haeckel had said about Kant's insistence that the ultimate inner cores of things—things-in-themselves—were forever closed to human perception and understanding?

Of course, it was also possible that intelligent alien life could be all too human in motive, enough like the intelligent species on Earth to deliberately want to remain secret, to visit Earth only in a hands-off way. Or maybe alien intelligences were much younger than humans and incapable of deep-space travel or communication, or much older, and burned out, or perhaps totally telepathic and ethereal, and thus not in need of any tangible technology at all.

But these seemed rather too neat alternatives to a more obvious reason that humans knew no technological intelligences other than their own: guess what, there were none.

But Aaron was not dogmatic about that. He accepted that all

theories and reasoning and ideas were fallible, including his own.

So a hulk of empirical evidence making itself known to their sensors, apparently shattering his lack of expectations about alien intelligence, thrilled him. Even as a part of him held on to an underlying feeling that the hulk might be something else.

But what?

Nikki was able to ascertain the following about the hulk: It seemed not of Earthly origin, or at least not made of materials known to twenty-first-century civilization, though it was of the same general size and spherical shape as their ship, which is why they thought of it as a ship at all; it had nothing that looked like writing or pictures on either its exterior or what could be scanned of its interior; it seemed indeed to be drifting, as no sort of propulsion or steering could be discerned in its motion; it apparently had no form of DNA life or robotic intelligence on board, though the scans picked up traces of some compounds that could have once been protein.

Which was why Aaron had taken to calling it a hulk.

"It seems we have a dead ship floating in space," he said at the meeting of the assembled crew the next morning. He'd been awake for more than twenty-four hours now, as had everyone else.

"Could it have been the source of the anomalous signal they picked up from here back on Earth before we left?" Kathy asked.

Aaron winced involuntarily. The anomalous signal made him think of Sarah, and how she had helped get their voyage over the last hurdle to its launch. . . .

"Impossible to say," Nikki replied. "It's not doing anything now."

"How do we know it's a ship?" Jack asked.

"We don't know for sure," Nikki said, "and we can't risk changing our course now to take a better look. But that's our best guess. Certainly it could be something else entirely."

"Maybe a ship from another civilization that came here planning to get back on the boomerang, and look what happened to it," Bo said.

"Or maybe a ship from a technological planet we've yet to see, closer to the star—a discarded early model of a fleet that will soon be here to greet us with fruit and flowers, and toys for Noah," Kathy offered.

"I like Kathy's scenario better than Bo's," Aviva said.

"I do too," Bo said, "but what do you suggest we do?"

"Dispatch one of our robotic planet probes to the, ah, artifact. Can we do that? Do we all agree this is worth the expenditure? We may wind up with one less to land on the planets or investigate other objects we might find later on," Aaron said.

Bo nodded his head yes. "Programming the probe is easy. And I think it's worth the vehicle."

"I'm certainly in favor of that," Kathy said.

"Me too." Aviva nodded.

Aaron looked around at the rest of the group. Hiro, Nikki, and McLaren gave their assent. So did Jack, but he didn't look very pleased.

"Jack?" Aaron prodded.

He made a noncommittal gesture. "OK with me if that's what you want. Advanced technological artifacts are not really my area of expertise."

"Excuse me, but what the hell is?" Bo said.

Jack smiled serenely. Most of the others laughed uncomfortably.

"Right," Aaron said. "Let's all get some sleep, then, and reconvene tomorrow morning for breakfast. I have a feeling we're going to have a lot of sleepless nights ahead."

He was awakened four hours later by a call from Nikki.

He thought he was dreaming, till the pitch of her voice settled unmistakably into the reality center of his brain like a plate clattering into coherence on a polished table.

"Sorry to wake you," she was saying, "but an urgent private message just came in for you from David Percival."

Aaron fumbled with his phone and the absurdity of an urgent message sent almost four years ago. "OK," he said groggily "put it on my screen and I'll be back to you after I've seen it."

Aaron hadn't heard from Percival since the day they'd left. A few bland birthday greetings from Naomi and his children—always arriving a day or two too early or late—were indeed the only private messages he'd received at all from Earth and Mars on the voyage. He'd written a long confidential report to Alexei Primakov after the Ivanoff crisis. He'd wanted not so much to denounce Ivanoff as to let the people back home know how unstable the crew had become, in hopes that better care would be taken in choosing the next one, if ever there was one, in case Aaron didn't return to review this voyage in person. But after writing the report, he'd realized that things had gotten better with Bo, and a report about a near-mutiny on the first starship might do more harm than good back home for the prospects of another star voyage. So the report was never sent.

Now Aaron punched up Percival's message on his screen, unscrambling it with a personal code that even his grandmother wouldn't have known: her middle name, anagrammatized, and with two arbitrary symbols added before and after.

Percival's urgency became clear right away.

"The political situation's deteriorated at home," Percival's tense face told him. (So what else is new, Aaron thought.) "JFC's wing of the party was hurt by some new revelations uncovered in secret documents from the nineties." (Aaron rolled his eyes and reiterated his thought.) "Naomi felt her campaign needed some good news, and has claimed to have received some communication from you indicating that, even though you're still less than halfway to Alpha Centauri, your sensors have confirmed the existence of intelligent life in that area. I and the others, of course, know this isn't the case—the message she produced from you lacked the special signature icons we agreed upon, and your getting confirmation of anything regarding Alpha Centauri from more than four light-years out isn't very likely. So far, we've kept our mouths shut, because, as ever, we don't want to do anything to injure the future of the space program. But obviously we're not very happy. I guess sleep with the devil and all that—but damnit, this isn't science anymore, it's a bloody travesty. Anyway, we know there's nothing you can do about this, but I wanted you to get this message before you actually arrived at ACA. Who knows, maybe you'll find something there to make an honest woman out of that political bitch."

Aaron stared at the screen for a long time. What struck him most was the irony, the perverse coincidence, of his receiving this information about Naomi's lie just after encountering something that might make that lie true. And Percival alluding to that very possibility at the end of his message. There was an old book by Arthur Koestler about coincidences, in which he argued that there really were none—just connections that were not apparent, or for some reason disguised. Aaron was inclined to agree.

But given what they had so far actually scanned and analyzed of the hulk, it likely wouldn't provide anything close to a confirmed discovery of intelligent life in the area—certainly not an intelligence currently alive. But this wouldn't be the first time that someone in the mean streets of science and the real world had shot first and asked questions later and come up a winner. Hadn't Aaron done this himself on this very expedition?

He found he didn't share Percival's outrage about what Naomi had done. Yes, it was a mockery of science, but then again all science he had ever known had partaken of such mockery, be it political power or money or any of the other lubricants of human progress. Even in the supposedly purer precincts of academe, how many times had he kissed a dean's ass to get some esoteric course running, had he trawled for students like a lobsterman to meet a minimum enrollment?

The true champion of truth was not the one who tried to pursue it free of political and commercial interests—for such pursuit was bound to end in failure—but the one who aimed to wring what truth could be had from the excipients that inevitably coated the truth.

So he wasn't angry about Naomi. Queen Isabella Senzer, Jack sometimes called her. Whatever her motives in helping their voyage, she had made their voyage possible nonetheless.

Noah had said this was a fairy tale. Naomi's story was a fairy tale—a gleaming white lie that might bring other voyages out here, voyages undertaken when maybe technology had indeed advanced enough to give them a confirmed ticket home. That was certainly preferable to Aaron and his people disappearing like some lost colony of Virginia without a trace—or worse, with no word other than that they had found nothing of importance. So Aaron would let this fairy tale stand, leavened with just a bit of reality.

He composed a short message. It described what little they actually now knew about the hulk, implying without specifying that it was the source of the message Naomi had claimed to receive from the *Light Through* four years earlier. Her face would be saved. Science and truth would be served. Percival and Primakov would understand.

Aaron could straighten things out with a later message, and more if and when they returned. In the meantime, he would help Naomi imbue their voyage with a touch of myth by relaying a story of contact with alien intelligence—which was more than the mute hulk had so far conclusively disclosed.

Aaron called Nikki and told her to send his message back to Naomi and Percival. "Now let's all get some sleep this time," he told her.

But science and fairy tales and Iroquois myths about rivers flowing both ways in space were querulous bedfellows. He fell asleep thinking that the farther they progressed in this voyage, the less he could tell if he was dreaming or awake.

five

Planet reports began arriving two days later. First a few dribs of much sharper data, then the vivid storm itself. A billion K of details per second, images and instant analyses from all conceivable angles. The ship soaked up data like a paper towel. Nikki said she could feel it list with the weight of this new knowledge.

Four bodies danced into clarification on the screens—two gas giants like Jupiter, one hot little pill like Mercury, and in between them a Mars-type planet that was maybe a shade more like Earth than was Mars back home. Same general layout as Sol's system, with the Mars-type planet 1.19 AU from Alpha Centauri A—in contrast to Earth, 1 AU from Sol, and Mars, at 1.53 AU.

These were the gems whose glint the Hubble II had first seen back in 2016, when Proxima and its flares had obligingly moved out of the way. These were the minuscule dots that had beckoned throughout their voyage.

Planets. The one home of life, and intelligence, thus far known to humanity.

They were in shorter supply in the galaxy than the first discoveries by the Hubble I in the 1990s and the new millennium had suggested. Many of the planetary hints seen by that generation's telescope had turned out otherwise under subsequent, more powerful scrutiny.

Planets were a rare and wonderful thing. Alpha Centauri B—the orange sun—had none. And neither did dim, tiny Proxima.

But the crew was not entirely thrilled with ACA's bounty. They hadn't counted on finding life they could talk to out here. Their wildest practical dream had been to find life they could eat, lean against, sleep under. But from the looks of this pale blue Mars around ACA, they'd likely be leaving here tired and hungry.

If they were able to leave at all . . .

"We travel all this way just to find another Mars," Jack said, "more of what we already see in space when we look out on a clear night from our own planet. There's a poetry in that."

"More than that," Kathy said. "We've confirmed with in-person observation that Sol-type stars come with planet systems similar to our own. The fact that there's no really Earth-type planet here in ACA may be just coincidence—we could well find three Earths in the next G2 V our species explores, and no Mars at all."

"You're both right," Aaron said. He closed his eyes and explored Kathy's after-dinner brandy with the tip of his tongue.

"So our decision now, I assume, is to what planet do we devote our best attention," Jack said. "The gas giants are the most likely to have something we can use as fuel, and Mars the Second has the most chance of harboring some happy little bubble of molecules we can label as living, right?"

Aaron nodded. "For twenty years our snail space program has been doing little else but probing every corner of Mars for something more than a faint pulse of life—"

"Like trying to arouse an unconscious woman," Jack mumbled in his wine. Kathy heard him and smiled.

"—so we finally manage to escape out here," Aaron continued, "and we're about to start doing the same damn thing. There's some kind of lesson there."

"Poetry," Jack said. "Like I was saying. The singularity of life. Parallelism. Euclid's parallel postulate—two straight lines never meet."

"Stick to poetry," Kathy said, leaning over and refilling Jack's glass.

"Our problem is that we *have* met that para-Mars out there, in our own Mars," Aaron said, "and that means it's not likely to do us much good."

"Well, at least we know how to look for life on a Mars-type planet," Kathy said.

"Not really," Aaron said. "Other than the microbes and that dust-mite thing, the closest we've come to life on Mars is that stupid face of Elvis."

"Maybe we'll find the Jordanaires on this new Mars, and have a Memphis session across the stars," Kathy said and raised her glass of claret for a toast.

"Who the hell are the Jordanaires?" Jack asked, and he clinked his glass with the other two.

Nikki walked into Aaron's office with an expression on her face he had seen at least once before. "There's something strange going on with the data for Mars Two," she said.

"How so?"

"Well, what I'm seeing is . . . the planet seems to be more like Earth than the first reports indicated."

No point in asking her if their equipment was functioning properly. "Be more specific."

"OK," Nikki said. "The first stats we had on this planet showed it was maybe one-twentieth more like Earth than Mars back home is. Now it seems at least one-tenth more like Earth—it has several bodies of what look to be water on the surface, rising levels of oxygen in the atmosphere, and—"

"So is that bad?"

"Well, no, it's not bad," Nikki said. "But I just don't see how we could have missed that."

"Any signs of life?"

"No," Nikki said. "Not yet."

"Could it be some sort of drastic seasonal change?" Aaron asked. "Who knows how those things work out here, with the two extra suns and all."

Nikki considered. "Well, I guess that's a possibility. But I'd call it more of a transformation. . . . I don't know; it seems too sudden for a season."

"Same sort of thing we saw when ACA suddenly bloomed with oxygen and hydrogen," Aaron mused.

"Seems like that, yes, could be," Nikki said. "But what's the connection?"

"I don't know." Aaron shook his head. "But it's time we saw what's happening on this Mars-across-the-stars in ultimate firsthand—on the planet itself, with our naked eyes."

Aaron had long ago decided that McLaren would be the one to lead any personned exploration teams on this trip. He had the highest combined total of intelligence, loyalty, and physical resilience—each quality crucial to the success of such exploration.

McLaren was delighted at the prospect.

"But understand," Aaron said. "This planet will be no bed of roses to explore. Not because its environment is hostile—our instruments can handle that. But it seems to be undergoing some kind of change, blossoming overnight with forests and lakes we didn't see before. I don't know, maybe that's the way the seasons unfold out here. But until we can track it, understand it, have some idea where it's going, it's dangerous. Unpredictability is our worst enemy."

"Let's be frank, sir," McLaren replied. "We both know that getting down there will provide some missing pieces to this puzzle, and the safest way of doing that would be to send a robotic team. But we also know that even the best robot team would lack the flexibility and imagination of even the stupidest member of our species. Robots make decisions about where to look and what to do based on what we program into them—they have no mechanism for pursuing or recognizing or even reporting to us some flicker of an insect or leaf they may or may not have seen in the corner of their eyes. And we also know that we may not have time for more than one in-depth interactive interview of that planet. Considering the stakes involved here—could you imagine if this planet was more of an Earth-type world in its summer, which could support us!—we've got to go with people on this one. And I'm your man for the job."

Aaron couldn't bring himself to disagree in the slightest.

But there was one person Aaron needed to talk to before giving the final OK to McLaren's leading the expedition to ParaMars—his current favorite name for this new world that was coming to resemble Earth more than Mars. There were many details yet to be decided, such as when to launch the probe, when to retrieve it—before or after their swing around the star? But Aaron needed to settle something first in his own mind—something that was no doubt none of his business, but weighed on whether he ought to put McLaren in a position of peril even greater than for those of them on the ship.

He called Kathy. There was no answer. He walked over to her quarters hoping to bump into her along the way. No such luck. He waited outside her door about ten minutes. He felt like a fool standing around.

He thought for a second, then used his keyword to let himself in. Might as well wait for her in the comfort of a chair. He'd done this before, as had Kathy with his quarters. They had few secrets to hide from each other, and those they had were by and large tucked impregnably deep within their skulls.

Noah's door was open, and Aaron could see he was sleeping with the peace that only someone whose age was in the single digits could possess in this situation. The camera over his bed that fed the momscreen was off, though. Odd that Kathy would go out and leave him alone, unmonitored like this. . . .

Then he heard Kathy's voice, soft and murmuring. "I was dreaming greenness," she was saying, "the smell of the lake in the late summer . . ."

His first instinct was to leave. Kathy sounded like she was talking in her sleep, and the . . . the sensuality, the intimate longing of it, seemed not right for him to hear in these eavesdropping circumstances. But it enchanted him, and kept him in his seat.

"The water so velvet," she breathed, "when it touched my skin . . ."

"You've got to accept that you may never have that again," a man's voice said, and it nearly yanked Aaron out of his skin. "Cape Cod is a long, long way from here—"

Aaron was out of the room and halfway down the corridor before the sentence was finished. Kathy hadn't been talking in her sleep—she'd been contentedly murmuring in the arms of someone she obviously felt very comfortable with.

Aaron couldn't say he was unhappy or even really surprised with the realization of who that was.

Now he had his answer about McLaren.

———————

"Let's talk names." Jack was in Aaron's office early the next morning, plopping into the old swivel chair and putting his feet up on the desk before Aaron had a chance to take his eyes off the screen and say hello.

"OK, sure," Aaron answered. "But of what?"

"You know what."

"You mean of the new planets out there?" Aaron gestured in the direction of the real-view window.

"Exactly," Jack said. "Let's do better than our forebears on this."

"Meaning?" Aaron knew what Jack meant, but had discovered long ago that it was always better to let Jack talk.

"Come on," Jack said. "Remember the IRT line in the Bronx? You'd ride down it and see the names fly by on the stations—Gun Hill Road, Burke Avenue, Allerton Avenue, Pelham Parkway—a bunch of ridiculous names, really, that had nothing whatever to do with the people who first lived there, nothing to do, for that matter, with us and the people who currently lived there. We've got to do better here."

Aaron's thoughts jerked back to the Bronx and the old IRT elevated subway and its shaky, clacking ride. God, that was a lifetime ago.

He focused again on Jack and his demanding gaze. Just like him to worry about *names* when a hundred more important things were yelping for attention. "You seriously think there may be another intelligent species out there?" Aaron asked.

"Well, someone other than the human species presumably made that hulk—"

"Not necessarily," Aaron said. "For all we know, some earlier human civilization got here first. Hell, for all we know, Naomi Senzer finally got funding for a faster-than-light drive scheme that tested out and she beat us to it." An unworthy little nightmare, the trumping of their voyage—not without its appeal in terms of their safe return and the breakthrough for humans in space, but highly unlikely. "And if the ship isn't of human origin, that still doesn't mean that it was built by any sort of intelligence from around here. Maybe we'll find out more if we get a chance to send another probe after we swing around the star."

"Let's get back to the name of the planet," Jack said. "What are we going to do? Officially call it New Mars? After what—the name for the planet in our own solar system, the Roman name for the Greek god of war? What connection does our voyage have to the ancient Greeks and their glorification of war?"

Aaron replied tiredly, "Like it or not, the science that makes this trip possible—not to mention your own research back on Earth, including the very mode of writing in the very books you pored over about Native Americans when you were a kid—all of this goes back to the ancient Greeks. They invented logic and science and mathematics. Probably anthropology and interest in ancient peoples too. All of it."

"Not quite," Jack said. "The alphabet was invented by Phoenicians and the printing press in China."

"Quibbles," Aaron said. "We got the alphabet through Greek culture, and printing had no impact until Gutenberg combined it with the winepress in Europe. But that's not to say that I disagree with you about New Mars being a stupid name."

"And?" Jack prompted.

"And, I told McLaren that I would leave it to him to name the planet. He's more than entitled—considering that there's some chance he may never come back from there."

"McLaren? You're delegating first contact to him? Are you sure he has the sensitivity?"

"You're full of good cheer this morning, aren't you," Aaron said.

Jack looked sullen, stood his ground. "When does he leave?" he finally asked.

"I had breakfast with him before you arrived," Aaron said. "He's set to go in about six hours. The plan is to pick him up before we make the loop-the-loop around ACA. The *Light Through* will be at its slowest speed—at a relative standstill—just before it makes the swing. Bo and Nikki have it figured that the shuttle's escape velocity from the planet will be just enough to make rendezvous with us. But that doesn't leave Roger much time on the planet. So we've got to do this right away."

"I don't suppose I could somehow sneak aboard?" Jack asked.

Aaron shook his head and smiled sadly. "I know how you feel—I wish I could go too. But I'm sending just one person to that planet. It's bad enough we're jeopardizing Roger. We've got lots of redundancy in our crew, true, and Bo and Nikki have done a great job taking over

Sarah's work, but I don't want to strain that fabric any further. The rest of Roger's crew will be robots, and not only because they have a better disposition than you. They're more expendable."

"Robots probably would've been kinder to the Incas than Pizarro's men," Jack said.

"Only if they followed Asimov's laws," Aaron answered.

Jack took the point, squeezed Aaron's hand, started to leave. He turned around at the door. "Does Kathy know yet?"

Aaron thought he felt himself flush just the slightest bit. "No—I was going to call her after I'd gone through this batch of reports on my screen." He stuck his nose close to the screen to regain his composure. "If you'd like to tell her, though, I could use the time to work out some details with Nikki...."

"Sure," Jack said. "Sorry to be pressuring you about all of this. You're by and large making the right decisions." And he left.

Aaron's mouth hung open. This was the first time in his life he had ever heard Jack apologize for anything.

Aaron got no sleep the night McLaren left.

He thought again about Sarah. About Russell-Shaw. Death.

Bertrand Russell was a stallion most of his life; GBS practiced abstinence. What conclusions could you draw from that?

Sex had nothing to do with long life.

Jack was more like Russell.

Aaron had had no real understanding of death when he was younger. People just disappeared when they died, whether he loved them or not. He felt no internal connection between what caused them to die and their disappearance. Even with the *Challenger* disaster, no matter how many times he'd seen the crew's last walk to their shuttle, those awful waves to the wide-eyed video cameras, that sickly, silent explosion, Aaron could feel no real link between events on the screen and the deaths of flesh-and-blood people. He of course understood intellectually exactly what had happened. But on a gut level he could never actually picture the astronauts dying in that shuttle. He sometimes chided himself with the thought that maybe that's why he was a philosopher.

But that emotional distance had begun to dissolve as he got older, even before he'd found a place in the house of the dreamers on Mars Vestibule. A lifelong friend had been diagnosed with a deadly brain tumor, a guy he had known all his life, just like Jack. He'd watched him deteriorate; he'd watched him die. A kid he had played sweaty handball with in the playground—calm and powdered now in undertaker's makeup, Aaron recalled.

He finally seemed to be getting the message: Someone has a horrible incurable illness—he or she is going to die. Someone is thrust into dangerous circumstances—that person may well die. Wanting it not to happen isn't enough. What you want has nothing to do with death and its ways, Aaron realized.

Ironically, it was easier, for some reason, to put a group of people at risk than a single person. The numbness of numbers. He could lead a mission of nine that might never come back, and not lose too much sleep over it.

But he'd whittled this planet team down to one, McLaren, who would have no comrades-in-arms there except chips and optics, faithless shining connections that for all of their gleam were little more than sheerscreens on stilts.

Even with the best equipment in existence, and the most carefully devised plans, McLaren's life was at the mercy of a universe that had often shown itself not terribly impressed by human equipment and plans.

Six

Nikki and Kathy had a theory the next evening.

They wanted everyone to hear.

"We were looking for a common denominator," Kathy said. "What happened here on the ship three months ago when the oxygen and hydrogen suddenly appeared around ACA? What happened on the ship last week when New Mars suddenly began looking more like Earth?"

"We'd chewed over the data to a sticky pulp," Nikki said. "The only place we had left to look was in here—at our own states of mind."

"And we found that three months ago was the height of our collective desperation about not knowing how we would make the return trip. Some of us were very concerned much earlier; I know that," Kathy said, looking at Bo. Her face was creased in understanding. "But three months ago was the peak of our *collective* concern. Even Noah was asking me every day then how we'd be getting back to Earth." He was in his room now, kissed good night and snuggling under the covers, visible to Kathy on the ever-shimmering mom-screen. "Our nets had the highest incidence of notes about this then, more than four out of five. And when our need for an answer to this problem was keenest, it appeared in the form of possible fuel—oxygen and hydrogen around ACA."

"You're saying we *wished* that into being?" Bo asked, and answered his question with an exasperated shake of his head.

"No," Nikki said, "at this point, we're just talking correlation, not causation. Saying that one thing causes another to happen is a complicated claim—is the first variable a catalyst, a direct causative agent, are there other possible connections—and goes a lot farther than just noticing that one phenomenon was present when another occurred. But we think this is a start."

"But the oxygen and hydrogen turned into steam," Aaron said. "It was worthless to us as fuel."

"Right," Kathy said, "because by that time we were much more upset that we were heading to the wrong star than we were about our return trip."

"And New Mars turned into New Earth about the time we were most concerned about finding a decent place to live out here if we couldn't return," Jack mused. "I like it. A universe so sensitive it has the courtesy to rearrange itself in accordance with our needs. If that's the way it's done out here, I'm all for it."

Bo laughed with no mirth. "Sure. We click our heels together three times and get whatever we want. Ding-dong, the wicked laws of physics are dead."

"Bohr was as much the author of that kind of thinking as Baum," Jack said.

"Not really," Aaron said. "Bohr and Heisenberg and their quantum mechanics at least tried to point to a new set of laws. It was counterintuitive, the idea that mere observation of a subatomic particle could alter its spin, but it was scientific, and supported by mathematics. Anyway, I'll confess: I hate that QM stuff of mind over matter—it offends every materialist cell in my brain—even on the subatomic level. But we'd be jackasses to just ignore this pattern. How about we figure out a way to test it?"

"We're going to do a few quick thought experiments—literally—while McLaren's still on the planet," Nikki said. "Have people earnestly hope for a field or a stream or a dogwood tree near McLaren, and see if he notices anything interesting. Probably far too simplistic a procedure, but as long as he's there we might as well try it."

"Well, my biggest hope about Roger McLaren is that he's back here with us safe and sound," Aviva said.

"A toast to that," Hiro said, and raised a cup of sake.

Bo smacked his lips and grunted approval. "His equipment's functioning perfectly so far. His window for rejoining us opens in two days and will close about ten hours later. Assuming we still think it best that he rejoin us before we make the swing around Alpha."

"No other choice," Nikki said. "We know much more about our speed and exact position on this side of the star than the other side."

"Agreed," Aaron said. "So you'll proceed with your research, and we can proceed now to do justice to Hiro's sushi."

It was soft pink shrimp, wrapped in some kind of a seaweed–bay leaf hybrid that Hiro had engineered, spiced with a new kind of wasabi.

It was crisp and vibrant.

Aaron didn't feel that way the next morning, when Bo lumbered into his office and spoke in his usual blunt manner. "He's stuck. No doubt about it."

Aaron slammed his palm down so hard on the table his elbow hurt.

"I feel the same way," Bo said.

"But the images he sent us yesterday were so beautiful—the new lakes so clear—"

"That's the problem," Bo said. "Too much water."

Aaron looked at him without comprehension.

Bo continued. "There's a fearsome storm raging over his part of the planet now. Worse than anything ever seen on Earth. We didn't calibrate for it when we sent him down there. New Mars was mostly desert just two weeks ago—"

"N'urth," Aaron interrupted. "He named the planet 'N'urth' in his transmission last night, a combination of *new, Earth,* and *U*r—Abraham's home—"

"Whatever." Bo waved his hand. "The storm system down there is too much for his optics to handle."

"Has the storm knocked out his launch capability?"

"As far as we can tell, no," Bo replied. "But flying into that would be suicide—those winds would tear the shuttle apart."

"Can't those robots put in some shielding? Goddamn worthless robots—"

"There's not enough time anyway," Bo said. "We'll be well past him and on our way around the sun in a few hours. And even if he did launch and manage to stay intact, the storm would make it nearly impossible for him to rejoin us—it would be like trying to hit a moving target with a weapon that's shaking all over in your hands."

"We come all this way and we're still at the mercy of the damn weather. How about those thought experiments Nikki and Kathy were talking about—maybe they can wish the storm away . . ."

Bo looked at Aaron as if he were crazy. "They already tried that. Had no effect. You're not serious about that, are you? Even if this planet-size QM business is really happening out here, it can't be that simple."

"I'm serious about anything that could help," Aaron replied. "Maybe the thought experiments somehow brought the storm into being. *Something* is causing those changes down there."

Bo shook his head. "No one was wishing for storms. Sometimes bad things just happen. Look, at this point, I'd take help from the Wizard of fucking Oz himself, but—"

"He was an impostor behind a curtain," Aaron said.

Which was precisely what he felt like. The curtain was pulling back now, revealing Aaron naked and clueless to his crew, himself, as the universe applauded and filed out the exits. He had no answers. He barely had cogent questions. What was the best he could wish for Roger right now? That their swing around ACA not result in a launch speed back to Sol, so that they would have time to pick up McLaren after the turn, assuming the storm on the planet had subsided by then?

That could save Roger, and leave them all to die here.

Aaron and Kathy walked hand in hand with Noah, as the three went slowly through Hiro's misty rain forest loop in the single-spiral Haupt Corridor—so named because its trees and fronds very much resembled a little piece of the Haupt Conservatory in the New York Botanical Gardens exactly as it had been back in the twentieth century.

It would almost have been too spectacular to bear, Aaron and Kathy each holding this star child's hand in this place in this space, had not Roger now been well beyond their reach. They had maybe three hours before they plunged into ACA's kiddie cart derby, to be whipped around to their destiny—and the impending event was clearly riding them rather than vice versa.

"I'm too old for this job," Aaron said. "My brain's working, but nothing's coming out."

"You've already proven Naomi wrong a dozen times on this trip," Kathy said. "Don't start agreeing with her now."

Aaron smiled weakly. "I lost Roger. And I haven't a feeble megabyte of insight as to what exactly will happen to us just three hours from now. All of Jack's talk about Wise Oak, all the scientific equations about swing trajectories, all of your and Nikki's ideas about planet-size QM—it's getting harder and harder to separate the science from the fantasy out here."

"Can I try the swing?" Noah said.

"With any luck we all will," Aaron said, and hugged the boy's neck.

"I'm not sure there ever was as much difference between them as people like to think," Kathy said. "You know the first Biosphere projects in the nineties were *savaged* by the media because some oxygen or something was smuggled into the Biosphere, which was supposed to be totally self-sufficient. But the media missed the point—as always. The important thing was that those Biospheres were moving ahead—demonstrating that to a large extent they could be self-sufficient. The fact that the science was imperfect, or the experiment was contaminated, less than complete, in the long run was no big deal. This ship proves that." She pulled down a big fern frond, and inhaled with satisfaction.

"Well, imperfect science is great when it helps human lives," Aaron said. "That's the way it is most of the time, and I love it. But not if it kills McLaren." He ended in a hoarse whisper, so Noah wouldn't hear.

"Noah, could you pick that flower for me, sweetheart?" Kathy pointed to a delicate white lily of some sort a few rungs above on the corridor. Noah scampered off. She turned to Aaron. "He knows more than we think," she said quietly. "He's very tied in to all of this. I sometimes think that Noah thinks my thoughts before I think them."

Aaron looked at the boy picking flowers.

Kathy continued, "I know how you feel about Roger. I feel the same. But this is what he wanted—and we may well get him back yet on the other side of the star. And he'll live on in Noah."

"In spirit—"

"In DNA, too," Kathy said.

"What? I mean, I thought..." Aaron was certain that Jack's had been the voice he'd heard in her quarters the night before he'd sent

McLaren off to N'urth. He'd never have agreed to let McLaren go if he'd known—

"You think I'm involved with Jack now, I know," Kathy said.

"Well, I . . ." Could she or Jack have heard him eavesdropping that night?

"I guess it's pretty obvious, no matter how discreet we try to be. You can't really disguise that sort of thing, with close friends," Kathy said. "Especially in these close quarters."

"It's OK." Aaron finally pulled his senses back into focus. "You don't have to explain."

"But I wanted you to know," Kathy insisted. "Things were different between Roger and me five years ago. We were very close. And I talked to him a long time the week before he went on his mission to N'urth—we talked about Noah and what Roger really wanted from his life. He wanted to go on that mission. He wanted to go for himself, and for Noah, and for . . . well, to help fulfill this whole trip out here. So the decision was his, not just yours. And he knew fully what he was doing."

Aaron smiled again, ruefully. That was more than he could say for himself these strange days.

Kathy moved close to him, touched his cheek with her hand, kissed his lips softly. "You're doing everything you can," she said.

ACA filled up the screen, far bigger and brighter than the sun had ever shone in the sky at Orchard Beach in the Bronx, but Aaron knew there was no chance of heatstroke or sunburn. They were protected by a cocoon technology proven in nearly twenty years of near-sun encounters with Sol. *That* part of their science, at least, was well tested.

So why was he sweating?

"Temperature's eighty-four," Bo said, mopping his forehead with an ancient, grimy handkerchief.

"It's supposed to be steady at seventy-two Fahrenheit—what's going on?" Aaron asked and looked at the clock on the wall. They were some three minutes from whip-around—the instant that would be their greatest proximity to the star—and about the last thing they needed was a heat-tile failure. Damn, that had almost happened on the very first Space Shuttle flight—the *Columbia*'s in April 1981—but it couldn't happen with the eight layered levels of interredundancy they had here.

Bo shook his head. "I don't know. The tiles are performing perfectly. I think we're closer to the star than we expected."

"How could that be?" Aaron demanded. Everything up to a few seconds ago had been exactly on course.

"We're checking it," Nikki said, fingers playing the keys of her console at what looked like near-light speed to Aaron's strained eyes.

"Ninety-six," Bo said, "ninety-six degrees and rising at a quicker rate now."

"God, it's hot in here," Kathy said. Her skin was the color of spoiled milk, her mouth ringed with big droplets of sweat. Her eyes drifted upward and she swayed. Jack was over to give her support. He didn't look too good either.

Aaron was glad to remember that Noah was in his room with Aviva—the middle of the night for him. Maybe it wouldn't be so hot in there. . . .

No, that wouldn't do Noah any good. If the ship was in trouble—

"One hundred fifteen now," Bo rasped. "Whip-around in forty-five seconds."

Aaron had a vengeful headache. He took a greedy, shaking breath—the air felt devoid of oxygen.

"Nikki? Anything?" Aaron's voice croaked. His throat had a fine deposit of sand in it now, shipped in somehow for this occasion from the deserts of Mars or someplace . . .

He thought to lean against the wall for support. He might have been slipping.

"Nikki?"

His neck throbbed. He jerked his eyes around to look at the clock—twelve seconds to whip-around.

He went down. He tried not to. He didn't want to.

His eyes burned and he struggled to keep them open and he thought he saw Kathy sprawled on the floor. Her mouth and her eyes were half open.

Was Jack trying to say something?

Ah, the sweet floor—thank God, the floor—thank you, it feels so good. He hugged it. He was grateful and shuddering. But then it turned on him, punched his nose. His face was running, bleeding, with some kind of blinding liquid ...

He was able to turn his head, lift it an inch. He saw ACA huge and red and all-consuming on the merciless screen.

Nikki cried out something in the redness.

And he wanted to ask her what she meant, but the red dress was too bright for him to speak.

Seven

Aaron opened his eyes.

Kathy was on the floor, not far from him, not moving.

He crawled over to her. His legs felt, not broken, but too sore to stand. He put his ear to her mouth. Her breath felt moist. Thank God.

"Kathy," he said softly, and touched her lips with his finger. "Kathy," he said again, a bit louder.

She moaned. Her eyeballs rallied briefly beneath her lids, but they stayed closed.

He maneuvered himself next to her, so her head was close to his. Her breast was against his chest.

He stroked her face and kissed her forehead.

She was wearing some sort of a two-piece outfit. He saw a soft band of exposed skin above her belly button. He reached to touch it with a trembling hand, but stopped.

"Kathy?" he said again. He suddenly realized that he couldn't remember why she was sleeping. He wasn't sure if he was sleeping. Wasn't it the middle of the day? Hadn't the sun just been out?

He moved his lips over her face and closed his eyes, just making contact with her skin, gently parting her dry lips with his tongue. He felt her arms around his back, her tongue probing his, and—

She pulled away. "You give pretty good mouth-to-mouth resuscitation, Aaron," Kathy said dreamily.

He opened his eyes and felt blood rush to his cheeks. "Kathy, I, ahm, I'm sorry, I . . ."

"Shush," Kathy whispered. "It's all right." Her eyes were still closed. Maybe she was not yet fully conscious. Aaron wasn't completely clear about his own state of consciousness. Then it got very dark again. . . .

"We're on the other side of the star, and we're alive," someone's voice boomed out much too loudly from across the room. It was Bo's. Aaron realized Bo was talking to him.

Aaron got up on one quivering elbow and looked in Bo's direction. He, Jack, and Nikki were huddled around a control panel. Jack looked over. "You two all right now?" he asked. "You were out like lights— longer than the rest of us."

Aaron looked at Kathy. She looked OK—she was coming out of it. He was sure this was no dream now, although a few seconds ago he hadn't known if he had been dreaming or awake.

She sighed and opened her eyes. She squeezed Aaron's hand and smiled at him. Her eyes were soft and wide. They looked happy, and—

Suddenly they flared in absolute fright. "Noah! Where's Noah? Is he all right?"

"He's fine, don't worry." Jack came over, bent down, put his arm around her. "Aviva said his room got a little hot, but apparently not as bad as here."

She sagged with relief. Jack helped her up and hugged her. "Is everyone else OK?" she asked. "What exactly happened to us?"

"Everyone's fine," Jack reassured her, and extended a hand to help Aaron up.

"Like I said, we've cleared the star and we're alive," Bo said, squinting at a screen.

"And?" Aaron got to his feet, walked over as steadily as he could to see what Bo was looking at. The tone of Bo's voice said Aaron wasn't going to like it.

"And we've got maybe one-tenth of the speed we had before rendezvous with ACA, and we're losing even that," Bo said. "So much for your star swing." He bowed in bitter mock graciousness. "We'll be lucky if we have enough momentum to clear the first little planet here, let alone hurtle four light-years back to Earth."

Aaron rubbed the back of his neck—it still ached. "You were

saying something to me, I think," he said to Nikki, "before I blacked out—"

"We all blacked out," she said. "You and Kathy just a few minutes more. We apparently passed much closer to the star than we expected. And that killed our chance for the boomerang."

Bo hissed. "What chance? We might as well have done a rain dance to put out the fires on those nuclear furnaces out there."

Jack started to speak—

The com chimed. "Noah" lit up on the panel.

Kathy took the call. "Are you OK, honey?" She tried to sound casual, but Aaron could hear the anxiety still thick in her voice.

"I'm great, Momma," he said. "But I wanted to talk to you and the com wouldn't let me."

"We were busy working, honey. I'm glad you're OK."

"I'm fine, Momma. But I was wondering..."

"Yes?"

"Will we have time to visit Roger on his planet before we go back home? We're right next to it now, aren't we?"

"Yeah," Bo said half under his breath, shaking his head and staring at another screen with swirling colors. "But there's no sign of McLaren on it now as far as I can see."

The green forests of N'urth's northern continent filled the room-screen in Aaron's office the next morning.

Aaron drank in the green like medicine for the red that still burned in his eyes. He imagined he might see some sign of Roger if he looked at the screen long enough.

"You can't be serious about this," Bo was pleading. "We haven't heard a peep from McLaren since we went around the star, our telemetry can't find him, and if you rush down to that planet, who knows if you'll have the optics to get back off."

"Listen to him, Aaron," Nikki said. "The planet's changed a dozen times since we first tracked it. You don't know what you're getting into down there."

"It's been stable since we turned the star," Aaron said, eyes still fixed on the forests.

"Why are you so stubborn?" Nikki asked. "We're not saying forget about McLaren. We're saying wait a few more days to see what our readings turn up—"

"No." Aaron turned his full attention to Nikki. "We need a closer look at this planet right away precisely *because* McLaren's disappeared on us. If we can't get back to Earth, N'urth may be our only chance for survival. I'm open to other options, but I don't see any at hand. Any more information on the alien ship?"

She shook her head. "We've scanned it head to butt more than twenty times now, before and after the star, and it comes up lying dead out there every time. We could send another probe to look around at closer range, but I don't see even a flicker of energy in it."

"It's a peculiar thing," Bo said. "Usually the closer a probe gets to its target, the clearer and more detailed the image. But this hulk looks just as blurry as the first time we saw it—even from the vantage of the robot probe, right up its ass. It's like the probe didn't really reach it, even though it seems to be there."

Aaron sighed. "All right. So any ideas on what the hell almost shoved us into the star?" Hiro had come up with the wild idea that maybe the hulk had sent out some sort of energy beam to push them closer to the star, to somehow keep them from leaving. That at least would have had the virtue of making the hulk a place they could search for intelligence, maybe fuel, maybe an answer. But Nikki's readings said otherwise. And Bo—

"I don't know," Bo said. "Our calculations were all on key. I checked them out again. We should have rounded the star at a completely different angle—I don't know what went wrong."

"I'll be honest with you, Bo," Aaron said. "I know I pointed a gun to everyone's head four years ago to keep us on course to get here— but I did that because, all in all, I thought it was the best thing, the right thing to do, not because I subscribed whole hog to the star-swing theory. After all, it was only a theory, never tested before. But I wanted to give it an honest test, so at the very least, even if it failed, our failure could be of value to the people back home. What burns me now about what's happened to us is that it's as if some goddamn mysterious hand pulled us off course. We never even got a chance to try the swing!" Aaron pounded his fist near the edge of the screen display of the forest of N'urth. He was doing a lot of fist pounding these days. The trees in the image rippled as if in a strong September breeze.

Bo and Nikki just looked at him.

"So," Aaron said, "it comes to this." He gestured toward the swaying trees. "This planet looks like our best—our only—chance now. And I'm going there now. Not tomorrow. Now. In a few hours. Understood?"

Aaron and Kathy were arguing.

"It's insane to take the boy."

"I'm taking him."

"He's four years old, for crissake!"

"I'm taking him."

"I don't get it. You've been concerned to a fault with his safety until now. Why would you want him on the goddamned planet?"

" 'To a fault'? Thank you, Captain Philosopher, but after our brush with the star, the *Light Through* seems no safer than a fireball."

"True enough," Aaron relented a bit. "But what about the psychological risks to Noah? Who knows what condition we'll find Roger in, and Noah could get really upset seeing his father that way."

"Noah doesn't know Roger's his father."

"All right, but still—"

"And I feel in my soul that Roger's alive," Kathy continued. She raised her voice. "Noah wants to go more than anything else in this universe. . . . I can't deny him that. Not out here."

"This is your opinion as a scientist or a mother?" Aaron asked. Kathy wasn't making much sense as either. It was almost as if Noah, not Kathy, had just been pleading his case. But neither did Aaron want to deny her.

Noah was on Aaron's lap, Kathy on his mind as well as on the data chairs across the cabin with Jack, and Hiro was at the controls as their shuttle made planet-fall.

Hiro was an inspired choice—a nutritionist with excellent shuttle craft piloting experience. Once he landed them safely on the planet, he could feed them. Another benefit of their macroneural-net logic of interchangeable jobs and redundancy.

That left Nikki, Bo, and Aviva back on the *Light Through*. They had the collective smarts to run it if somehow N'urth decided to take Aaron's party permanently to its bosom. As for getting back home, the three on the starship certainly knew no less than Aaron at this point.

The shuttle landed in a clearing near a river that shouldn't have been too far from Roger's last transmission. They'd had a close look at this part of N'urth on the way in, and saw no sign of him.

"You know what it feels like to me," Kathy said as Hiro did a quick diagnostic to make sure everything on the shuttle was as it should have been after the landing, "it feels like Earth in our time, but with no human habitation. But most of the other life—like the trees and birds we spotted—seems pretty much the same. Strange, since a lot of that life was the result of human habitation back on Earth."

"Earth with no industry," Jack said. "Maybe there is human habitation, but not so out of balance as to scar the land. Like Iroquois New York in, say, fifteen hundred."

"No," Kathy said. "The trees look like—I don't know—like they were planted. In large numbers. Like in the New Millennium Renewals. Trees in the wild have a much more straggly, closer-together look."

"Look, Momma—those flowers are beautiful." Noah pointed through the real-view window to a purple patch of what looked like mountain laurel. They were beautiful indeed, Aaron agreed.

"Your boyhood dream of a Bronx before apartment buildings and the El come true here, eh, Jack?" Aaron said.

"Again not likely," Kathy said. "See that stand over there?" She pointed to another part of the scene outside. "Those trees look like those 2009 imports from New Zealand."

"Sometimes dreams come partially true," Jack said.

Would be nice if yours about Wise Oak had, Aaron thought. But he didn't say it. He knew Jack was feeling the pressure—his own internal pressure, far worse than anything anyone else could dish out—about his river that flowed both ways flowing just one way so far, just as Aaron was beating himself up about the boomerang theory that he'd never been sure would work in the first place.

But he also understood that Jack wouldn't have minded being taken off the hook for the return trip, wouldn't have minded settling for a good place for all of them to live, here on N'urth. At this point, what they saw through the window indicated that they were off to a pretty good start—all the greens and blues and earth tones, all the colors of home. So fine a morning, so welcoming an awning...

"OK, you're all set to go out and explore," Hiro said. "The oxygen and other factors test out just as we'd expected—lots of good clean fresh air for you. And I sent an e-mail back to Nikki letting her know that we landed OK, and reminding her not to leave the miso—"

"I'm sure it's under control." Kathy laughed. "Let's get outside and look around."

Her laugh was a tonic for everyone's nerves. Now they all looked at Aaron. "Well, yes, let's go outside. That's what we're here for, isn't it?"

He moved to pick up his chamelocase, a svelte little product of Amish neural ergonomics that always felt as if it weighed three ounces, regardless of the real weight that it actually carried. The philosophic consequences of that were too heavy for even him to consider. He just loved what it did for his arm.

"Uncle Aaron?" Noah asked. "Can I take along my pail and shovel?"

"Sure—just don't build any apartment buildings." Aaron winked at Jack and picked the boy up and sat him down on a chair, where they struggled to put on his hiking boots. Putting on little kids' boots was for some reason one of the most difficult things in the world, apparently, wherever that world was located.

They were ready to open the hatch about ten minutes later. Hiro did a final set of readings. Everything looked good. He would stay in the shuttle, in constant contact with Kathy, Jack, and Aaron—Nikki, too, if necessary.

Roger was still missing. Everyone knew that, everyone was worried. But everyone also felt good.

Aaron let Noah be the first one out—in Kathy's arms. There was no point in trying to convince either of them to stay in the shuttle. Jack and he followed. Two guys hugging either side of eighty, Aaron thought—OK, let's say the Russell-Shaw factor and gene therapy reduced their effective age to sixty, maybe late fifties, but even so—and a four-year-old boy and his mother. Some exploration party. A new universe indeed.

"What were Roger's first words here?" Kathy asked.

"Lost in garbled transmission," Hiro answered over the com.

"Why don't you say something," Jack said to Kathy. "Hiro will make sure it's recorded."

Kathy spoke in a quavering voice, unusual for her. "Here, second planet of Alpha Centauri A, is the best of what Earth has to offer you. The love and wonder of a little child, born on no planet, on a ship from Earth. Consider that, please, and not just our science. And don't forget the father of this boy who came to you last month. You wouldn't be so crude as to hurt him." And she started crying.

"I love you, Momma," Noah said, and wrapped his arms around her thighs.

Crunch . . . crunch . . . they crunched along on what seemed to be a path of maples and oaks and the occasional white birch on a high ridge by a river. The air had the smell of leaves soon to fall.

"Bronx Park East," Aaron said.

Jack nodded.

They kept walking. They didn't stay in one place long enough to examine any flora or fauna. Time for that later.

Noah wanted to investigate—"Are there wild fish in there, Momma?"—but they wanted to get to McLaren's landing site as soon as they could. "I think there could be," Aaron said to Noah, "but we'll check that out on the way back, OK?"

"OK," he said. "This place is great!" He bounded ahead and picked what looked like a mauve buttercup—a flower whose color bore no resemblance to any buttercup Aaron had ever seen in the Bronx. For some reason, this point of discrepancy was a comfort.

"Remember," Kathy called out, "it's OK to pick but don't put anything in your mouth." Noah had gloves on, tied to his sleeve and unremovable.

Noah laughed. "Why would I do *that*, Momma?"

Kathy turned her attention to the environment-taster she held in her palm. "The readings are just as they were on the shuttle—Earth-type proportions even down to the pollen levels I'm picking up here."

Jack breathed in. His face looked more lined in the real, yellow sunlight of ACA than it had in the ship's simulation of sun, but the lines were deep grooves of satisfaction. "This is my Geiger counter," he slapped his chest and said. "It tells me everything around here is good."

"Maybe too good," Aaron said, unable to resist giving voice to that qualm now.

"I was thinking the same thing," Kathy said. "What are the odds that this planet would be so like Earth, and in so short a time? I mean, we knew we'd find something like this—we know how the planet's changed in the past few weeks—but seeing this with our own eyes, actually walking around here, it seems unbelievable."

"Well, we seem to be seeing a metamorphosis here, not evolution," Aaron said, "where the end point in all its detail is already determined—to be just like Earth. But even so, I don't see how a transformation into something more like Earth, if that's what's going on here, could possibly result in such specificity of species. Unless the original material that's being acted on—the original planet—has properties we don't know about. Who knows, maybe this is how organic forms develop in this neck of the cosmos. Maybe there's less variety in DNA than we thought. Maybe matter just evolves faster here."

"Dreams are like that," Jack said.

"Like what, Uncle Jack?" Noah asked.

"Dreams can bring whole worlds into being in the wink of an eye," Jack said.

"Are you scared of dreams?" Noah asked. "You sound a little scared."

"Well, I guess I am a little," Jack said, and put his hand on Noah's shoulder.

"But I thought you love dreams," Noah persisted.

"Depends on whose they are," Jack replied. "I think we could live very well in yours."

"How much longer to McLaren's site?" Aaron asked Kathy.

She looked at her taster. "Damn," she said.

"What?"

She punched some numbers in and looked around. "We just passed it. I just confirmed with Hiro."

They all looked back over the steps they'd taken. The only places where even so much as a blade of grass was bent were the spots on which they'd trodden.

Aaron called Hiro. "You *sure* about this?"

"I just checked again with Nikki," he answered. "Her readings are pinpoint specific. No doubt about where McLaren's site was."

Aaron shook his head in disbelief. "No wonder we couldn't find a trace of him from the ship." He gestured to Jack and Kathy to come closer. Noah was scrutinizing some brown seedpods.

"OK," Aaron said quietly, "we're going to stick our faces into every pebble and piece of moss near McLaren's site and see if we can find some sign of what happened to him. The instruments register nothing, but they're not infallible. And, Hiro—please keep an eye on us and make sure we don't disappear too."

Now how's he gonna do that? Aaron could hear his conscience impersonating Nikki's voice in his ear.

Kathy pulled Noah away from the seedpods. They walked the fifty feet or so to the exact place where McLaren's craft was supposed to have landed.

"Does the grass around here look a little newer?" Kathy asked. "I don't know, a sort of softer green?"

"Wishful thinking." Jack looked around and up at the sky. "More likely due to a shade differential. Is that Alpha Centauri B over there?" He pointed to a bright orange star near the horizon.

"I believe it is," Aaron said. "Looks almost like the taillight of a plane." He contemplated the orange star a little longer. Then he got down on his hands and knees and began crawling around, eyes an inch or two above the ground. Kathy and Jack did the same. "Noah, you can help too," Kathy said, "but look just with your eyes and let us know if you see anything that seems like it doesn't belong here. But just tell us—don't touch it." She leaned over to Aaron and spoke in his ear. "I don't want him gashing his finger on some jagged piece of rubble from Roger's shuttle that cuts through his glove—if that, God forbid, is all that's left of it here."

Aaron nodded. "Not likely the instruments would've missed something like that, though," he whispered. He took no satisfaction at all in realizing that Kathy's optimism about Roger was no longer what it had been on the *Light Through*.

"OK," Noah said, already half turned to the ground. Aaron caught a graveness in Noah's expression that made him think the boy had picked up on their desperation despite their attempts to hide it. Noah also looked older here than he did on the ship.

Each of them concentrated on a different part of the little clearing.

Kathy was on her belly, snakelike, examining the soil and flora with her eyes and a variety of tiny infrared and other optical equipment. "Beautiful, beautiful," she said from time to time.

Jack was on his back, running his fingers along the underside of shrubbery branches. "Soft as a newborn's skin," he said.

Aaron had his nose to the ground. The loamy smell was intoxicating. "This doesn't seem like any kind of illusion, certainly not digital," he said to no one in particular. "The detail at these close quarters on every sensory level is too real—trees and sunshine and broad strokes like that are one thing, they're easy to paint, but I'm seeing old-fashioned little wormholes and fungi here."

Only Noah reacted. "Wormholes make me laugh," he said, and he laughed.

Aaron had an odd feeling that each of them was a bit too far away from the others. Noah was closest to him, stroking a big smooth quartz-like stone, trying to get a sense of its texture through his glove. So much for Kathy's injunction. But even Noah seemed distant—Aaron thought he should tell Noah to stay closer, to stop touching . . . but the earth that was near Aaron's mouth and nose and eyes was much more real to him. It was inside his lungs, his body. Soothing him, warming him, healing . . .

"Uncle Aaron," a tiny voice said. "I think I found something . . ."

Whose voice was that? What does it want from me? Aaron wanted to merge with the earth, every itch in every cell of his being caressed and intermingled with it—

"Uncle Aaron—"

What?

Something cold—fingers—touched his neck.

He forced his eyes open. Noah.

"Uncle Aaron . . ."

Aaron looked up at Noah, and the sky above. He felt woozy. The sky looked off yellow, like a dream thrown up, turned inside out. Aaron pulled the com to his mouth with great effort and called Hiro. His tongue moved like fast-drying concrete. "Are we OK? Are we still here?"

"Of course you are," Hiro said. "Why?"

"We're coming back," Aaron said, and got to his feet. "Let's go," he said loudly. Neither Jack nor Kathy moved. Noah took his hand.

"Uncle Aaron—"

"You go over and, ah, wake up Uncle Jack, OK? I'll see what's doing with Momma."

He walked quickly over to Kathy and touched her shoulder. She turned over. Her eyes were open, and she looked at him, but her pupils were dilated as if she were stone drunk or deep in sleep. If he'd been the physician, not she, perhaps he'd have had a better guess of what she was seeing through those floating eyes.

"Kathy," Aaron said, "come on; we're going back to the shuttle." Her pupils shrank back into focus. "Beautiful things down there," she said slowly, and reluctantly shook off some internal pleasure.

Jack was on his feet, about as unsteady as Aaron felt. "What just happened?" he said. "We didn't find any trace of McLaren?"

"I don't think so," Aaron replied. "Let's get back to the shuttle and sort it out."

Kathy put her arms around Noah and gave him a kiss. "Let's go," she said.

"OK," Noah said. "But I think I found—"

"Right," Aaron said. "You were trying to tell me that before, weren't you?"

Noah nodded, looked embarrassed.

"What's the matter, honey?" Kathy said.

"I touched it," he said guiltily. "And I put it in my pocket because I didn't want to lose it."

"That's OK," Aaron said. "Can we see it?"

"Sure," Noah said, relieved that he apparently hadn't done any-thing too wrong. He pulled a thin gray rock out of his shirt pocket, flat as a silver dollar. "This looked different," he said. "It wasn't like the other rocks I saw."

And indeed it wasn't. It was a camouflaged data disk, with McLaren's personal hologram signature affixed.

———

The hike back to the shuttle was uneventful—or rather, they were so focused on the disk that they barely noticed their surroundings. A soft, misty rain began to fall. It had an appealing pineapple scent.

Aaron clutched the disk in his pocket. It was well beyond being waterproof. It was total-environment proof—a classic ecodesign that mimicked an insignificant natural object, a rock, and thus made it resistant to natural and untutored human interference alike, as well as invisible to even the most sophisticated scanning. This in turn made it nondisruptive to any pre-computer-literate society that might accidentally find it, and untraceable by any advanced society that might *want* to find it—the perfect memopad for an ecocop obliged to steer clear of both the last Stone Age tribes that still lived along the Amazon and the high-tech *infomatiques* from the local government/rancher combos that hunted them down. McLaren had cut his teeth on these disks, and he continued to use them like Aaron's father had clung to his fountain pen. That, and McLaren's desire that no intelligence other than theirs read this disk, had likely led him to use this medium.

Jack caught Aaron's eye. " 'Better for the Borneo man to find a Carpenter disk than a Coke can,' right?" Jack intoned the ad that appeared on millions of scholarly computer screens, referring to the people whose collision with Western artifacts Edmund Carpenter had studied in the 1970s, and who long since had gone on to make computers themselves in the outpouring of electronics from all points Far East.

Kathy made five copies of the disk and telecommed its data to Nikki as soon as they got back in the shuttle. Nikki had to have a copy in case the shuttle somehow blew up or disappeared before they had a chance to look at the disk and communicate with her. She would keep the telecommed data in quarantine until their programs certified it free from viruses. Of course, the data could have a virus undetectable by any of the programs on the shuttle or the starship. Certainty of virus protection was an impossibility even back on Earth.

What could be the source of a computer virus way out here? Aaron had no idea. He'd often thought that the twenty-first century suffered from computer-virus paranoia. But better safe than sorry—or, at least, a little safer—when it came to the *Light Through*'s computer system. They'd all be dead without it.

Hiro called the disk directory up on their biggest screen. It showed nothing on the disk except a paltry 3.37 K of ASCII data. "Run the virus programs again," Aaron said. "Viruses have been known to cloak data." The programs checked not only for viruses but all kinds of hidden data. They came up clean.

"It looks like just the three K of text," Kathy said.

"OK," Aaron said. "Let's see what Roger wanted to say to us." Kathy called the text up on the screen.

First, apologies for this text rather than a full audiovisual report. I didn't have the time. I plan to leave thousands of these scattered around the planet—a lot near my landing site. If you're reading this, my plan worked. If not—well, no point talking about that, because then you won't be reading this.

Here are the highlights:

1. I know I haven't been able to communicate with you since you turned the star. Obviously this has something to do with this planet, which I'll get into in a bit more detail below.

2. I've been able to keep in good scan-touch with you throughout, though. I saw you had a pretty close call with ACA—Nikki and Bo, cutting it a bit close, weren't you? I also see you're barely moving now that you've made the turnaround. Well, at least you're alive.

3. Back to N'urth and its strange properties—I hope you like the name. As best as I can tell, the planet's in its last stages of becoming more like Earth. I think it's sort of working like a rewinding tape—you know, the closer it gets back to the beginning, the faster it moves. Anyway, the storm phase is what finally confounded my telemetry, and kept me stuck here, as you likely guessed. But then I had a little brainstorm: If I was right that N'urth was transforming more and more rapidly to be like Earth, and I could estimate the rate of change—the acceleration—then maybe I could program my telemetry to accurately reflect what the specs of this planet would be like tomorrow.

4. That's in fact what I did yesterday, and the specs so far look like they'll be right on key today. Probably my recalibration—which made my instrumentation totally out of synch with what was going on here on the planet even yesterday—made me even more incommunicado. In any case, I still can't communicate with you. But the good news is that the specs look like they'll be better than ever today. And the storms are over too. If everything stays that way, I'll be able to leave altogether.

5. Now, sir, if you're reading this, don't start shouting, but if I'm able to lift off this planet I'm going to check out the hulk with my own eyes. I can hear all your good reasons against that, and that's why I'm not going to even try to communicate with you about this beforehand. Let's face it: the hulk may be our last chance to get some fuel to return home. Someone's got to inspect it close at hand. I'm here, I have a shuttle, I've got to be the one to do this. I'll be in touch with the *Light Through* as soon as I leave the hulk, assuming I can communicate then. With any luck, I'll be back on the *Light Through* shortly after with a full report.

6. One last thing—for those of you who may be reading this on N'urth now: The planet's obviously unstable. It looks like I was right about the planet's weather today, but who knows about later. I can't even be sure that looking like Earth is the end point of its transformation. The gist is: It may or may not be suitable for us to live on. We can discuss that when I get back to the ship. But I'd advise any of you on the planet, now that you've read this, to get off as soon as possible. This world seems to, I don't know, grow on you—maybe literally—and until we understand that better, I think we're better off staying away.

—R. McLaren

P.S. Oh, yeah: Give Noah a big hug for me.

Noah had a huge smile on his face. He'd read and likely understood most of Roger's note. Aaron scooped him up.

"Are we going to go to the hulk now to see Roger?" Noah asked.

"No," Aaron said. "We're going back to our big ship."

"Incoming call from Nikki," Hiro said, ear to his com. "She's heard from Roger! He's OK!"

"On his way back from the hulk?" Kathy asked, taking Noah and kissing his face. The joy in her voice was like a bell ringing.

"I . . . just a minute," Hiro said, scrunching his face in concentration. He pulled his com away and hurried over to the console. His fingers rushed over the keys like a millipede's legs.

"What's happening?" Aaron asked.

Hiro finally looked at him. His shook his head like a surgeon who'd just lost a patient.

"Our telecom's down," he said. "Completely gone."

Eight

"Telemetry?" Aaron asked.

"No good also," Hiro said. "Same basic problem as telecom. We're not only dumb, we're deaf and blind."

Aaron was on his feet, pacing. "So tell me why we just can't take off and fly out of here with no telemetry? Many's the time I crept along in my car on fogged-in roads in Pennsylvania—so thick I couldn't see an inch past my windshield—and here I am telling you about it."

"That was before computers," Hiro said. "You weren't driving with no telemetry then—your brain was on-line. And you were able to make tiny adjustments in your speed and steering as you went along, based on all your previous experience as a driver. Here, our shuttle isn't really guided in flight by our brains—it gets its guidance from its net, and its store of previous patterns. Far too much information for our human brains to handle. But when the patterns in the stored net are too much at variance with what telemetry sees out there—when there's too much of a conflict for a match of any kind—the system shuts down. We could override it and take off anyway, of course, but that would be crazy in these circumstances. We'd have no way to control the shuttle; it'd be a miracle if we even made it through the atmosphere."

"Finicky system," Jack said.

"No, not finicky," Hiro said. "This isn't just a new weather pattern or cloud formation out there. The net would probably be able to handle that. It's almost a new planet—even the ground is giving different readings from when we arrived. Too much for any net to process."

"That's what we were feeling out there," Kathy said. "The ground was alive." She closed her eyes and breathed in deeply.

"Any way you can take a stab at anticipating the changes in N'urth, like Roger did?" Aaron asked.

"I can try," Hiro said. "But Roger's ingenious guess was that N'urth was becoming more like Earth. And he knew what that was like, knew its general patterns. But now this planet seems to be moving beyond Earth—post-Earth—it's like Earth jumping over the Industrial Revolution. Who could know where that will end?"

"I have an idea," Jack said.

He had everyone's rapt attention.

"A few years ago—actually, a few years before I joined you on Mars Vestibule—I was involved in an interesting modeling project at Columbia University. The idea was to create a simulation of what our world would have looked like in 2015 if we could erase all negative traces of the Industrial Age. I convinced them that North America, circa 1500—one of my favorite years, as you all know—would be a good baseline. We researched and projected lots of very explicit details on the climate, weather patterns—"

"We were doing that in my room last month, right?" Noah spoke up. He'd been brooding in a corner for most of this.

"Right," Jack said, "and you can help me with this now. Let's see if we can program the 2015 no-industry model into the shuttle net— maybe it'll be enough of a match for what's now really out there for us to leave the planet. I've had a feeling I've been walking in some kind of post-industrial version of Wise Oak's world ever since we got here."

"There's got to be some sort of deeper explanation for that," Aaron mused. "Can't be just coincidence..."

"Let's worry about that later, and see if we can use that model to get out of here now," Hiro said. He joined Jack and Noah—a master computer chef and his two assistants—and the three started working the keyboards.

Kathy put her head on Aaron's shoulder. "At least Roger's OK," she said after a while.

They took a food break about two hours later. "We have a fifty-eight percent match to what is out there now," Hiro said. "A lot better than zero, but still very risky."

"I'm drained," Jack said. He looked exhausted.

"You did a wonderful job." Aaron reached out and put his hand over Jack's. "All of you. What are our options now?"

"We can keep refining the programming," Hiro said. "But the planet's still in flux. We may get lucky and be at sixty-eight percent tomorrow, or the bottom could fall out and we could plummet back down again to no match."

"The problem is that our Columbia model tried to leave in place some good natural consequences of the industrial era—like trees transplanted from faraway places—and since there apparently was no actual industrial era on N'urth, it's hard to take those factors into account as we try to educate our net here," Jack said.

"All right," Aaron said. "I say we try to leave—right now."

He looked around the table. Noah was dozing in Kathy's lap. She shook her head yes. Jack and Hiro nodded also.

The shuttle took off.

It shook like a leaf in a lightning storm.

But it held its course and cleared the planet.

Everyone settled into a few hours of desperately needed sleep, and Aaron thought: So why the hell would N'urth be transforming itself into a post-industrial New York?

And if the planet proved ultimately unsuitable for their habitation, they'd still need to get back to Sol and Earth.

How?

Maybe McLaren would know. . . .

"Patch her through to me," Aaron said. "No, put her on groupcom so everyone can hear." No point, anymore, trying to keep information from Noah.

A hash of pinging garble filled the cabin, like popcorn in a microwave gone wrong.

"Something off with the telecom again?" Aaron asked. They were well away from N'urth and any influence it could have, a few hours from rendezvous with the *Light Through*.

Hiro shook his head. "No—sounds like sun static interference. Maybe augmented by Proxima's flares. I'll have it clear in a moment."

"Aaron, how are you, all of you?" Nikki's voice came through, crackling but comprehensible.

"We're fine," Aaron said. "Had a few rounds of aggravation on the planet, par for the course, but we're OK now. I'll fill you in when we get back. How's McLaren?"

"He seems to be OK," Nikki said. "We've been out of contact with him for the past thirty hours—horrible sun static out there."

"Yeah, we know," Aaron said. "But Hiro said you heard from him. He's not back on the *Light Through* yet?"

"No, not yet," Nikki said. "His bioreadings seemed OK, best as we can tell at this distance. We got just one strange line of text from him—no voice. It may have been garbled in the static too."

"What was it?"

" 'To understand this tyop, change the arrangement of its letters.' "

Noah laughed. "It's a joke," he said. "He's tied up."

"I'm not sure we got that," Aaron said. "Could you send it through in print on the screen?"

The screen glowed: "To understand this tyop, change the arrangement of its letters."

Hiro studied the display. "Could a 'tyop' be some sort of particle Roger discovered there? Some subatomic something—like a tachyon—that changes when we try to observe it?"

"Possibly," Kathy said. "More likely some kind of garbling, with the rest of his message cut off. You got nothing more from Roger?"

"No," Nikki said. "We lost contact right after that. Medscan data showed a ninety-three percent match with the last readings on him from the planet—that's well within the normal range. His shuttle was operating as it should, about halfway on a vector between the hulk and us. I'd expect him back here in about two days."

Jack was thinking about something else, shaking his head. "Not likely to be noise," he said. "The rest of the message says to change the arrangement of the letters. So McLaren was deliberately pointing to the first part of the message, and telling us that to understand it, we have to change it. That's deliberate information, not noise."

104 / Paul Levinson

"So let's change it," Aaron said.

"Well, *tyop* is the obvious word to change," Kathy said. "There aren't many words that begin with *ty*—"

"*Typo*," Jack said. "*Typo* does."

Kathy leaned over and typed onto the screen, "To understand this typo, change the arrangement of its letters." She relayed it to Nikki.

"Excellent!" Hiro said. "But—"

"Precisely," Jack said. "We seem to have made progress, but we're no better off than we were before."

"The story of this whole goddamned mission," Aaron said.

"Why would Roger send such a peculiar message?" Kathy asked.

"Maybe his commentary on our mission, indeed," Jack said.

"No," Aaron said. "Not Roger's style. More likely he was trying to tell us something . . . about the hulk . . . or about our whole predicament."

"Like: 'Don't try too hard to unravel the mysteries, for you'll get nowhere'?" Kathy asked. "What then? We just let ourselves be carried along?"

"Roger's phrase sounds familiar," Nikki said, "like something I read years ago in one of Hofstadter's books—he called them self-effacing emergent propositions, or something like that."

"*Meta Magical Themas,*" Noah said.

"What?" Kathy and Aaron asked.

"That's what the book is named," Noah said. "I screened through it in the library. I thought it had fairy tales."

"You sure you're four, and not really forty?" Hiro shook Noah's small hand in amazement.

"Noah's right," Nikki said. "The proposition deteriorates into meaninglessness even as it briefly sticks its head above its initial incomprehensibility. Our understanding gives it life and final death at the same time. That's why it's self-effacing—sort of like, I don't know, a male spider dying in the very reproductive act."

"Charming," Aaron said.

"But that still doesn't explain why Roger would communicate something like that," Kathy said.

"He was making a joke," Noah said again.

"Something may have impaired his ability to communicate," Jack said.

"How so?" Kathy asked.

"Well," Jack said, "I remember reading something once about a new kind of high-level autism that's been identified, in which people speak in short, riddlelike statements. The upshot was the Delphi Oracles and all may have been autistic—that sometimes people see so much, have so much to say, that their pathways become overloaded and all they can produce are cryptic little statements."

"But the statements have meaning?" Aaron asked.

"Yeah, they do. Lots of meaning, too much meaning, that's the point," Jack said. "But sometimes even the context is so far beyond everyone else that no one is able to understand them."

"And McLaren got that way from what? His visit to the hulk?" Aaron asked. And he thought: or who knows, maybe a delayed effect of his time on N'urth.

"Well, it's a strange star system," Jack said.

"Well, it is," Aaron agreed. "But we're running way ahead of ourselves here. All we've got so far is likely a fragment of a longer, normal message from McLaren that got cut off in transmission."

"Just a theory," Jack said. "Just an idea to scratch that linguistic mosquito bite."

"It does itch," Kathy mused. "His first message, the one he left us on the planet, was so clear. . . ."

"How long before we're back on the big ship?" Aaron asked Hiro and Nikki.

The docking felt good. Being back on the *Light Through* felt good. Aaron marveled that he felt more at home on a small starship of biospheric engineering than a planet that reminded him of Bronx Park East in May. Something not right about that. Or maybe the inside of this ship was after all more like the apartments he'd spent more time inhabiting than anyplace else in the Bronx.

The resemblance of N'urth to Bronx Park—down to the subtle nuances of color and leaf form—was stunning. Was it real or in his mind? The question, of course, was wrong. External reality and mental projection were ever inextricable. People see the world—organisms take in reality—only via the colors and shapes and forms that their senses allow them to perceive and their brains can process. To a color-blind person, Bronx Park and N'urth both would be shades of gray. . . .

Nikki and Aviva and even Bo greeted the returnees with joy. Noah scampered up and down into everyone's arms.

"Nothing more from McLaren," Nikki said.

Aaron nodded and looked at her. He'd just been talking with her on the com a few minutes earlier, and he got that odd feeling he used to get sometimes when he'd drive up to the house of someone he was talking to on the cell phone: the sense of a voice suddenly snapping into a full flesh-and-blood personage—the representation, the communication, instantly imploding back into its point of origin.

"We need to talk," Nikki said to Aaron, out of the others' earshot. It was clear that she wanted a private conversation.

Aaron advised everyone else to get some sleep, and he walked off with Nikki.

"This is about McLaren?" he asked as they walked toward her office. "He's been out of touch a long time for just sun static, even with flares from Proxima."

"No, not McLaren," Nikki said. "We're getting through to him now on audio and text, but he isn't responding. Probably just a little something out of key with his transmitter. But he should be back here in a few hours anyway."

"Good." Aaron sighed with relief. "So what then?"

"Well, it's about our QM explanation about the strange developments," Nikki said. "That oxygen and hydrogen display around ACA before we got here—and now what's happened on N'urth, maybe even why we almost got pulled into ACA."

"Ah, yes," Aaron said. "And Noah was the reason you didn't want to say anything about this in front of everyone, or even on the com to me, where it could have been accidentally heard by someone else?"

"Yeah," Nikki said. "I didn't want Noah to hear—or Kathy."

They reached her office. Nikki pressed in the entry code, and pointed Aaron to a comfortable chair by a circular table.

"Tea, Aaron?"

He nodded. Nikki slipped a cup of hot, shimmering liquid over to him along with the sheerscreen. The room temperature was perfect, but he felt chilled and tired and was glad for the fragrant tea steam in his face.

He sipped and read.

"Kathy and I pretty much worked all this out before our little slow dance with the sun," Nikki advised quietly, like a voiceover commentator. "But I put the finishing touches on—a few relationships splashed into place—while you were down on the planet."

"I see."

"The bell curve is about as clean as I've seen," Nikki said. An icon in the form of an ochre-painted fingernail traced the line on Aaron's screen. "It came into focus as soon as I realized we were dealing not with a group but an individual causative agent here—and one for which we had no background stats in any of our records, no baseline figures from Earth for comparisons. That's what made his patterns so hard to identify at first."

"Hard to believe," Aaron said, but it was indeed all there. "You know, I never cared much for subjective QM even on its well-established subatomic level—"

"We know," Nikki said.

"—but, OK, physicists want to say that two particles collide like billiard balls, travel away from each other to great distances, and you examine one and it affects the spin or momentum or whatever of the other—this offends my sense of rationality to the bone as a philosopher—but, OK, if it makes the physicists happy, if they've got the equations and the evidence, I still think there's likely some sort of other hidden-variable explanation, maybe some sort of faster-than-light signaling, but, OK, I'm willing to play with mind over matter and mysterious quantum fields of influence at that level. But on our *life-size* level? On even *bigger* levels? How? How can what we want of the universe possibly make it happen that way? How can a child's desires create hydrogen and oxygen out of nothing—turn a Mars-like planet into something that feels like Earth?"

"I don't know," Nikki said. "Maybe part of the answer is that the rules of cause and effect, of mind and matter, are somehow different in this part of the universe. Maybe our approach to ACA at half-C, our slowdown, our being caught between the lingering gravitation of Sol from behind and the burgeoning ACA in front, maybe this accordion somehow acted as an amplifier to QM forces that back near Sol operate only on subatomic levels."

"How?"

"I don't speak *how,* Aaron," Nikki said. "All I know with confidence is the data. Look." She caused more fingernails to light up on his screen display. "Here."

An icon pointed at the appearance and disappearance of the hydrogen and oxygen.

"Here again."

Aaron saw the blossoming of N'urth.

"And watch here."

Before Aaron's eyes was the *Light Through*'s near-collision with ACA, a vivid virtual rendition.

He began to perspire.

All of this correlated far too well for coincidence with Noah's wishes, confided to Kathy, Aviva, him, everyone on the ship, expertly gleaned from days of interviews by Nikki, and set out in a "wish" graph that accompanied each of the renditions on the screen. Extremely convincing.

"But Noah didn't want us to crash into the star," Aaron said.

"No, of course not," Nikki said. "I think he just didn't want us to whip around the star as we'd planned and go on our way back home. He was afraid we'd leave McLaren behind. He wanted to see the new planet. He's a four-year-old, for God's sake. He just wanted what he wanted and had no idea what the consequences would be."

"He picked up our concern that N'urth wasn't enough like Earth to support us if we had to stay there," Aaron said, "so he, what, somehow stimulated the planet to grow into the Earth he knew—parks and sanctuaries on his viewscreens, stories from Jack about the Iroquois, a make-believe purple flower or two thrown in for good measure, as any little kid would do? Difficult to believe that a single brain could have such sway over matter."

"It shows maybe we don't know enough about the matter out there," Nikki said. "Or not enough about that single brain."

Aaron gulped the last of his tea, lukewarm now. "So Kathy knows most of this, some of this . . . ?"

"I think she knows a lot of it. She'd have to—she's his mother. That's why I wanted to talk to you about this first. I mean, she's his mother, and she'll naturally want to protect him. But we've got to protect the ship in case Noah wants something else. In case—"

"I understand," Aaron said. "I'll talk to Kathy."

"Good," Nikki said. "I know you're very close to the boy. He's obviously extremely intelligent and means us no harm. If maybe you could explain to him what's happening here, before something else happens—"

"You think another transformation is on tap?"

"Well, he's been talking a lot since he got back about visiting the hulk. But so far all the readings are steady."

The com chimed—call for Aaron, routed from his office. The letters "Ivanoff" appeared on the screen.

Aaron put him on holaround. Ivanoff looked worried.

"Bo," Aaron said.

"McLaren's back, a little sooner than expected," said Bo.

"Wonderful!" Aaron replied.

"Not so wonderful," Bo said. "He's not talking."

"Not talking to you?" Aaron asked. "I don't—"

"Not talking to me, not talking to Hiro, not talking to anyone. Period. The man's totally unresponsive."

Nine

Aaron knocked on Kathy's door the next morning. She let him in, with a weak smile.

Noah was asleep in the other room. An endless loop of Drifters' songs spun softly in the background—minor chords, glistening edges, save the last dance for Russell-Shaw . . .

"I saw something in his face," Kathy said. "He wants to talk to us, but for some reason he can't."

"Jack may be right," Aaron said. "God knows what he encountered on that hulk—it may be beyond any human ability to convey."

"But it's so *frustrating*," Kathy said, and started to sob. "It's one thing to explain his behavior with our theories. But to see him—just sitting there—*wanting* to talk to us but just not able . . . It's not fair. All of my training, and I can't do a thing to help him."

Aaron touched her cheek, brushed away a tear with the fleshy part of his thumb. The droplet was warm. "It's way too soon for despair," he said. "Roger could be fine tomorrow." He took her hand. "He seemed the most responsive to Noah."

"Predictable, based on Jack's theory," Kathy said, breathing in slowly and exhaling. "Noah represents the least pressure to Roger, probably because Noah couldn't understand what it is that Roger wants to tell us."

"Whereas all the rest of us presumably could?"

"I don't know," Kathy said. She squeezed his hand. Something changed in her expression. "We need to talk about Nikki's equations, don't we?"

"Well, yes, I would have last night, but with Roger in the shape he's in—"

"And you feel uncomfortable talking to me about my son, because he is, after all, my son, and my mother's feelings might get in the way of what's best for all the other people on this ship," Kathy said.

"It's not like that," Aaron said.

"What's it like, then? Tell me," Kathy said.

Aaron looked at her. "Very complicated," he said. "First, I'm still not sure I completely buy Nikki's theory. I'm an old-fashioned cause-and-effect chauvinist—I think it takes physical energy and materials to move mountains, not just minds—and I find it hard to swallow that Noah's mind did all this. Maybe there was something else in the brew that Nikki's correlations overlooked. But, second, if Noah did do it, I wouldn't say at all it's something we need to be afraid of—maybe just the opposite. We're very low on fuel now. With N'urth so unstable, we're running out of options. I'd hoped the hulk might give us something, but McLaren's condition is hardly a good portent for that. If Noah's mind does have some power over physical reality, maybe we can use it for our benefit."

Kathy shook her head and smiled again, in a rueful way that hurt Aaron's eyes. "I think that Noah's lost any special ability he might have had."

Aaron looked at her. He thought about putting his arm around her, giving her consolation. But for what, exactly?

"Can we start at the beginning?" he said softly, at last.

"Oh, Aaron," she said, "there are so many things about me and Noah you don't know. I wanted to tell you. . . ."

"It's OK," he said. "We're all entitled to what little privacy we can find in this fishbowl."

"They're the things you realize, think you realize, in the middle of the night," Kathy said. "Then the next morning you're awake, you go about your business, and you're not sure. Maybe I was imagining it . . . maybe I was crazy. I didn't want you to think I was crazy."

"No chance of that. No chance."

"But now I'm sure of what I was feeling. I know it was real," Kathy said.

"It's OK," Aaron said.

"He's an extraordinary child," Kathy said, beaming as if she were talking to herself rather than to Aaron. "I knew, I think, long before he was actually born. I could feel the presence of his mind inside mine—like an urge, a wonderful urge I had to follow. Not to really do anything—but, I guess, to think of things. And it was . . . intensely pleasurable."

"What things?" Aaron asked as gently as he could.

"Cosmic things, good things, really hard to describe. When I felt in touch with him like that, I felt that somehow all was in synch in the universe. Those words are too sweet—not sweet enough, I don't know—the feeling can't be described by words. Words make it too brittle."

"And after he was born?"

"The urges became more specified. Nursing was unbelievable, like nothing I'd ever read about. The milk would start to flow before we were in the same room. And I'd know for sure that that's exactly what he wanted. And the feeling of feeding him, of nurturing him—of knowing that what my body was producing was still giving him his energy, his life—was, again, beyond description. Because I could feel not only my own pleasure, but his too—and the whole thing was exponential. And it changed me. I've felt closer to the cosmos since then. More open to it."

"And the later effects—on the star and the planet—were like Nikki said?" Aaron asked.

"Yes and no," Kathy said. Her eyes were closed now, as if she were reading a screen on the inside of her lids. "He never really created anything out of thin air. It was more like he selected—magnified—forces and systems already in place. He pulled processes into prominence on the star and the planet—processes already there. Like my nursing—I don't think he would've been able to get any milk from you." She opened her eyes. "I didn't fully understand it. I still don't. You saw some of it, like the way he made me feel that the best thing was to take him down to N'urth. I could see in your eyes then, when we were discussing it right here, that you understood something was going on."

Aaron nodded slowly and thought for a few moments. "Convincing you to feel a certain way is not the same as changing a climate."

"To him they were," Kathy said. "Thoughts and matter were both in his grasp, equally manipulable by his mind. From what I know of physics, it's not so impossible. Just quantum mechanics writ large out here."

Aaron considered. "Why do you think his powers are gone now?"

"I felt it down on N'urth," Kathy said. "I felt Noah's need to stay there—that's what he wanted, as much as he'd wanted us to have fuel when the oxygen and hydrogen appeared; as much as he'd wanted us not to get lost when they combined into steam and we saw we were on course to ACA after all; as much as he'd wanted all the other things. That's why he wasn't affected by what we all felt down there. He was the source. But he changed down there. Something about N'urth—not finding Roger there, I don't know—made Noah get a little older. Or maybe he'd have outgrown his power wherever he was. But Noah is different now. More articulate, less inchoate. He's gone from wanting and creating to understanding."

Aaron exhaled slowly. "Hard to believe any kid could have such power. Hard to believe anyone could. And yet I hate to think that it's gone." Here they were floating eight years away from home with maybe a month's worth of fuel at most. No damn breaks on this trip. A possible avenue that he'd thought impossible to begin with now closed up ahead because its Peter Pan grid had decayed from old age. At age four.

Kathy was crying.

Aaron put his arms around her and held her close.

Acker Bilk's "Stranger on the Shore" was playing in McLaren's room. Kathy said she'd tried more than two hundred recordings in the past few days, and McLaren was the most responsive with this in the background. She thought maybe this was because "Stranger on the Shore" had been playing the night Noah was conceived.

The reedy music reminded Aaron of the JFK assassination and a girl with no name and the best tight skirt he'd ever seen. But the dance was ending and she was too far away, on the other side of the room. And Bilk's clarinet breathed on.

Aaron was too far away to get to Roger now too. He'd talked to him so many times since he'd returned, always with the same null result.

"I know how hard it must be for you," Aaron said. "If you could just meet us a little way, just give us a clue of what we need to do to . . . free you."

Roger slumped down in his chair. Aaron saw tears in his eyes.

"This has to do with that ship out there, right?" Aaron pointed toward a viewscreen, darkened now. He had no idea if the hulk was really out there in that direction. "You saw something there; something happened to you."

McLaren stared at him.

"Noah may have unusual powers—may have had them," Aaron said. "Kathy and Nikki think he somehow set the molecules in motion that made N'urth change so fast. I don't know. Maybe his talent also helped him discover the disk you left there. We felt so good, all of us, when we read your note. Your first note. And now you're so close to us again—I just wish you could be a little closer."

"No," McLaren said.

Aaron nearly jumped out of his shirt. "Great to hear your voice!" But was that *no* or *note* or *Noah*?

Aaron put his hand on Roger's shoulder. "If I ask you questions, is there any way you can shake your head or move your eyes to indicate a simple yes or no?" Kathy had been through this with him already a dozen times, but he'd just uttered a word and Aaron had to try.

McLaren stared through him.

"Don't worry; it's OK," Aaron said. "We'll find a way."

Aaron lay in bed a long time with eyes wide. Above his head was a beautiful star chart constructed by Aviva. Sol and Alpha Centauri A sparkled like two bright beads at either end of a colorless string, running through the middle of a fabric made of cyberspace. Why shouldn't the human race tie together *real* space?

That's what had motivated this trip. . . .

He felt a soft wet brush—like a tongue—on his chest. . . . He must've been sleeping. The tongue and the lips drifted slowly up his chest to his mouth, and he smelled hair, *her* hair. . . .

"Kathy . . ."

Her body was on top of his, nipples taut and pressed against his chest and shoulder, her thighs over his . . . and he was inside her.

Her mouth was warm and open and her tongue flicked around. His hands slid from the nape of her neck down her back.

He had some vague recollection of a Japanese philosopher who counseled love without orgasm as a way of enhancing and sustaining pleasure. But before Aaron fully realized what was happening, the good old American way had prevailed. . . .

Kathy sighed in contentment and nestled her head against his shoulder. "I've wanted to do this for a long time," she said.

"Me too," Aaron said, and ran his fingers along her scalp. "I wasn't sure if I was dreaming when we almost fell into the sun."

"You weren't dreaming," she said dreamily. "Something about you old guys. I feel drawn to you."

"*Guys?*" he said half jokingly. "Oh, yeah. Jack."

Kathy tensed a bit and pulled away. "Come on. You've known about Jack."

"I'm too old to be jealous," he said, "gratitude is the more appropriate emotion." But he did wonder whether her attraction to Jack and him might be another expression of this QM business. Maybe that's what Noah wanted. . . . But he didn't feel like going down that path now.

Kathy snuggled. Her eyes fluttered closed on the side of his face.

"So," he said. "Why tonight?"

"The time was right tonight," Kathy murmured.

"Yeah." He kissed her softly and closed his own eyes.

"The time was right," Kathy said, even more sleepily. "We need another baby."

"You're being foolish. I'm not mad—at you *or* her," Jack said.

They were talking on top of Haupt early next evening. Each had a glass of clear red wine. Cool stars shone through the real-view window over their shoulders, making a light show of the wine and vying with the palms and pineapple plants in Hiro's garden for their attention.

"There's old Sol." Jack motioned with his wineglass to a star shining brightly near the Cassiopeia–Perseus border. "Biology's the best science we've got to get back there now. I've had a nonexistent sperm count for years."

"You love her?" Aaron asked.

Jack looked at him with exasperation. "You aren't listening. That's not the point anymore—if it ever was, anywhere."

"You're betting that the laws of physics are different out here than in our solar system," Aaron said to Kathy later that night, "and somehow your children can control them."

"You have any better ideas at this point?"

"We're talking three to four years for our baby to attain the kinds of powers Noah had over stars and planets. *If* she attains them. *If* Noah in fact really had them," Aaron replied. Morning-after tests had confirmed the conception as well as the gender of their child. They'd already named her too—Alicia—after his grandfather Al and Kathy's grandmother Alice. And because this whole strange journey had had an Alice in Wonderland quality from before day one. Wormholes and rabbit holes seemed much the same in this part of space.

Back on Earth, even on Mars Vestibule, Aaron never would have gone for being a father again. Not even by proxied sperm. But now that it had happened, he had to admire the boldness of Kathy's move. It sang to him on lots of levels. Emotional, physical, even political.

"You think Alicia won't be like Noah?" Kathy asked.

"She's a girl and he's a boy," Aaron replied. "Who knows what effect that has on this? Then Roger's DNA and mine aren't the same. He's Irish, good Gaelic stock with maybe one or two Norse insertions, in the same place going back at least a thousand years. I'm Jewish— my people came up to Spain, then across Europe to the *shtetls* in Russia and were raped by droves of Mongols and Cossacks along the way. Our genes are very different, Roger's and mine, and the interaction of his specific genes and yours could well be responsible for Noah's abilities, if he had them."

"You still doubt them?"

Aaron said nothing. Then, "I'm not sure. They certainly haven't been demonstrated with any scientific rigor."

"Maybe Alicia will make a believer out of you. . . . Look, I agree we're on very shaky ground here. I know Noah had those powers.

Maybe no one else will. But maybe any child born on board out here, or just away from Sol, will have grand QM capacities."

"So what's our next step?" Aaron finally allowed himself a small smile. "Encourage Nikki and Aviva to get pregnant too?"

Kathy returned the smile and kissed him. "Not tonight."

So far, Jack was the only other one Aaron felt he could talk to about this. "We've got to do something sooner," Aaron said the next morning. "We'll certainly be shit out of luck and fuel and stuck here long before our baby's even born unless we come up with at least a short-term solution. We can't afford to leave everything up to what powers Alicia may or may not have four years from now."

"Only three possibilities I can see now if we want to do something other than let fate take its course," Jack said. "Back to N'urth—"

Aaron shook his head. "No, that's the worst—my sense is we barely got off there in one piece last time."

"Agreed," Jack said. "So we can take a closer look at the two gas giants out there, but Nikki says they don't seem to have much, if anything, of the kind of gas we need to drive home."

"Right," Aaron said. "Leaded in an unleaded tank."

"Worse: helium in an unleaded tank," Jack said. "So that leaves what the hulk out there might give us."

"Which so far seems like McLaren with a fused central circuit," Aaron said.

"Perhaps," Jack said. "Maybe even likely. But so far the hulk is the option we know least about. I can't see turning our back on it."

Aaron weighed the possibilities.

Jack continued. "I'm just saying the hulk is the only real option we've yet to explore. We can't be sure that it rather than McLaren's long stay on N'urth is what caused his problems. So its drawbacks are less than N'urth's—since we all felt the planet's strange impact down there—and presumably more than the gas giants'. But the big gasbags have nothing for us. So when you add up the risks and possible rewards, the hulk wins."

"Let's talk to the rest of the crew about this."

Ten

"How is it that I know you've come here to object to our trip to the hulk?" Aaron asked Nikki and Bo, who had come to see him in his office. "Yesterday afternoon you said you liked the idea."

"We're objecting, but not to the trip," Bo said.

"To what, then?" Aaron invited them to be seated.

"The personnel," Bo said.

"Oh?"

"You're too valuable to do this," Nikki said. "Look what almost happened to you down on N'urth."

"We've been through this before," Aaron said. "First, I don't want to risk anyone else's mind on that hulk. You see what's happened to McLaren. Second, this may well be a one-shot, all-or-nothing fling. Who knows what we'll find on board. Whoever's on the scene may have to make immediate life-and-death decisions affecting everyone else on our ship. It's proper that that's me. It's my job to make those kinds of calls."

"We agree with almost all of that," Bo said. "Which is why we can't entrust it to a philosopher past eighty who believes in Indian voodoo and some half-baked genetics about George Bernard Shaw."

"And the operative epithet there is what, Bo—philosophy, age, voodoo, Russell-Shaw?" Aaron knew it was all four.

Nikki reached over and put a calming hand on Bo's. "Aaron, with all due respect, I—"

"You agree with him, I know," Aaron said.

"Not that you're too old to be trusted," Nikki said. "But Bo's best qualified to evaluate the fuel possibilities on site on that hulk. You know that's true."

"Fuel's not the only concern," Aaron snapped back.

"Now *you* look," Bo said. "You badgered us into letting you go down to N'urth. You badgered us into continuing the trip out here when we knew there wouldn't be enough fuel to get back. You can't hold this mission by the balls forever. Other people have a right. Our lives deserve to be in *our* hands sometimes—not always yours."

"He's right, Aaron," Nikki said.

Aaron looked at them. Time to compromise. Roger was in no position to help in this argument. Kathy had Noah—and Alicia—to think about. And what Bo and Nikki were saying was not without merit. "All right. But only you go," Aaron said to Bo. "You stay," he said to Nikki.

"But the shuttle needs at least two if we don't want to leave it docked on the hulk," Nikki said. "Robots aren't reliable enough, given what we don't know about the hulk, to maintain the shuttle in near-hulk space."

"We'll send along Hiro, then. He's a good pilot. I'd rather our food suffer for a few days than our computer operations." The truth was, and they knew it, that he was more concerned about both of them unchecked in what could be a pivotal decision situation on the hulk than he was about their computers here on the ship, which could be tended to just fine by Hiro and Aviva. But he hoped that the proposal of Hiro rather than Jack or himself for the shuttle would sweeten this just enough for Bo and Nikki to take it.

Aaron wasn't completely sure of Hiro's loyalty or judgment either—certainly he wasn't as consistent as Roger or Kathy or Jack. Aaron still wasn't completely clear whose side Hiro had been on in Bo's attempted mutiny. But Hiro had never overtly opposed Aaron. And it really didn't matter anymore. Aaron had to trust someone who could fly, someone who might be acceptable to Nikki and Bo.

The two looked at each other. Fortunately they seemed to see that half a loaf could provide some sustenance too. "OK," Nikki said, "we can live with that."

"We'll need to do this right away," Aaron said.

"I'm ready," Bo said. "I'll call Hiro."

"We'll stay in constant contact now," Nikki said.

Bo's response took a long time to reach them. Constant contact was more holes than contact out here. He was within boarding distance of the hulk. The *Light Through* was at what Nikki had reckoned to be a safe distance—about half the distance from Sol to Earth—should Bo's intrusion cause the hulk to blow up or do something dangerous, like emit radiation. Probably much more than a safe distance for anything they could logically expect might happen, much less for what they could not.

Nikki's words took about four minutes to reach Bo, and his reply the same to get back. Eight again, Aaron noted. The number of years it had taken them to get from Mars to here. The number of minutes it had taken him to hustle across Bronx Park in a copious sweat on his way to the 205th Street subway station as a kid—late as always for whatever his first class happened to be at City College down on 125th Street. Late again.

"OK," Bo said. "I'll tell you what I see as I see it."

The hulk had precisely the maddening lack of clarity Bo had earlier described—no matter how close the probe, how powerful the computer scan, its image defied complete resolution, as if it were actually much farther away than it otherwise seemed to be, or was somehow not one but an infinite number of spherical vessels piled one on top of another. The rungs of an old Slinky toy, always slightly out of synch . . .

Each of the crew dealt with the tension in a different way. Kathy was on the couch with her knees up and her legs tucked under, listening to Leslie Gore on an open speaker, as Aaron recalled a friend's sister doing in 1964. Nikki was on the computer, stroking the keys as if she were playing with a lover's fingers. Aviva was looking deeply into the screens, pixels no doubt swirling in fantastic new arrangements in her head. Jack was looking beyond all screens, into space somewhere, perhaps seeing things the rest of them could not. Noah was napping. And Aaron stole a glance or two at the Alpha Centauri suns, A and B—a pair of gleaming persimmons in the real-view window now, one feisty yellow, one purest orange—when he wasn't watching everyone else.

But McLaren wasn't staring or listening or tense at all—he was beyond tension, outside it all, in a world in which eight minutes and eight years and eight seconds were likely one and the same.

"OK, I'm going to inspect this thing with my own eyes," Bo said. "My best telecom readings here are exactly what all of our earlier reports said. No sign of life or fuel or anything."

Nikki jabbed a key that said "OK" to Bo. "How the hell did it even get there without leaving a trace of its fuel?" she wondered aloud to the rest.

"That's what Bo's there to find out," Kathy said.

"Why are we all assuming that the ship was self-propelled?" Jack said. "Just because ours is? Maybe something else towed it out there."

"Nice of you to speak up now," Aaron said, "after we've been discussing this for weeks."

"Only just occurred to me," Jack said.

"And it is a good point," Kathy said.

"Sure, it is," Aaron said. "Let's add it to the list of explanations. It's some kind of illusion—we're living in Noah's dream. No—it was created by Noah, but it has an existence of its own now. Or, it used a propulsion system invisible to us, or one we can't understand. Maybe a self-consuming propulsion system, like a battery that collapses into something that looks nothing like a battery after it's used up. Or, it didn't really move in the sense we understand motion at all. Actually, it stood still, and created space and time structures around it, including—let's go for broke—ACA and its family. And now a new one: It was brought here by some kind of action at a distance, a celestial tow truck. Any other candidates?"

"Maybe it was shot out of a cannon, like a projectile," Jack replied. "There are dozens of possibilities." He looked at Aaron. "You don't enjoy playing with possibilities like you used to."

"Only those that have a chance of getting us home," Aaron said. "A spent projectile or a barge that needs a tugboat does us no good at all, without the gun or the tug."

"Magic in a cosmic tit," Nikki said. "That's what Bo always said our fuel to get home was. Question is whether we'd be able to milk enough reality out of it. I sure hope that hulk ran on something better."

"The man has his own eloquence," Jack mumbled. "Give him credit for that."

"So far she's like a nightclub on Christmas morning," Bo said, as if on cue. "Empty. Nothing."

Jack half laughed and grunted.

"How much longer should we leave him there?" Aviva asked.

Nikki gestured to a bank of teeming, tiny schematic screens. "He's already eyeballed more than eighty percent of the ship," she said. "Not much more to see there. We've got it all recorded. We'll be able to fine-scan it all. But so far it looks like more of the same blurry images on the inside as the outside. Empty and unclear."

"Maybe the ship, inside and out, was designed to defy any precise observation," Aviva mused.

"Like a protective cloaking or camouflage," Nikki responded. "It's certainly a possibility."

Aaron sighed. "This is likely our last rational shot."

"Doesn't mean it's our last shot," Jack said.

"I know," Aaron said. "I know." He looked at the time, and at Nikki. "How much longer do you think he'll need to see the rest of the hulk?"

"Three to five minutes," Nikki said.

"All right. Bo." Aaron spoke deliberately into the com unit, though it would have picked up his voice wherever his mouth had been pointed. "I want you to leave the hulk and return to us as soon as you hear this. Hiro, as soon as Bo's back on board, please leave the vicinity of the hulk and dock with us." No point in risking Bo's life—or mind—any more than need be.

Kathy put her hand over Aaron's. He could tell from her touch that she knew he was losing his faith in the possibility of their coming up with a way to get back to Earth. He could also tell that for some reason—maybe their child—she still had hers. This gladdened him. But it didn't make the future of the *Light Through* seem any more under their control.

And then there was Jack, who seemed neither especially hopeful nor hopeless. He had the air of a man who'd cast his fate to the wind, and now was content to wait for the next breeze.

Aaron wondered how all of them could be right.

Three things made themselves known upon Bo and Hiro's rejoining the *Light Through*: Their ship seemed to have a bit more fuel aboard than previously calculated (good news). They seemed to be heading, for no apparent reason, back toward ACA (not good news). And Bo was not the person he was when he left to enter the hulk (not necessarily bad news—but unsettling because of the obvious parallels to McLaren).

Hiro was talking at a meeting. "I heard your message to return. Certainly. But I don't know about Bo. He showed up on my shuttle with a hurt look in his eyes. He says he has no recollection of receiving an order from you to return."

"Hurt?" Kathy asked.

"Yes," Hiro said. "Hard to describe in words. But his expression reminded me of a peach bruised under the surface, in such a way that the skin wasn't really broken or even darkened, yet there was something different in the sheen—something speaking of a blow earlier received."

"A blow to the psyche," Kathy said.

"Perhaps," Hiro replied. "Yes."

"But why'd he return to your shuttle at that time if he heard no order to return?" Nikki asked.

"I don't know," Hiro said. "That's the problem. I agree—it seems too much to be a coincidence. Maybe he heard your message but then forgot it."

"But you don't believe that," Aaron said.

"No," Hiro said, "I don't." He closed his eyes and reached for the right words. "I think it looked to me like he was operating in reverse. Like he was retracing his own steps . . ."

"But not because of my message?" Aaron persisted.

"No, not because of your message. And not of his own accord. It was like some force had pushed him back again to the shuttle."

"A force from the hulk?" Jack asked.

"I don't know," Hiro said. "Maybe, but my instruments picked up nothing."

Nikki agreed. "We've gone over the shuttle's data a thousand ways to Sunday, and there's no trace of anything from the hulk."

"In other words, no change in the hulk from the first time we saw it. Dead, dead, dead," Kathy said.

"Yes," Nikki said.

Jack said, "Meaning, no sign from the hulk that was picked up by our instruments."

"Well, right," Nikki said, "but what's the point of talking about something that we can't in any way perceive, even through our instruments?"

"OK, please," Aaron said. "Let's not get into another debate about Kantian epistemology. Yes, there may be something about that hulk, but our instruments can't perceive it, and if our instruments can't pick it up, and we have no knowledge of it, there's no point in talking about it now. Let's move on."

"Oh, there's definitely something strange about that hulk," Kathy said. "Turned Roger into an autistic, and took away a piece of Bo's memory. No doubt about that. Bo wasn't down on N'urth at all. So if his mind's going the way of Roger's, that could only be because of the one new experience they both had in common: that hulk."

They met again the next morning.

"He's not exactly like Roger," Nikki said. "Bo's grown sullen, withdrawn, introspective. He's sleeping a lot. It's like he saw or sensed something there that his mind can't quite handle. Something that drew so much energy from his mind that it had to shut down a part of itself to continue to function."

"It overloaded Roger's completely," Kathy said.

"He was likely there longer," Aaron said.

"Paradoxes are like that," Jack said. "From the point of view of information theory, they can drive you crazy—they perpetually invite you to bring more information to a situation than you can possibly handle. Every time you come up with a solution, you come up with its unraveling. 'This statement is a lie'—if it's true then it's a lie, but that means it isn't true, which means it's a lie, which means it's true—"

"We can't send anyone else back there," Aaron said. "Whatever paradox Bo experienced, if that's what it is, he'll have to tell us about it."

"He may not be able to," Jack said, "if he's still caught up in it in some way."

"*We* may not be able to," Kathy said, "if we're still experiencing it—if we're a part of it."

Nikki sighed. "Now you see why I don't like talking about things we can't measure. At least we have a clear indication of our increasing fuel."

"Really increasing?" Jack mused. "You sure?"

"As sure as I can be that anything I'm seeing or reading is real," Nikki replied. "We apparently have more fuel in our holds than we did last week—weight, gauges, ship's performance—all are in line with the increase."

"Impossible," Aviva muttered.

Hiro asked for another meeting after dinner that evening.

"I think the food's different too," Hiro said.

"What do you mean?" Aaron asked.

"The amount of food is more like last week than two days ago," Hiro said. "I realized this just this afternoon."

"You mean the quantity of food has increased—like our fuel?" Aaron asked.

"Yes," Hiro said.

"Is the increase in the living plants and organisms, or in the food already harvested?" Jack asked.

"Is that important?" Hiro responded. "Don't know for sure. The increase I'm certain of is in our food stores—in our harvested food, ready to eat. We keep about three hundred—"

"That's OK," Jack said. "We don't need the numbers. But you say you don't know if the live nursery stock increased?"

"Well," Hiro said, "let's see. I looked at them also a few hours ago, and, no, I'd say they haven't increased at all. They're as they should be."

"Hmm," Jack said. "OK, how about some of the more inert hydroponic equipment—you know, the tubing, that kind of thing?"

"What are you getting at, Jack?" Aaron asked.

"The difference between living and nonliving material," Kathy answered for him, "or maybe between living and formerly living matter."

"Not sure what you mean about equipment," Hiro said "You mean is there more of it, less of it? I'd say it's the same."

"I mean is it showing wear and usage as it should be?" Jack said.

"Oh, I see," Hiro said, "though I don't know what that would tell us. No, I don't know about wear on the equipment. I'll have to check."

"I'm with Hiro in not knowing what this is telling us," Aaron said. "We've got anomalies in mental phenomena, in McLaren and Bo. We've got strange occurrences in physical material, in food and fuel increases. But not in living organisms? What's that add up to?"

"Nonliving material, living material, thinking material," Jack said, eyes focused on nothing, or on something well beyond the room. "Someone made that distinction in a paper I heard at the AAAS way back in the ancient 1980s," he said to Aaron. "Three different realms. Three different properties. Maybe three different responses to the river that flows both ways."

"Nikki," Aaron said, "I'm still not getting what Jack is talking about here. But do a scan of everything you can get a light on in this ship. Let's see if there are any other . . . increases."

"OK," Nikki said. "But I can tell you right now about at least one other thing that's increasing: our approach velocity to ACA."

"Can't we control it?" Aaron asked.

"I'm trying," Nikki answered.

"Are we on a collision course this time?" Aaron asked.

"I don't think so," Jack replied.

Eleven

Water combed the beach in green foamy swirls. The tide was receding, each swirl claiming a minute-hand less of the sand. Close up revealed a thousand hermit crabs and nearly as many snails scurrying for food or sun or whatever they craved on the drenched, exposed shore.

Could have been near the rocks at Montauk, or maybe the Brewster Flats at the start of low tide on Cape Cod Bay.

Except it was a beach on N'urth. They were approaching the planet again, on a course that Nikki was unable to change.

A world without a moon . . .

So how come it had tides?

And how could Noah, who'd never seen Montauk or Cape Cod or anything similar on Earth, have had anything at all to do with its configuration?

Aaron had looked over their library holos very carefully, and the fact was that, as extensive as the library was, it simply had no images of this kind. It did not, after all, have an image of every possible scene on Earth.

So how could Noah have copied this? How could he have copied that which he never saw?

Aaron sighed and looked at the time. It was after midnight. Nothing more he or anyone apparently could do about the *Light Through*'s new trajectory. Nikki was sure, at least, that they wouldn't hit the planet. She and the rest of the crew were trying to get a few hours of sleep. Aaron had tried and couldn't. Might as well put the time to some use.

He sat down at his screen and opened a file: "Memo: re: Noah's Method."

He didn't have the answers, but whatever he had he needed to write down. Now, while there still was time. He'd do it in philotext—a philosopher's hypertext tool he'd helped develop more than twenty years earlier. It allowed the careful thinker to put together all kinds of reasoning chains on the screen.

Of course, the chains were rarely stronger than their weakest links, and most of the connections he had were very tentative. But even if he had only unanswered questions to send back to Earth, they were a lot better than nothing.

> QUESTION: Assuming Noah had the powers Kathy believes, how could he have copied images of Earth he never saw?
> ANSWER: He didn't copy.
> INTERPRETATION 1: Noah was not responsible for N'urth.
> INTERPRETATION 2: Noah was responsible, but not via copying.
> If INTERPRETATION 1 is the case, then
> INTERPRETATION 1a, Who or what else was responsible?
> Or, INTERPRETATION 1b, What was N'urth that it behaved this way?
> Since INTERPRETATION 1a and 1b require additional information not currently available, let us table Interpretation 1 for now.
> That leaves Interpretation 2: Noah's power utilized some technique other than copying.
> ELABORATION: He was a builder, a creator, but not via blueprints. For blueprints in some sense look like what they engender, are recoverable via reverse engineering from completed structures.
> CONTEXT: Deriving a blueprint for a house already built is trivially easy.
> OBSERVATION: Nothing about understanding N'urth is trivially easy.

BACKGROUND DETAILS: Here is this new planet. Here
is everything that Nikki and Kathy say Noah has done.
But no one has the vaguest idea of how he actually did
it. Here is Kathy carrying my baby, which she thinks
might be able to do something like this again, something
that might help us, yet no one knows what that "this"
even was.

Aaron frowned. No, that wouldn't do. Alicia didn't belong in this
report—not yet.

He deleted the text beginning with "Here is Kathy..." and resumed typing.

Perhaps someone does know. Maybe McLaren. But he
seems incapable of communication now.
NEW QUESTION: What did McLaren see?
ANSWER: Impossible to say.
QUESTION REFINED: What did he understand?
ANSWER: Same.
CONCLUSION/PATH: Back to Noah.
QUESTION: Did Noah bring these realms into being? Yes
or no?
ANSWER: Not known, but not via blueprints.
FOLLOW-ON QUESTION: How, possibly, then?
PATH: Back to McLaren.
FACT: McLaren wrote, "To understand this tyop, change
the arrangement of its letters."
STATEMENT CATEGORY: A recipe for self-effacement.
FOLLOW-ON CATEGORY: A warning? Maybe.
BEST CATEGORY, ONE WORD: Recipe.
ANALOGY: Living recipes.
BEST ANALOGY, ONE WORD OR PHRASE: DNA.
ELABORATION: Maybe Noah worked by creating self-
actualizing, evolving recipes—

Kathy walked in.
"You can't sleep either," he said.
She nodded, came over, put her arms around him.

"I can get back to this later," Aaron said.

"No, you finish up." She kissed him. "Want something to eat?"

"I'm fine," Aaron said. "I'll just be a few more minutes."

Kathy left the room and Aaron returned to his screen.

It was blank.

"Damn." Aaron checked the four places where his file should have automatically been saved. Only one had the file—it had been saved there a split second earlier. The other three places bore no indication of a file at all. Aaron called the file back to his screen. It disappeared in the directory.

"What the hell . . ."

Then it vanished on his screen as well.

Aaron shook his head in frustration. Just what he needed now— a wonky computer. A cyber-corollary of Murphy's Law: Computers always seem to act up at the worst possible time.

Well, there was nothing he couldn't re-create later in his philotext. He'd mention this to Nikki in the morning. He put his computer to sleep and went in to join Kathy.

He thought he could hear Alicia's heartbeat, with his head next to Kathy's belly, but it was only the blood in his ears. She was barely old enough to have a discernible heart, let alone a heartbeat.

Thump . . . thump . . . They would miss N'urth, but were still speeding at full, irrevocable force toward its sun.

Jack thought they weren't on a collision course.

Why not?

Jack needed more time to work out the theory behind this, but he thought they would swing around the star, just like before, close as Aaron's ear was to Alicia. Close but untouched, he'd told Aaron.

Iroquois insight? It didn't matter. Nikki seemed unable to affect their course in any case.

N'urth's stats were holding steady—no real change there since their visit: a couple of hurricanes in the southern hemisphere, a quake halfway between the equator and the northern pole. Nothing obviously untoward. Maybe the place was really stabilizing. Made it all the more tempting. Aaron hated to pass it by. But who could say what was brewing below its surface? Who could say what it would be like tomorrow?

McLaren's stats were sadly holding steady too—no real change in him since the day they'd picked him up in his shuttle. The last thing anyone could want was that Roger would stabilize in his current condition. Aaron hated to even think about what lay below Roger's surface. But he expected that, sooner or later, if he wanted to help Roger, he would have to figure it out.

Jack thought they had a chance. The legend come true.

"I can almost hear Alicia's heartbeat," Aaron said to Kathy.

She put a cool hand on his head and pulled him close.

The second twirl around the star was nothing to write home about. It was close to ACA, all right—the same exact distance as last time—but they were able to manually boost the eco-cooling system so that everyone on the ship was comfortable.

Just as Jack had said.

Aaron invited Bo to lunch in his office the next day.

"You're looking much better," Aaron truthfully said.

"Thanks," he said. "I'm feeling good too."

"But we still don't have enough fuel to get home," Aaron said.

"Right," Bo said, "nowhere near enough, our increase has been small—we have now pretty much what we had when we first approached the star."

"Yet you're feeling good," Aaron said. "Feeling good even though we have nothing like enough fuel to get back home now. That's not like the old Bo at all."

"Right," Bo said. "I'm feeling good. But that *is* like the old Bo. Because fuel's no longer the issue. We're not running on fuel anymore."

"But Nikki says that—"

"I know what Nikki says," Bo said. "It's an ingenious idea but it's wrong. That star or hulk couldn't have done anything to our fuel to make it increase *because* it was consumed. Goes against a much-too-basic law of physics. Consumption is consumption. Less may be more in psychology, but not in reality."

"Nikki's backup explanation is that the instrument readings are wrong," Aaron said.

"She's been listening too much to you," Bo said. "Meanwhile, our ship is still moving. In the right direction. If we were really out of fuel, and the readings incorrectly reported an increase, we'd be drifting on inertia in space by now."

"Well, the momentum from our new swing back around the star—"

"Isn't enough to move us anywhere," Bo said. "But even if it were . . . Open your eyes—our velocity's increasing much faster than any of the boomerang equations can explain. Something else is going on out here."

"So what's your explanation for this?"

"I don't know why this is happening," Bo replied, "but I can tell you *what* I think is happening: We're rolling back in time, back in time and place to Sol, where we started."

Aaron scoffed. "Jack's saying the same thing. I'm surprised at you. That's no more scientific than Wise Oak's vision."

"I don't deal in visions," Bo said. "I work with tangibles. And if they point in a certain direction, I go with it. Frankly, my backward-in-time theory feels a lot more scientific than all that stuff about Noah. Time and space and speed have been linked together by physicists for years. Who knows, maybe what you think was caused by Noah's powers was brought on by our approach to the point where we'd soon be reversing in time." Bo shrugged. "So tell me, how are *you* feeling these days?"

"Good," Aaron said. "I'm fine."

"I'm glad," Bo said. "I mean it. Are you feeling any younger?"

Aaron laughed. "Even if we *were* rolling back time, not enough of the rollback's occurred for me to really feel it in that way—eighty and eight months is as much a decrepit age as eighty-one."

"Give yourself time then," Bo said. "Maybe you'll see what I mean."

"But if we are rolling back in time, how come we remember what happened on the far side of the star?" Aaron asked. "I remember clear as day when we picked you up at the hulk."

"Everything's a haze with me about the hulk," Bo said. "Maybe it affects different people differently. I didn't say I had all the answers yet."

A chime indicated an urgent incoming call. "One minute, Bo." Aaron turned his attention to the console.

"How much you wanna bet that it's one you've already seen before," Bo said.

No, it couldn't be that simple. A time reversal, if that was what was going on, couldn't be that straightforward—nothing on this trip had been.

"I'm out of here, Bo—we'll pick this up later." Aaron rushed out the door.

Kathy was having some sort of abdominal pains.

Muscle spasm, false alarm, please; that's what he was praying for.

The seconds it took Aaron to reach Kathy's office seemed longer than their whole damned trip.

But every once in a blue moon or an orange star, prayers are answered.

"It's OK." Kathy pointed to the screen, where a zoegram of Alicia, no bigger than a fist, floated in holographic insouciance. "She's fine. I'm OK. Whatever caused the pain is gone. These things happen all the time back on Earth."

"Yeah," Aaron said, "but most people on Earth aren't going through what we are now." He helped Kathy off with the equipment and off the table. He hugged her.

Alicia's recorded three-dimensional image was still afloat on the screen. "She's beautiful," Aaron said. Then it winked out.

Aaron muttered something about computers and tapped the machine.

Kathy pulled him over and put his hand on her stomach. "Who cares about the image? Alicia's just fine in here."

"Yeah," Aaron said, and smiled at the baby within.

"You were worried that the time rollback could hurt Alicia? I've been talking a lot about the fine points of that with Jack and Bo."

"I don't know," Aaron said. "If we really are in some sort of rollback, then Alicia could be the first way that we'd notice its effect on people. She'd—she'd cease to exist in a few months. And then Noah. He'd get younger and younger and then just disappear halfway back to Sol? I can't bear thinking about that."

Kathy zipped up her blouse, then sat down to put on her shoes. "No," she said, and rubbed her stomach. "Alicia's fine. I'm sure of that. And Noah's better than ever. His special capacities are gone, but his intellect's as powerful as ours already—maybe in some ways stronger."

"You thought his GQM powers were fading before any of these rollback effects even began," Aaron said.

"Right," Kathy said, "so their disappearance doesn't seem connected to whatever's going on now. Although—I guess a last gasp of Noah's QM powers could have brought on the time reversal, if that's what it is."

"Maybe the time reversal will bring them back," Aaron mused. "Hard to tell which end is up, just what's caused what, at this point. Jack thinks the strings that tie matter together are really rubber bands. It certainly then wouldn't be implausible that on a ship hurtling at half the speed of light to a star that flips the ship on its ass and bounces it backward in time, that on a ship like that a young boy's brain, in its developmental stage, under that kind of expanding and contracting pressure of time and space, could achieve some sort of quantum mechanical power over matter, and then lose it. Bo was just suggesting something that could fit in with that. Nikki was talking about our slowdown from half-C being like an accordion in space even before the time rollback. Who knows."

"Too bad it didn't have that effect on older brains too," Kathy said.

"Thanks, but mine's too far gone for any power in the universe to have any effect on it, I can tell you that," Aaron said.

Kathy smiled. "I was serious. You know, there could be a lot of good in this rollback—in addition to getting back home, of course. You and Jack would lose a few years; Roger could get his right mind back. And . . ." Her smile vanished.

"Let's pray it doesn't work that way," Aaron said. "The kids are more important."

"They're OK. I told you," Kathy said. "You're OK too." She reached up and kissed him full on the lips.

That pleased Aaron. She's getting used to me as the father of her baby, he thought. Our baby.

"Let's see her again," Aaron said. "Would that be OK?"

"Sure," Kathy said, and grinned. She undressed and they hooked up the equipment they had just disconnected.

They watched Alicia's live zoegram, an image of life sprung from its place.

Aaron carefully put his hand through the edge of the gram, and brought it to rest, palm up, under Alicia's shimmering soul.

"No doubt about it now," Nikki said to the assembled group the very next morning. "Unless all of our instrumentation on every level of redundancy is wrong, we've rolled back in time about five months. If the pattern continues, we'll soon be well on our way back to Sol."

"Just to be clear about this one more time: The instruments are not just replaying the readings they had five months ago; they're accurately and completely reporting increases in fuel and all the other stuff now?" Aaron asked.

"It's really happening, Aaron," Nikki answered. "Jack and Bo were right."

"We're going home," Bo said. "*You* were right," he said to Aaron and Jack. "I'm big enough to admit that. The river flows both ways. Not as a boomerang in space, but in time."

"Apparently," Aaron said. "But what does that mean? If we wind up back at Mars Vestibule eight years ago with no knowledge of what we've experienced, this whole trip will have been a complete waste of time—literally. Maybe we can send out some kind of record of our experience . . ."

"If what's really going on is that time is rolling back for us," Jack said, "then sending out a record won't do us any good—it'll be subject to the same time rollback."

"Meaning?" Aaron asked.

"Meaning that the record will stop existing shortly after we send it anywhere," Nikki said. "It will have become part of a later time that no longer exists. Same applies to any messages we try to send to Naomi back on Earth—they'll never arrive. Same for any messages we already *sent* to Naomi or anyone—they'll get caught up in the rollback too. By the time we get back, no records that we exported from the ship during the voyage will be in existence. They'll be gone—if this rollback is really going on—just like our sixteen years."

Aaron thought about how he had agonized over what kind of message to send back to Naomi in response to Percival's. He thought about his philotext analysis. Even the recording of Alicia's zoegram. All gone, or soon to be. Aaron exhaled slowly. The consequences of this were daunting. "OK," he said. "I think I'm getting it. But if we're really in a time rollback, shouldn't we be seeing replays of the messages we've *received* here in the past years? I mean, if we received a message from home on our way here—like the one I got from Percival five months ago as we were just entering this system—shouldn't we be seeing that message again now, as we pass through the same time point on our way back?"

"Right," Nikki said. "Makes sense—I hadn't thought of that."

"Yet we haven't received that message again," Aaron said.

Nikki looked uncertain. "I don't know—maybe the time rollback isn't entirely uniform."

"That's what I've been trying to say all along," Jack said. "Though I'm not sure how this message phenomenon fits in."

"Well, look," Kathy said, "the very fact that we can talk now about receiving a message five months ago shows that our cognition is not being rolled back."

"That, and Roger's condition is the same, regrettably," Hiro said, as if Roger weren't in the room. Then Hiro realized Roger was, and bowed his head apologetically in Roger's direction. Roger stared someplace toward the center of the table, with an expression that said he understood either everything or nothing at all.

"I wish I could help you," Bo said to Roger. "I think a tiny part of my brain is like yours—I've got a hole in there somewhere, but I can work around it."

Roger looked away from him.

"So we seem to be in some sort of...fuzzy rollback in time," Aaron said. "The material indices are mostly clear. But the living and cognitive gauges are contrary."

"Right," Jack said. "There's probably something more going on here."

"The macro QM business again?" Kathy asked.

Aaron knew she was thinking about Alicia and her possible powers. Kathy had told him that so far Alicia didn't seem to have the same intrauterine sway over her as Noah, though Kathy couldn't say exactly when Noah's persuasions had started.

"Not likely," Nikki said. "Whatever was going on then seems to have stopped—completely."

"Yes, of course it would," Kathy said. "As far as Noah's impact is concerned. After all, if our cognition is not being rolled back, there's no reason that we would be recapitulating any mental phenomena from five months ago. And GQM is obviously cognition driven. No, I was thinking..."

"About Alicia?" Nikki completed the thought.

Kathy nodded.

"Well, I guess we'll just have to see," Nikki said. Aaron knew that she was less than pleased about even a long-shot prospect of another child with Noah's erstwhile possible powers in their midst. He'd talked to Kathy months ago about keeping Alicia secret for a while, keeping his fatherhood secret for a while, maybe for forever, from some of the group. They'd gone over all the options, and decided that secrets like that didn't make much sense in this ship.

Others likely shared Nikki's mixed feelings about Alicia, but Aaron had no intention of taking a poll. He caught Aviva's eye, though, and she was smiling at him. A genuine, open smile. It warmed him. He looked up at Noah's image, projected on Kathy's mom-screen. He was sleeping so peacefully. You wouldn't believe, looking at that image, that he had had much power over anything....

Aaron smiled back at Aviva. *Thank you. Glad you're here. I've probably paid less attention to you than to anyone else on board, but I'm glad you're here.*

"Any chance this could somehow bring Sarah back to us?" Aviva asked. "I mean, I can't see exactly how that could happen—her just popping back into our ship, alive, from deep space—but still..."

Jack shook his head slowly. "No, I don't think so. Life and intelligence seem to be moving one way in this rollback—forward. Our lives are going onward, our memories continue, we're all getting older against the backward flow, while nonliving materials, our ship, the fuel and nonliving things in it, are going the other way, *with* the reverse flow. So I can't see how the nonliving material of Sarah could make the leap over that gap and become alive again. I guess it's possible her body could rejoin the ship—and I guess anything is possible here; we'll just have to wait and see—but I think her life is gone from us, gone for good."

Aaron shuddered.

"In the meantime, even the results of the GQM are disappearing," Nikki sighed. "N'urth is beginning to look more like Mars again than like Earth."

Aaron focused on what she was saying. He suppressed another shudder. Good thing they hadn't decided to stay down there.

"It should be that way," Jack said. "N'urth should be affected by the rollback—it's a material system, comprised of some living components, but a material system on the whole nonetheless."

"Like this ship," Nikki said.

Jack nodded.

"But our ship's going back in time, and we're alive, and N'urth's going back in time too, but it's losing its living systems," Nikki said.

"Right," Jack replied. "Because the *Light Through* in its past state was designed to support life—us—but the planet down there was not."

"But there was life down there," Kathy said.

"Yes," Jack said. "But the planet itself is a primarily physical system. All planets are. The idea that they are somehow unified living organisms—the Gaia hypothesis—is just a metaphor."

And the river that flows both ways isn't? Aaron thought. Maybe not. This time rollback seemed to be making Jack's river more real and less metaphoric by the minute.

"But the hulk's still there," Kathy said. "And it's apparently material."

"Yes," Hiro said, "which shows the hulk is not a result of our GQM, not something that emerged with our visit. It was there, like Alpha Centauri A itself, before we ever arrived."

Bo grimaced. It was a quick, involuntary gesture, but deep.

"Typo," McLaren blurted out.

"What did you say?" Nikki asked.

"He said *typo*," Kathy said. "*Tyop* to *typo*. Maybe progress."

They all looked at Roger, hoping he'd say something more. He stared impassively on.

"Maybe not," Kathy said, and went over to him and rubbed his back.

"Maybe not for Roger—as yet—but maybe for the universe," Jack said. "Maybe the rollback is a recipe for human settlement of the cosmos that respects the harmony of being, one that returns things to their proper place after we leave. Cleans up our litter. A self-restoring system. A recipe—as you were exploring in that vanished philotext you told me about, Aaron—a rearrangement of letters, of the materials they represent, from humanly created confusion to natural coherence. Tyop to typo. A recipe that, as they used to say, is EC, ecologically correct."

"A typo's coherent?" Nikki asked.

"Good point." Aaron nodded. "But even if it is, how, given this time rollback, can we even communicate this revelation back to Naomi and everyone on Earth?" If there was just some way they could position information, records, analyses like his philotext, to jump this time barrier . . .

"Why don't we just tell them when we arrive?" Bo asked.

"Won't work," Aaron replied. "If we really are returning to Sol via a time reversal, then for everyone at home it will seem like we never left in the first place when we return. They'll have only our word for what happened out here. Why should anyone believe us, with no proof or records?"

"You're recordocentric," Jack said. "Lots of unrecorded recipes throughout history have been lost to us. Whole cultures. But somehow their messages still got through."

"Like your Wise Oak," Bo said. Not sarcastically. Not confrontationally. Just said. Aaron marveled.

"Yes," Jack said.

"We've got to do better," Aaron said.

"We already have," Kathy asserted. "We have children. Their very existence speaks louder than any recipe or record that we've been away from Earth. And the rest of us will look sixteen years older."

Assuming we're all still alive, Aaron could not help thinking.

Bo nodded sympathetically. "But I'll be honest with you," he said softly, intensely. "I don't really care about recipes and proof. All that matters to me is getting home—all of us. I'll tell you a little story, a true story, from my own family. My father had no money. He could have borrowed some from a bank, he could have bought a home for us with a mortgage, but he had to figure out all the possibilities first. And so he spent his life figuring and figuring, and he died living in a putrid, peeling flat in Saint Petersburg. That's where I come from.

"Meanwhile, my uncle also had no money. But he didn't give a damn. He borrowed some money, moved his family to Sheepshead Bay in Brooklyn, and bought a nice house. My father said, Miklosh, you're crazy. How will you be able to pay back the mortgage, pay for the house you're in? And my uncle said, I'll get in the house first; I'll live in the house and figure out how to pay later. Meanwhile, I'm enjoying my house—I'm in my home.

"And that's all that counts now. Getting back home. We'll have the rest of our lives to figure it out later."

Aaron held Kathy's hand as they looked out at Alpha Centauri in the real-view. Kathy was very pregnant now. ACA, on the other hand— the sun they had traveled eight years to encounter—was a quarter of the size it had been the last time he had looked. It had merged together with its orange sister now, rejoined her, into a single zygote of light.

"Are you sorry we did this?" Aaron asked, moving his hand right over where he thought Alicia's head might be. "It looks like Alicia won't have the powers that Noah had." Noah was on the other side of the room, reciting something to Roger—the letter Roger had written to them on N'urth, which Noah had memorized.

"For all we know, Alicia *had* the power, and created in a few hours the whole time rollback that we're now a part of," Kathy said.

"No limit to the number of wildflower hypotheses we can pick from here." Aaron hugged her and kissed her on the neck. "Part of the charm of this whole affair. I should learn to enjoy it more."

"You should," Kathy said. "Who knows what kind of feelings and powers a baby in the uterus really has—especially out here in space. But science aside, I'm thrilled with our baby." She nuzzled against Aaron.

"There's no doubt now that none of us is getting any younger," he said. "The time rollback has no effect on us—just the nonliving things around us, things most likely to follow the arrow of time wherever it goes. Let's say the Russell-Shaw longevity factor makes me the equivalent of sixty. People die younger than that. Look what happened to Sarah. I hope Alicia knows her father."

"Don't be ridiculous," Kathy said. "You're mixing together too many things. Sure, a twenty-year-old—Christ, a little child—can get killed by a car whose scanners are off, can die of unexplained natural causes. There's no protection in the universe against that. That's what happened to Sarah. Could happen to me. Could happen to you. But the *odds* are, the great likelihood is, that you'll live not only to see Alicia born, but her children. Same as me."

Aaron nodded. "I have no grandchildren back on Earth. I was very unhappy about that—never really accepted it, never was resigned to having my line die out, melodramatic as that seems. But what could I do about it? Argue my philosophy of life with my eco-minded kids? They said it was just my vanity. Now . . . now everything's changed. We'll be returning with a baby young enough to be *their* granddaughter."

"The important thing is we're returning," Kathy said. "All of us, and our baby. You should be happy about that."

"I am." Aaron put her hand to his lips.

"As for the rest," Kathy continued, "the ripples you might make coming home an unexpected father in your high eighties—well, that'll be the least of the ways we'll be shaking up the people back home when they see what we've done on this trip. We'll show them. All the Earth-glued losers. We'll show them the future."

And their eyes never wavered from Alpha Centauri.

Part 2

Omega Centauri

Twelve

Noah

Aaron looked around the Seder table. "Everyone knows why we're gathered here this evening," he said, and talked about the meaning of Passover, the Jews as slaves in Egypt, the meaning of the wine and the matzo.

And Noah, nearly ten years old now, thought about the Stones—the Rolling Stones—one of his favorite groups, and their song "2000 Light-years from Home." Well, they weren't that far—Earth was just two light-years away now—but what were a few more decimals among friends?

Around this table sat everyone in Noah's world—everyone he'd ever known in this universe. Aaron with his plush felt yarmulke on his bushy white head, Jack with the little frown that was really the smile that Noah knew was always there, and Noah's biological dad, who still couldn't talk to him with words. . . . And Uncle Hiro and Uncle Bo and Auntie Aviva and Auntie Nikki—"*auhntie,* not *antie,* Noah—even an honorary aunt doesn't want to be called an *ant*"—were at the table. And of course his mother. And, oh, yeah, Alicia too.

". . . and the *charoseth* symbolizes the mortar that the Jewish people used to build the pyramids when they were slaves in Egypt," Aaron said, and passed the stuff around the table. It was a mixture of apples, cinnamon, nuts, and wine—delicious, a lot better-tasting than the ancient mortar must have been. Everyone smiled and nodded their appreciation to Hiro.

Alicia was asking the four questions. "Why is this night different from all other nights?" she asked.

"Because we're still way out in deep space, traveling backward in time?" Bo asked.

Aaron laughed. "That's as good an answer as any," he said.

Of course, for Alicia and Noah, space wasn't different—it was the same. Planet life would be different. And as for traveling backward in time, that's all Alicia had ever known. And even Noah had no real memory of what the ship was like when the fuel and food stocks and everything else got less and less as they were used, not more and more.

"Noah, would you like to take over the reading now?" Aaron asked.

"Sure," he said. Noah read aloud about the four sons—the wise son, the wicked son, the stupid son, and the son with no capacity to inquire. The wise son already understood the reason for the Seder, so the Seder was not necessary for him. The wicked son, with his arrogance that none of this was true, put himself outside the group, so the Seder wasn't for him either. (Noah always felt like him, because he didn't really believe the ancient stories.) The stupid son's questions could be answered very quickly and simply, so no entire, convoluted Seder was needed for him. But the son who had not the capacity to inquire— he posed a problem because no one could know *what* was on his mind. So he was the reason for the Seder, and the telling again and again of the Passover story.

Noah knew what everyone was thinking when he talked about the son with no capacity to inquire. They were thinking about his real father, about Roger. Noah took Roger's hand under the table and squeezed it. It's OK, Dad, he thought.

He could tell Roger the story of their voyage, like the story of Passover. How Aaron had half tricked the government to get this voyage going. How Uncle Bo had almost mutinied halfway out but Aaron talked Auntie Nikki into overriding Bo. How the crew lost someone they loved—her name was Sarah. He could talk about the hulk, about their rollback voyage home. But Noah felt certain that Roger already knew all of that, and more.

"Let's eat," Aaron finally said, and passed a plate of Hiro's chicken soup that Aaron swore was better than his grandmother's. She must've been one great cook, Noah thought.

Nikki and Bo and Aviva and Hiro were gone by eleven. Roger too. Alicia was sleeping on the couch. Aaron and Jack and Kathy were talking around the table, aware that Noah was there but talking as if he weren't, a scene he'd been part of so many times.

"You're worried because you can't do anything," Jack said to Aaron. "Worried not so much because there's a clear-cut problem, but more because you couldn't do anything if there were. We've been over this before."

"That's right," Aaron answered. "We have no effect on the universe around us now—anything we do hasn't happened the very next moment, so every cause is robbed of its effect."

"Has a nice ring to it," Kathy said dreamily. She finished off a glass of sweet red wine.

"May have a nice ring," Aaron said, "but it means we've lost our power, utterly, to influence anything beyond this ship other than in the infinitesimally immediate term. Even here, inside the *Light Through,* there are lots of things we can't do. We just all go along with the reverse flow. And, yes, that always worries me."

"We didn't have all that much effect on the universe going out to Alpha Centauri in the first place," Jack said.

"There's always some loss of control when you're going into the unknown," Aaron replied. "But that was a different situation entirely."

Jack shook his head. "You express a culture that puts itself above the flow, that thinks it can reorder events to suit its purpose—"

"*I* can do things," Noah blurted out. "I can make events have consequences. I plant seeds and they grow."

That was a mistake, Noah realized. He should learn to keep his mouth shut. That way he learned a lot more. This way, he attracted everyone's attention.

Sure enough, Kathy started to say it was his bedtime—

Fortunately, Aaron broke in. "You're right," he said softly and reached over and rubbed Noah's back. "You do have some power to make new things happen, because you weren't part of the time we're rolling back on. But so far, as best as we can tell, your power—and Alicia's—is strictly local."

"And seeds are living systems," Kathy said.

"I know," Noah replied. "We can do things with living systems. All of us. And I can make other things happen here too, inside the ship, but anything that I try to do outside the ship—like sending out a test marker—is gone the next minute too."

"Right," Aaron said, "because those markers are subject to the ship's backward displacement in time."

"I know," Noah repeated. "I understand. But here's what I was thinking about: *I* could go out in one of our shuttles. Since I wasn't part of your trip out here—we're past the part of space where I was born, right?—don't you think I could control some more things from that shuttle? Because I wouldn't be part of our ship's backward, uhm . . ."

"Space-time field," Jack said.

"Yeah," Noah said.

"Out of the question," Kathy said.

"You might have more control out there," Aaron said, "and then again, you might just disappear. Because that's not your time. Here, the ship's internal temporal field—comprised in part of our own living processes—seems to protect you. I know, it's complicated, and we don't fully understand all of it yet either. But that's what your mother, and all of us, would be worried about if you left this ship."

"And also," Jack said, "why would you even want to try that? Our rollback is going fine just as it is—we're right on course back to Earth, to the instant we first left on our voyage."

"I don't know," Noah said. "I guess I want to find out what I could do out there, free of this ship. The *Light Through* is the only place I've ever known—I really have no idea what's going to happen to us when we return."

Aaron said: "You're right about that. I think we all feel that way."

"Out of the question," Kathy said again.

They finally agreed to a limited shuttle jaunt from the ship, with Hiro as well as Noah aboard. The shuttle went about 100,000 miles, then suddenly bounced back to the ship—"like a rubber band contracting," Hiro kept saying—though he was pumping the shuttle in the opposite direction.

"The ship's space-time field is too strong," Aaron said to Jack and Kathy, when they thought Noah was asleep in the next room. "The shuttle couldn't overcome our reverse momentum. Could be Hiro's connection to the past is stronger than Noah's freedom from reverse, or maybe Noah's freedom just doesn't extend beyond this ship."

The ship had an area, a field—both inside it and a certain unknown distance around it—that was traveling back with it to the past, Aaron reasoned. Everything in that field was part of the time rollback. But it was even more complicated, because in addition to the ship's field, Aaron thought people on the ship had their own reverse-flowing fields around them too. Everyone except Noah partially and Alicia completely—because Noah wasn't around for half of the trip out, and Alicia wasn't at all. Except now Noah's was probably completely gone too, because the ship was way past the point in deep space where he was born. So: Noah goes with Hiro on a shuttle in a direction away from the ship, trying to break loose of the ship's reverse pull if he can. They go a fair distance, and then: *pop,* they snap right back to the ship. Probably because the combination of the ship's backward pull along with Hiro's outweighed Noah's if it still existed.

"Inconclusive," Jack agreed.

"How's this gonna end?" Aaron asked. "I feel like we're prisoners of this process. We get back to Mars Vestibule the instant that we left. The sixteen years that have just passed for us traveling at half the speed of light, out to Alpha Centauri and back, haven't happened yet for anyone else, haven't happened for the nonliving systems on this ship. And then what? Every message that we've sent, every bit of evidence on this ship, is gone? I just can't fathom our situation when this ends."

"We've been over this already," Jack said. "Recorded scientific evidence isn't the only kind of evidence."

"We have Noah and Alicia," Kathy said.

"Naomi can say we smuggled them on the ship," Aaron said.

"DNA evidence will prove that they're ours—yours and mine and Roger's," Kathy retorted. "None of us knew the other that long before the voyage."

"That won't prove a thing to Naomi," Aaron said. "Maybe you

and I had a torrid affair eight years before the voyage; maybe Roger and you were secret lovers four years before that. There's no way we can prove to Naomi that we never met each other back then, that we were away together in space for sixteen years."

"We'll look older," Kathy said.

"Naomi could say we had plastic surgery to make us look that way," Aaron responded.

"That woman can say anything she wants," Jack weighed in. "But Noah and Alicia are indeed the key. We've got to look to them for our answers."

"I'd feel happier about that if we had some indication of the kids' survivability off this ship, on their own, without someone like Hiro connected to the past, protected by it," Aaron said.

"Don't even think about it," Kathy said. "We're not sending Noah or Alicia out on any shuttle without an adult on board."

"Once we get back to Sol," Aaron continued, "Noah and Alicia will have to live off this ship, in a time in which they never existed."

"You'll frighten him if he hears you say that," Kathy said.

Getting past Bo and Nikki's security rigs three nights later was child's play for Noah, even though he couldn't remember ever feeling like a child. He had the shuttle fueled and coursed and ready to go within an hour. The false readings he'd programmed into the central system would tell anyone who scanned his quarters that he was sound asleep in bed. And the shuttle's readings would say it was in stasis.

But he intended to take this shuttle just beyond where Hiro and he had been, and keep it there for two days. That would prove to Aaron and everyone that Noah had real freedom from this ship. He knew that would make Aaron happy. Aaron was worried that the kids wouldn't survive this voyage, but Noah would prove to him that they could.

Noah initiated the final computer check and launch sequence. He took a sip of orange juice. The computer purred in his ear that everything was all right, then—

A screech nearly punctured his eardrums. It was some kind of alarm. He called up visual—someone else was in the shuttle bay!

Damnit! Noah jabbed a key to stop the launch, got out of his seat, and opened the shuttle hatch. He'd been so careful to make sure no one had followed him.

He walked slowly out the door, ready with an explanation. There'd be hell to pay for this with his mother. . . .

"Mommy's gonna be very angry at you," a voice said.

"Alicia, get out of here," Noah said. "It's way past your bedtime. You should be sleeping."

"You should be too," Alicia said.

OK, Noah had to be calm about this. No point in screaming at a six-year-old. "Look, I have something really important I have to do here tonight. And it's important that Mom doesn't know about it. Can I count on you to keep this secret? Please?"

"Mommy says you'll *die* if you go out there," Alicia said breathlessly.

Noah laughed. "That's ridiculous. You know Mom—she overreacts about everything."

"What's 'over carrots'?" Alicia asked.

"Well, you know—she always says things will be worse than they really are. Like when she says you'll get high blood pressure when you're older if you don't eat lots of carrots now."

Alicia smiled. "Or when she yells that your brain will rot away from playing too much virtel?"

"Right," Noah said. "So you shouldn't really listen to her when she says this is dangerous." He pointed to the shuttle, its door open and inviting. "It's nice and safe in there."

A big mistake.

Alicia's eyes seemed to open even wider. She looked at the shuttle and the viewscreen beyond for a long time.

"Can I come too?" she asked.

"No!" Noah said. "I mean, it's perfectly safe and all, but you're not even six yet."

"So?"

"So that means Mom needs you here on the ship." But Noah realized what he was saying wasn't very convincing. Maybe he should take Alicia along after all. . . . That would keep this a secret long enough to let them leave. And if what Aaron was saying was right, having Alicia on the shuttle would give it another person who wasn't tied to the past. She was a pain lots of the time, but she came from even less of the rolled-back time than Noah. Maybe her field, or whatever it was, could be just what they needed to break away. . . .

But he still didn't want to take her. And it wasn't just because he was afraid she'd get some of the glory.

Noah had to admit that maybe it was because deep inside he believed there was a tiny little chance that the shuttle would never return from this hop. Or maybe return with its passengers dead.

He didn't want to die. He didn't want his little sister to die.

Noah opened the outside panel on the shuttle and poked in the seal-up and return-to-stasis sequence. The lights went off inside.

"What are we gonna do now?" Alicia asked.

"We're going back to bed." And he took Alicia's hand and they walked out the door and quickly down the halls. . . .

Noah slid under the covers and closed his eyes, and ruefully remembered what he'd heard Jack say lots of times about this ship.

She was like Mother Earth. She didn't want you to ever leave her.

Thirteen

Jack

It's like running down the stairs, Jack thought, something he hadn't done, come to think of it, since he'd first stepped onto this starship.

You can't really focus on each stair, can't really think about what you're doing, or you'll trip and break your neck.

That was Aaron and him. Jack never thought much about their relationship, he just did it, and that's probably why it worked. Running down the stairs. Though sometimes plotting to get a hold of their future, to survive, felt more like running *up* a huge staircase. Or maybe up an endless down-escalator ...

Their conversation today in Aaron's office had certainly hit a down note. "I'm not afraid of dying," Aaron said. "I've been prepared for that from the beginning. If the Russell-Shaw effect gives me another twenty good years, I'll grab them. Bertrand Russell was boffing 'em practically into his nineties, and had all of his marbles, and George Bernard Shaw was sharp as a whip until then too. I'm not crazy, I like the taste of life. But if it ends a little sooner that's OK too. High eighties is a good life. A little short by today's standards, true, but what the hell do standards count for in our situation? And let's face it, by the standards I grew up with—you and I grew up with, Jack—by those standards, knocking on ninety years ain't bad." His hand was shaking as he pulled a teacup to his mouth. His teeth looked more yellow than Jack remembered them, but who could recall the last time he'd looked at Aaron's teeth? Likely due more to tannic acid than age.

"I know," Jack said.

"It's the kids," Aaron said.

"I know," Jack said. They had been worrying for years about what would happen to the kids. Jack guessed all the people on the ship had, in their own ways. There were no exits from the children's voyage that didn't promise to be painful.

"I can see them just . . . blanking out of existence when we get back to Mars," Aaron continued. "Somehow, as long as we're on this ship, we have enough . . . I don't know, enough *presence* of our journey out. Enough of that field remains for Noah and Alicia to live. To flourish. But once the time rollback is complete . . ."

"We can't be sure what will happen," Jack said.

"But every other scrap of what we accomplished on this trip is long gone now," Aaron said. "All of our records, our data files, our physical evidence. All we have are our recollections. Our children. How can they buck that stream? I don't see how they'll fit, how they can exist, in a world in which they never belonged."

"They're strong," Jack replied. "I mean, their life forces are strong." But he understood Aaron. This time rollback may have been a vindication of Jack's—Wise Oak's—vision, but it was no less a grave danger to the children, for just the reasons Aaron was saying.

"Yeah, strong," Aaron said, "but stronger than time itself? I don't even know what that means."

"What's the alternative?" Jack asked. "Setting them loose in a shuttle? That's why I was thought-playing with the idea of letting Noah go out for a jaunt on his own last week." Jack also knew about Noah's and Alicia's near-launch on Tuesday—a little birdie named Alicia had told him. But she made him promise not to tell anyone, and Jack always made a point of keeping his promises—the younger the children he gave them to, especially. And he saw no value in burdening Aaron any further now.

"No, that's not the answer," Aaron said. "That's no less risky to the kids than our Sol reunion. We have no idea what might happen to them out there."

"What's the answer then?"

"Living things aren't yet affected by this backward arrow," Aaron said. "Let's say we drastically increased the biomass, the lifebulk, on the ship—that might throw us off course a bit."

"Increase the biomass? How? By impregnating all the women?" Jack smiled.

He was glad to see a slight, return gleam in Aaron's eyes. Good, he hadn't lost his sense of humor.

"We'll be in our solar system in two years—not enough time to produce enough babies to make a difference," Aaron said. "No, I was thinking of something a little lower down the scale—like getting Hiro to get the plants to run amuck."

"Balloon the biomass with plant life, and this might somehow alter the time rollback?" Jack asked.

"We're being sucked back into the mouth of time—the belly of time—who the hell knows," Aaron said. "I'm saying that if our biomass—the only damned thing we seem to have any influence over here—can be made to explosively increase, maybe it will give this time-snake an upset stomach, and it'll spit us out."

"To where?" Jack asked.

"I don't know," Aaron said.

"I've got to hand it to you," Jack said. "You spend the first half of the voyage telling Bo and company not to worry—that against all odds, we'll find a way to get home. And now that that's coming true, you want to figure out a way to spit us out again into space?"

"You afraid your theory will be proven wrong?"

Jack shook his head. Noah and Alicia meant more to him than all the theories in this universe, Wise Oak's included. That's what Jack's science *and* his spirit taught. That the living always deserve our best attention. "Bo and Nikki won't go for it. They'll say the safest thing for the kids is to get them back to Earth. And they could well be right."

"We don't need Bo and Nikki to do this," Aaron said. "Just Hiro."

"Then why are you telling *me*?" Jack asked.

"Same reason as always," Aaron replied. "I value your counsel."

A cool, stiff breeze cut through Hiro's garden. It took Jack by surprise—it always did; the ecoengineering always caught him off-guard and delighted him—and he shivered with pleasure.

Hiro smiled up at Aaron and Jack. He held a new type of glistening string bean in his hand. "Strange to say," he stood up and extended his other hand, first to Aaron and then to Jack, "but I'm going to miss this place when we return to Earth."

"How come?" Aaron asked.

"Control," Hiro said. "Here on this ship I have much more control over my environment, over my food species, than I could in any lab or farm back on Earth. Here I'm a Charles Darwin and a Luther Burbank and a Joichi Takada all rolled into one."

"You're better than those guys," Jack said. "They encouraged people to stomp all over their original environments. You're more constructive— you cooperate with the species you find."

A tinge of annoyance darkened Aaron's eyes. Jack had seen it before—what's Jack doing airing his damned politics at a time like this?—but Jack understood. Aaron couldn't help himself. And what Jack said to Hiro would make him better disposed to hear Aaron's request. Not to mention that it was also true.

"Thank you." Hiro bowed slightly in the body language that remained his people's. "But the truth is, I have very far to go to really surpass Darwin or Burbank, let alone Takada. He turned the huge Arab deserts into breadbaskets with his sea-watered wheat. I've done much less here." He gestured to his garden.

"But as you say, many things are possible on a starship," Jack said, "many things in this closed, floating world in which you have such full coevolutionary control."

Hiro nodded. "I appreciate the irony of a control that is fully co-evolutionary—completely a partnership—but I'm getting the feeling that this is more than a visit to inspect my new string beans and compliment my complementary philosophy."

"Yes," Aaron said. "We wanted to ask you how you would feel about trying to do something to stop our return to Earth."

Hiro laughed. "You're joking, right?"

"This whole trip has often felt like a joke to me," Jack said. "But, no, we're quite serious. We're concerned that to return to Earth and take Noah and Alicia off this ship might be to take them out of existence, because they were not part of the time-space in our solar system to which we'll return—they didn't exist anywhere then. They had no status in any realm on Earth or Mars Vestibule when our voyage began, except possibly the potential."

"If the reverse time flow ends when we get back to Earth—and why shouldn't it?—then the field on this ship will end too," Aaron added. "And that may be all that's keeping the children alive now."

"But if we don't go back to Earth, where will we go?" Hiro asked. "Back to Alpha Centauri? What's for us there? We found nothing but inexplicable paradox there. And we don't have enough fuel to go anywhere else."

"True," Aaron said.

"And we can't know for sure that the children *will* disappear when we get back to Earth—that's just speculation, like everything else," Hiro said. "So if we do something to interfere with our return, we may be risking everyone's life on this ship, including the children's, for no reason."

"That's true too," Aaron said.

"And besides," Hiro said, "I don't think we can actually do anything to prevent our return—we seem totally in the grip of the reverse-time tide."

"That may *not* be entirely true," Aaron said, and proceeded to tell Hiro his biomass notion, allowing how "a million more string beans might derail the train of time."

Hiro sighed. "For myself, I might chance it; it has its appeal," he said. "I have no real connections back on Earth—no wife or kids, my parents disapproved of this trip—and I've grown in many unexpected ways in my years on our ship. Mostly, I've come to see that the microcosms I tend to inside this ship are not so different from the worlds and suns outside—a breeze carries feathered seeds in here, a ship carries human ideas out there. I wouldn't mind playing cosmic gardener some more and going back out to the stars. But to make that decision for others—the rest of us on this ship—that's something else. Something I'd need to think more about."

Jack started to respond, but Aaron put his hand on Hiro's shoulder. "That's OK," Aaron said softly. "Your position is moral and I respect it. I just wanted to raise this issue with you now and see how you felt. We'll talk about it again. And I give you my word we won't do anything to disrupt the voyage behind your or anyone's back."

"Thank you," Hiro said, and bowed.

"You're still full of surprises," Jack said to Aaron as they walked back down the corridor.

"I realized something as I was making my point to Hiro," Aaron said—"something about the words we were using near the end of the conversation. Words can be very instructive."

"Oh?"

"You sometimes drive me crazy the way you use words. I wish I could get you to just tell me point-blank what your thoughts are on these crucial issues—they're only a matter of life and death—rather than my having to tweeze them out of you," Aaron said. "You've probably been trying to tell me about my insight with Hiro for a while now—it feels like something that would have already occurred to you."

"I've found it better to sketch a road," Jack said, "and let you walk a bit upon it yourself. That way you discover it on your own terms, rather than mine or someone else's. That way you bring your own perspective to the new idea, a fresh stimulus to its growth."

"Jack Lumet, Native American epistemologist," Aaron said.

"At your service," Jack said, and bowed. It was catching. "So tell me about your—our—insight."

"It has to do with the difference between trains and tides," Aaron said. "Hiro said we were moving on a reverse-time tide; I said we were on a train."

"Not surprising," Jack said, "in view of Hiro's being a naturalist and your being a philosopher of technology."

"Right," Aaron said, "but tides and trains have different properties. A train gets to its destination—whether initial or return trip—and can stay there, indefinitely, ever after. But the very essence of the tide is that, once it's arrived, it begins moving back in the direction from which it came."

"Back and forth forever," Jack said.

"How long have you been on to this?" Aaron asked.

The thought had occurred to Jack the instant he realized that they had reversed their course in the Alpha Centauri system. The ancient peoples he'd studied back on Earth had understood well the two-way, eternal nature of the tides—that rivers which flowed both ways continued to flow both ways.

"A while," Jack replied. "But like Hiro said, it's just another theory, another conjecture. I'd be surprised if it weren't the case, but there's still a near-infinity of information that we don't have about our situation. And I'm not clear how this affects the picture for the children." *And you, old friend, were having enough trouble grasping even the return flow of the tide from Alpha Centauri to Earth at first*, Jack thought. *But that's OK. Nothing about this trip was easy to grasp.*

"But the point is that if we increase our lifebulk," Aaron said, "we may well disrupt our natural counterreturn current—if that's what's happening—rather than promote it. More biomass in the river could split up the current into a thousand smaller streams, whatever that would mean for us."

"Yes," Jack said. "Or the increased biomass could make the current even stronger, and result in our overshooting the return to Sol. Who knows where we'd wind up, and what that would do to the counter-return."

"Yet you went with me to Hiro and supported my presentation of the biomass option to him," Aaron said.

"Yes," Jack said. "Because you were right to at least raise that option to him, in case we need it. And because I knew there was no chance he would agree just like that."

"OK," Aaron said, "so we have an option—increased biomass. But its disruption of our back-and-forth flow pattern—*if* it disrupts the pattern, *if* that pattern is in fact in operation here—has too many possible consequences to fathom. And we're not even sure if the circumstances that option might shatter—our return to Earth—are good or bad, at least for the kids."

"But you do want to keep the kids away from a complete remerging with Earth," Jack said. "We're operating now on the possibility that a return to Earth could kill the kids, aren't we?"

"I want them to live," Aaron said simply.

"The biomass option could well keep us from Earth," Jack said.

"But if we let things take their natural course," Aaron said and shook his head—"*natural* is about the last word I feel like using here— but if we let this proceed without intervention, without a biomass insert, then we would likely be in touch with Earth for just the most fleeting instant, the instant our journey first began, before the current reverses itself and we're back here on our way out again. That's the way tides work, don't they? The water begins to recede a split second after high tide. Just an instant delivery, and back to the sea again. The slightest of kisses in time," he mused.

"That could be one way it would happen, yes," Jack said. "The dividing line between changes of tide is infinitesimal."

"And the ship's field might well be able to survive such infinitesimal contact. A single starlit heartbeat. The kids might be able to survive it..."

"The biomass option is probably still a more likely way of avoiding Earth altogether," Jack said. "Let's not lose sight of that."

"I know, I know." Aaron clenched and unclenched his jaw, in the unconscious chewing Jack had seen him do for seventy years when struggling with strong emotions. "But I don't want to intervene if there's a chance that leaving things alone will work out. Interventions have unforeseen consequences. I've done enough intervention on this trip already," Aaron added.

This whole trip was intervention. That was the way of science and the West. Poke reality in the eye, see if it waters or glares back at you. Learn by perturbation. But Jack had to admire Aaron's sense of caution and proportion now. Jack realized, as he often did, that for a Eurostyle philosopher, Aaron had a keen awareness of the cosmic order of things, and when to leave those workings alone.

"So we do nothing for the time being?" Jack asked.

"I think that's right," Aaron said. "Yes. We keep our minds open for any change, for any glint of information that might be relevant. And we stand ready to try to disrupt our course, if need be, to take our case to Hiro again or whatever, at a moment's notice. But for now, at least until we understand more of what this rollback is, we do nothing to interfere with its progress. Does that seem right to you?"

Jack nodded, and squeezed his friend's shoulder.

A trickle of sweet saliva tickled Jack's chest. It was not from his mouth, but Nikki's, who lay sound asleep on him. He traced some unknown fractal design on her lips with the tip of his finger.

She said she was a private person. She didn't want anyone to know about the two of them. They'd gotten together after Bo's return from the hulk—he was a changed man, Nikki had said, coiled inside himself in a way that left no more room for her—but she didn't want her relationship with Jack to go public. That's the way she had played it with Bo as well.

Fine with Jack. He'd never been one to wrap a woman around his neck like a trophy pelt.

Who knows, maybe she thought she had a pipeline of information from him about Aaron. She could hope what she pleased.

For Jack's part, he had no problem distinguishing his semen from his spirit. The latter was sacred. No sighs in his ear, no thighs touching his could ever possibly move his spirit to compromise a friend—let alone a lifelong friend like Aaron.

Jack knew that most people misunderstood him—mistook his love for the North American Indian as a romance with Rousseau's noble savage. But that wasn't it. Jack's path was neither noble nor savage.

The Iroquois saw a river—a river so close to the powerful tide of an ocean that the ocean's salt and sweat went up more than halfway to Albany, New York. And then back again. And up again. Flowing both ways.

What did those people know of the stars? Was it more than what they saw from Earth? Did they somehow actually travel to Alpha Centauri and back, and discover that the space-time fabric that held Sol and Alpha Centauri together also undulated back and forth, like Muhheakunnuk, the River of Steep Hills, the River That Flowed Both Ways, the Hudson?

Highly unlikely, of course.

But who was Jack to deny it with 100 percent assurance?

He hadn't been there. At least, not before now.

Maybe it was just a theory of the Iroquois. Was Wise Oak's idea—that the yawning stretches beyond our world somehow obeyed the same forces as a river thread within that world—somehow less impressive because it wasn't published in some scholarly journal and called fractal logic? Was an idea wrong just because it came from a thinker five hundred years prior to MIT, CalTech, the Technion, OmniTech, CzechTek, MetroTech, all the fine and wondrous techs of the new millennium?

The modern world worshiped at the altar of empirical data—the myriad hard-as-zirconium facts that came from spotless, glittering equipment. Jack preferred to bow down and sniff the dirt of the past, to sift it with his hands and heart for an arrowhead that might point him in a better direction to understand.

Had not the ancient Greeks—the heroes of Aaron's philosophy and science, the despoilers of the Iroquois world through their descendants, the Romans, and their European progeny—had not those Greeks managed to come up with an atomic theory, via a technology scarcely more developed than the Iroquois'?

Aaron had found Jack's paper about the Iroquois and the stars on some pitted, backwater stretch of the Internet, and somehow Aaron had converted it into this ship. That was Aaron's special gift, his alchemy. Transform an idea into a starship. Magic. Aaron deserved all the credit.

But Jack shared the blame. They had created a world in which not just their ideas were obliged to die if they were wrong, not even just them, but their children.

Jack had never thought of children when the *Light Through* left Sol. He was stunned when he first learned that Kathy was pregnant with Roger's child—but he couldn't blame her. He felt the same need she did to gain some control over their realm, and children were a powerful way to do that. He'd likely have had some kids with Kathy himself if he were capable of more than just making love.

He felt now as if Noah and Alicia *were* his children—the children not of his sperm but of his ideas, his Iroquois ideas.

And yet those very ideas, implemented in the half-knowing fashion in which ideas usually are, had brought them to this juncture. Aaron was right to be worried. They were a long, long way from out of these woods. . . .

Jack fell asleep thinking that the chances were very slim indeed that they, their ideas, and their children would all manage to survive their rendezvous with Earth. Everything depended upon just how long that kiss in time would be.

Nikki made a low, throaty sound, as if in agreement.

Fourteen

Nikki

Nikki slipped out of bed and into her clothes and out the door.

She was glad Jack was still sleeping.

She stopped at the Connected Cafe for a glass of strawberry-orange juice—straight from Hiro's latest gengineered crop—and a steaming blueberry muffin and a cup of coffee.

She was glad no one else was there. She didn't feel like talking. She was on her way to see Roger.

So much of what had happened on this trip was due to Roger McLaren. The truth is, he had begun acting crazy even before his jump to that damn planet around ACA. Sleeping with Kathy, OK. He was only human. He was a man. Didn't matter whether the bed was on Earth or a starship light-years away. But getting her pregnant? What was he thinking?

Now Nikki held his hand. "So I bet you never expected to return to Earth a daddy," she said. This was the first conversation she'd had alone with him in months. She had tried one or another variation of this daddy opener lots of times, with no result.

Today was no different.

"Sure wish you could tell me something of what happened to you on that hulk."

Same reply.

Bo was no different. Neither man who had been to the hulk

wanted to talk about it. She guessed neither could. And that's why the truth of their situation likely was tied up in some way with that hulk.

She sat there with Roger for maybe an hour, just holding his hand. She looked at the soft, shimmering walls—intelligent surfaces, maybe more intelligent than Roger now. No, not more intelligent, but more communicative. Millions of tiny chip panels that could combine in countless ways into larger panels that could show Nikki any part of the ship, hook her into any part of the ship's grand network, a second skin far more alive and tingling with knowledge than hers. She had designed all of this for Roger—and for what it could tell her—in the past few years.

One thing the walls couldn't show her was the future—or past—or wherever the hell it was they were heading. In that respect, these highly intelligent walls were indeed as dumb as her own perspiring skin and everyone else's on this ship. As mute as McLaren.

She often wondered if he ever came out of his shell and embraced these walls when he was alone at night. If he used them to confide his inner secrets, express his demons, entertain what was locking him up inside.

She thought she would have—she would have tried to come out in the cupped hands of night, had she been like Roger. No one to hurt him then. Just these walls. But what did she really know about his condition?

As far as Nikki could tell, Roger had said nothing to the walls—no more than he'd said to anyone on the ship. Perhaps he talked to the walls silently, with a flicker of the eyes so quick, a shift of the lips so subtle, that no other eyes could catch it. At any rate, Nikki's computer connections that gossiped with McLaren's walls had nothing to convey. If McLaren's walls had ears, they were deaf to McLaren. Ears that could hear might as well be deaf if the speaker was mute.

"OK," Nikki said, "I'm gonna go now. We'll be back home on Earth soon. Just a few more years now. Maybe they'll know how to take care of you there."

Out here, a few more years seemed soon.

For Nikki's money, Kathy was by far the strangest person on the ship—and that was saying a lot, because the *Light Through* was crawling with weirdos everywhere you looked. She guessed that was to be expected. Who else but a nutcase would volunteer for a mission based on a scientific theory derived from an Indian? Or on a boomerang that had worked around the sun and the moon, at a sliver of the distance between Sol and ACA? But Kathy—that girl was in a class by herself.

Nikki found Kathy in the conference room, going over their final report on the grand QM phenomenon. Nikki had finally worked out an automatic, perpetual data copying process with Aviva—the idea was it generated a new copy just as the previous one was lapsing into oblivion in the time rollback. Didn't do much good for images, which went into overwhelming noise-to-signal ratio after the eighth copy. But so far, so good for just plain text. "I'm happy with it," Kathy said about their report, "but I doubt that anyone back on Earth will pay much attention to it now, even if it lasts the distance. No one cares about explanations for events that never took place."

"Well, sure," Nikki said, "but they did take place. The fact that we have no evidence of them now doesn't mean that they didn't take—"

"No," Kathy said. "We're really back in an earlier time now, before the events that we describe in our report happened. The fact that our lives and our minds still flow from that future doesn't change the fact that that future hasn't yet occurred in a physical sense, and may never occur. The physical space around us is literally as it was almost sixteen years ago—you know that; all of your equipment and readings are saying that—and that's because the physical, material realm that we're in, other than the lives and thoughts on this ship, *is* almost sixteen years ago."

Nikki shook her head in disagreement. "You remember when Newark Freenet crashed, fifteen years before we left?" she asked.

"No," Kathy said.

"Well, I was just a kid then, but I remember what happened. The crash was so bad that the only way they could fix it was to roll the on-line database back two weeks. So the next time I signed on, it's like it was two weeks earlier—everything after that was gone. The date was two weeks earlier, the newest messages were two weeks earlier, everything. But the *reality,* of course, the *truth* is that it was really two weeks later. It's just that on that database, the two weeks hadn't happened yet."

"This isn't a database." Kathy gestured to the real-view window at the far end of the room. "This is reality itself. That's the difference."

"But you don't know that," Nikki insisted. "You can't know that for sure. It's just as likely that there's an ultimate reality beyond what we're now going through, a core of reality in which our memories of the future are memories of events that *did* occur—*will* occur—"

"When?" Kathy asked. "You planning on going back to Alpha Centauri any time soon?"

"Well, no," Nikki admitted. She hadn't intended this to be so intense, but it was just as well. You learned more from intensities than superficial pleasantries.

"So you're saying that you're holding out some hope that our time rollback isn't what it is?" Kathy asked. "That somehow we'll live happily ever after back on Earth, with scientific recognition for what we discovered in the stars, with everything business as usual, all supported by some kind of ultimate, deeper reality? Everything falling neatly into place, as if there were no time rollback, and everyone on Earth aware that we'd been gone for sixteen years, aware of where we'd gone? That's what you want?"

"Yeah," Nikki said. "Don't you?"

"What we want is not necessarily what we get," Kathy said.

"So what are you telling me?"

"I'm telling you that what you want can't possibly be," Kathy said. "We can't return to Earth and be as we are when the Earth we return to is still sixteen years in the *were*. Something has to give. I don't know what. Maybe our minds rather than our lives, if we're lucky—if being like Roger is lucky. I don't know. But I do know we can't just squeeze lives and minds back into a sixteen-year-old tube of toothpaste. For all we know, our very return to Earth will cause the whole time-space structure to explode."

"You worrying about the whole universe now?" Nikki asked. But she realized Kathy was probably worrying most about her kids, which for a mother would understandably be most of her universe.

"Everything," Kathy said, "I'm worried about everything."

"Look, we have no way of preventing this ship from going back to Earth," Nikki said. "And even if we did, where else would we go? You want your kids to spend their lives riding around the galaxy, until we all die off and they're the only ones left on this ship?"

"I don't want them to die the year after next, I know that," Kathy said. "But you're right—this whole discussion is hypothetical. There's nothing we can do to stop this anyway."

Sure, tell me another story. . . .

Bo was right about these people. They had something they were working on, something about not going back to Earth, something that Kathy was glad and tormented about at the same time—some kind of last hope that she couldn't be sure would turn out right, something that of course they didn't talk about outside of their inner circle. . . .

What were they after? Who would choose life in a vacuum for even a chance to live again back on Earth?

She'd have to keep a careful eye on them.

Just as Naomi had urged about Aaron and Jack in that briefing she'd given some of the crew the week before they'd left.

Hiro was one person Nikki thought she could trust—not because she thought him absolutely trustworthy (she didn't know anyone she had that kind of faith in, including herself), but because he hadn't been part of the inner circle at first. That self-anointed inner circle . . . No, Hiro was just a short-order nutritionist long on good sense. He owed nothing to anything except his own talent.

"Nikki." He greeted her with a handful of string beans he had just picked from his garden. They looked a little too shiny for Nikki's taste—she was still partial to the dull-green things her grandma used to grow in her Southside lot.

"You perfecting your plants for reception on Earth?" she asked.

"Yes," he said. "Living things come through the time strain. The more we have, the more we can show what we've been doing these past years."

"*Time strain,* I like that," Nikki said.

"I mean time *strainer,*" Hiro said, embarrassed. "You know—the backward roll takes out nonliving material, not life or thoughts, because life and thoughts are antientropic. They always go against the flow of decay, whether time is moving forward or backward. So I think of what we're going through now as a strainer. And what's left after the straining are life and thoughts."

"*Strainer*'s good too," Nikki said. "You're nearly as good with words as you are with vegetables."

He smiled, and bowed slightly.

"You think we're going to make it, then—back to Earth," Nikki said.

He lost his smile and stood up straight. "Why shouldn't we?"

"Lots of things can go wrong before we get there," Nikki answered. "Lots of things can go wrong *when* we get there. Kathy's afraid that, in the end, the time of sixteen years ago might not be able to accept us when we return—I mean *physically*—that space-time could unravel, explode, at the instant we try to reintegrate with it."

"But we've seen no sign of that on our ship," Hiro said, "and we're traveling back in time right now."

"Yeah," Nikki said, "but that could be because we're also traveling at half the speed of light, or because we're actually moving back now in time. Kathy's fear is that when the process is complete, it could result in our ... being erased." Great, she was explaining this so well she was beginning to feel some of the raw anxiety herself.

"There are infinite possibilities," Hiro said. "Why focus on one particular horrible one?"

"Well, there may be a lot of possibilities, but in the end we have just an either-or choice—try our best to return to Earth, or not—and we can know which of those two directions to choose only by examining as many of the infinite possibilities as possible."

"You're wrong," Hiro said. "We have no choice at all. Our knowledge means nothing in this."

Nikki looked at him, taken aback by his uncustomary bluntness.

"What control have we had over anything in this whole voyage?" he continued. "From the minute we started, what choice did we really have? Our trip to the star was one surprise after another. And our trip back has nothing to do with any choice we made. It should be clear to everyone by now that our fate is in hands that have never touched ours."

"Whose hands?"

"Unknown," Hiro said.

"Yet you grow your string beans," Nikki pressed.

"If we get back to Earth, they'll be good evidence. If not, they'll be good to eat wherever we are. And, anyway," he smiled, "they give me pleasure right now, whatever happens later."

But Nikki knew her pleasure was far less easily obtained.

Fifteen

Roger

"Maybe they'll know how to take care of you there," Nikki said, and walked out of my skins—out of the space between the middle skin of my body and the outer skin of my walls—out into the halls that were nobody's skins at all.

I have a great interest in skins, in boundaries, in realms within realms. I once heard Aaron talking about McLuhan—I was attracted to the name because it sounded like mine. He had a view that a fish was the last being you should ask about certain properties of water, because the fish was totally submerged in it and had no sense of its boundaries, where the water began and the water ended. Don't ask a fish about the intersection of water with land and air. Even if it could talk, all it could really tell you about land and air is the death gasp of a fish out of water.

I was even worse than the fish. In so deep and out the other side that boundaries themselves were my water. Gasping, writhing, slapping my being on some shore as I struggled for a breath of unattainable understanding. Just a breath . . .

I'm not sure what that really means, but it feels right to me. I'm not even sure that words convey my meaning anymore—I use them only because they once worked for me, and I hear them still from people I know.

These words—my *think* words—have nothing to do with the words I sometimes say. Those words, my *say* words, are the twitching of a muscle long gone slack. They have nothing to do with the me inside my inner skin. I think they once had some connection to something I once understood, but I'm not sure. I could be wrong. Or I could've been wrong when I thought I was once understanding something.

I once was in a place where I saw so much, so fast, that I wanted to tell everyone. That's truly what I wanted. But they put too much pressure on me, the people on our ship that I wanted to talk to. I'm not angry at them. It wasn't their fault—they had no idea that I even had anything to tell them. But I could feel their need—*tell me, tell me, tell me.* I could feel their need to know clawing in my mind. I could feel it tugging at me all the time. And I knew also that I would never be able to answer properly.

For seeing is not understanding—it's gasping, not breathing.

The whole thing happened in maybe just a few seconds. I shut me off. It was the only way I could live.

Warm hands over mine—I can feel the warmth radiating deep into me, through skin, flesh, bone, most layers indifferent to it, some grateful, until it gets to the deepest part of me, where it licks the nerve like a cat's tongue on a glacier.

Kathy's talking... "Aaron and Jack think there's a good chance we won't actually remerge with Earth—we'll be sucked out on another trip back to Alpha Centauri the instant we return."

No news. It's been going on for a long time....

"I'm mostly relieved about it—I couldn't see how the kids would fit in; the time and place wouldn't be theirs. At least on our ship, they'll have a chance."

Yeah. The pious hope of every soul who's ever been on our ship.

"I'm still worried about the actual reversal point, though—the instant we shift from back time to normal, forward time, and start our journey back to Centauri. I won't breathe easily until we're actually past that."

Even then you shouldn't. If Naomi Senzer had even an inkling of what was going on—of the insane socket we'd plugged into—she'd get JFC to send a dozen warheads out to hit us as we left. I'm not sure I'd completely blame her, either.

Sometimes I have lunch with Alicia in Hiro's garden.

She talks to me.

"I made three wishes at the well but I can't tell you what they are." She giggled. Splashes of joy in the space-time continuum. "I'm just like you now."

The spider's web of words. This little angel had made three wishes—all of which were that I could talk to her, I bet—but she couldn't talk to me about them or they wouldn't come true. I couldn't talk because too much was true already.

Alicia tugged on my hand. "See? That's a picture of the forest, and here's the tree where we're sitting." She had scratched out in the black dirt a reasonable sketch of where we were, with a big twig standing in for the oak tree we were leaning against.

I picked up a little twig and a tiny twig from outside the sketch area. I bent the little twig in half and propped it up against the big, upright twig. Then I bent the tiny twig in half, and put it in the lap of the little twig.

Alicia jumped into my lap and hugged me.

Bo was still the biggest danger. Not that he or anyone would have much control over what would happen, but he was still the worst factor on board. Not because he was selfish—everyone is selfish in his or her way; even Albert Schweitzer did what he did because it gave him personal satisfaction—but because Bo had seen something on the hulk.

He's come to see me again now, along with Nikki. Nikki's beau Bo. Bo bo bubbly bubbles . . .

"McLaren," he says, and it sounds like it always does from his mouth, like a cough or a curse.

"I know the pain you're suffering, my friend. Don't worry; when we get back to Earth you'll have plenty of important people to look at you. Big men—specialists. They'll know how to make you better."

If I could speak, I'd say: You're not my friend. You never were and never will be. Just because you share a tiny drop of my insanity—of what made me this way—doesn't mean by the standards of any universe that you're my friend.

Perhaps he senses what I'm feeling. Because to Nikki he says, "I still get the feeling he doesn't like me—like we're what, criminals? I'm a criminal because I want to go back to Earth, to our planet. Talk about ass-backward consequences of this time rollback!"

Nikki puts a calming hand on his shoulder.

"We just want to live, McLaren, we just want to live," he continues. "That's all. I know you don't like me. Try to see beyond that. Think about it. That's all."

And they're walking out the door.

"I know what you're afraid of." Bo's head is back in for a brief refrain, whispering. "I'm trying to *prevent that from happening,* goddamnit. Why can't you see that?" He's sounding out each important word like I'm some kind of imbecile. "Think about it, McLaren, think about it. That's all."

And he's gone.

Believe me, I've thought about it. And it doesn't matter.

But if I could have talked, I'd have asked them what exactly were they so afraid anyone would do to change things?

The illusion Bo and Nikki had that anything *could* be changed was touching—so strong, so at variance with reality that the whiff it left in my room was intoxicating.

If only I could change what I'd ingested on that hulk.

Age so old, so worn from repeated use, that the very quarks of creation peered through like shredded skin beneath a derelict's shiny pants leg. No wonder some faint, odd signal had come from that direction. No wonder the hulk scanned as an alien construction—time in that quantity, times the radiation of the universe, would do that to any alloy. How many times had that hulk traveled back and forth, back and forth, from Earth to Alpha, from Alpha to Earth, from Earth to Alpha to Omega in an inexhaustible but supremely exhausting loop? How many souls had lived and dreamed on it, died pounding on the doors of hope on it—the whole of their cosmos, the only cosmos that ever heard them, on that ship?

I had even seen Sarah there—a much younger version of our poor Sarah, who had come upon this voyage to be released at last, to die, as she had told Kathy with her dying breath.

Our species had been old enough to dream the day it was born.

But never old enough for what became of those dreams on that ship.

They were sentient, they were human, though that hulk had been trafficking between the beginnings and the ends for far longer than there had been humans on Earth.

You see, I came to know many things on that hulk....

But what shut down my brain, infinite amps through a finite circuit breaker, was the glimpse that that ship was ours—and I hadn't the strength to stop it.

Sixteen

Bo

"How did we sink this low? What happened here?" Bo realized he was shouting again. Nikki ushered him into her office. "What's happened to science, Nikita?" He lowered his voice. "Are we the only scientists left here—the only people of reason? We're a starship captained by lunatics from the Middle Ages!"

"Aaron's a philosopher of science," Nikki said. "He used to teach—"

"That's my point," Bo said, " 'used to.' Aaron used to be a reasonable man—before he became boss of this ship. I'm sure Kathy was once a decent doctor too—before she started treating her patients with her pudendum. Jack was always a mystic. Believe me, my people have had plenty of experience with Rasputins; I can spot them miles away. We're a starship full of Rasputins. I feel sometimes like we'd be better off killing all of them!"

She gave Bo that look: *Bo, you're overreacting. Bo, take it easy. I agree with your frustration, but, Bo, there's no point in bursting a blood vessel. There's nothing we can do now.*

Right, and that was the problem.

They had to find something they could do in case those Rasputins tried to pull a fast one. Bo felt he couldn't live another hour if he thought for a minute that he'd ever have to see that hulk in his face again.

"OK, OK." He looked at his watch. "I'm relaxed now. I'll try to take it easy now. I'm going back to my room to take a nap."

She squeezed his arm.

He liked her. She had some intelligence.

Bo lay in bed thinking.

Man's first trip to a star would have been an insult to the cosmos without a Russian aboard!

Russia got the human race off the planet in the first place!

But when Bo had finally begun to understand the truth, the instability of that star system, what it did to all of those boomerang equations—yes, he'd wanted to go back to Earth, right then, like any sane man should. What, risk his life on what was left, the strength of some savage red man's theory? No, thank you. That's the problem with America. Yes, they have good science and good music, but they take their minorities much too seriously. What the hell did the Indians ever achieve that Bo should take one of their visions seriously—that he should risk his life on it? OK, they gave us corn. Bo liked corn better than potatoes; he'd give them that. But what did corn have to do with the price of the stars?

He couldn't wait to see Alexei's face when he got back. You weasel. You have a stain on your head just like Gorbachev. Not a physical stain. Something deeper. A stain of deception. Alexei had lied to Bo, implied things about the boomerang that Bo discovered were not true. Almost too late—everyone had deserted him when he'd tried to do the right thing halfway out to Alpha Centauri—but not too late after all. Alexei never expected to see Bo again—but he was wrong! Boris Ivanoff didn't volunteer on this mission to die! He volunteered to live! To travel to the stars and return to tell the story! And that they were now doing.

Yet Aaron the philosopher-king still was not happy! And that's what Bo could not understand. Aaron had promised a return home; he had let them drift into Alpha Centauri without a clue in his head as to how they would actually get home. And now they were going home—so what is he so worried about? We're all alive, aren't we? The kids are growing and healthy. So what if they all got back to Earth with no tangible records of their voyage? They would still have their memories. No one could ever take those away.

Bo had some memories he'd rather not have. Memories he had walled off like a cyst so they didn't destroy him, but that he'd been unable to discard, even in this backward ride in time in which so much else was lost.

McLaren understood. If only he would talk—but what was the use? Talking to that mute was like trying to get music from a stone.

Nikki maybe was right. Bo could be uneasy about this all he wanted, but what could he really do? He had no control of the ship.

The chime sounded. It was Nikki. Her face looked grave on the screen.

"Aaron's had a heart attack," she said.

Everyone was standing around Aaron's bed, fungi of life-support tubing coming out of him, Kathy crying her eyes out, everyone else like a grim Dutch Master. Bo couldn't say he was happy about this turn of events for Aaron—seeing a man die was never a pleasure—but all of this was yet more evidence of how these people lived in a dreamworld. Death and life—they're both part of the same dime, both part of life. You have to accept one if you want the other.

"Is he . . . dead?" someone's quavering voice asked of no one in particular. Bo thought it was Aviva.

"No," Kathy said through puffed, muffled lips. She was bending over Aaron now, her face and hair intertwined with his. "He's in bad shape, though."

"Only one person has died so far on this ship," Hiro said. "Let that be all."

"One's a lot for this day and age," Nikki said.

"This day and age means nothing out here," Jack said, more upset than Bo ever had seen him. "We're in an age by ourselves out here. Between the stress and the deep space and this time rollback, who knows what effect it has on the heart."

"Sarah died on the way out," Nikki said. "Before the rollback."

"That was a stroke," Hiro said.

"Same river," Jack said.

Shut up with that Indian bullshit already, shut up with it, Bo thought to himself. It was a fact of the cosmos, not a river. Bo had tried singing that Indian song with Jack when they first made the turn around ACA, but they had to be real now. They had to decide who would lead the ship.

Kathy was wailing again, holding Aaron's head in her arms.

There were tears in Bo's eyes too, though he couldn't say why.

Aaron had tried his best; Bo had to admit that, at least.

He looked around at everyone and marveled at how the nearness of death could equalize all other differences.

Two days later Bo was in Nikki's office, along with Hiro and Jack.

Kathy walked in with the news.

"He's stable," she said. "He's alive for now. But no telling how long he'll be this way—or if he'll even be alive tomorrow."

"Thank God he's at least stabilized," Nikki said, and put her arm around Kathy as she took her seat.

Bo thought he could understand what must be in Kathy's mind: *I'm the mother of two children. The father of the first is in some kind of autistic tailspin, the father of the second is nearly dead.*

"We, uh, we need to talk about leadership," Nikki said, trying to be deferential to Kathy's feelings but firm about the need to discuss this.

"Oh," Kathy answered, distracted, "I hadn't thought—"

"It's OK," Bo said, and put his hand on Kathy's. "None of us wants to think of this."

She pulled her hand away. More in unconscious recoil than deliberate rebuff, Bo thought, but that was even worse. It told him that strong as her sorrow was about Aaron, it didn't dilute her dislike of Boris Ivanoff.

"Who is the best candidate?" Hiro asked.

"Well," Nikki said, "I was thinking that Bo—"

"What?" Kathy looked at Bo. "I mean, well, sure, Bo would be OK," she continued, "but don't you have seniority here?" She said this to Nikki. Kathy couldn't be too happy about Nikki either, but, hey, anything's better than the stinking Russian. . . .

"Yeah, I do," Nikki replied. "But I'm too busy with programming now to take over Aaron's work."

"Isn't Bo busy too?" Kathy asked.

"Truthfully, no," Nikki said. "The automatic rollback that we're in makes engineering unnecessary—all they do is record increases in fuel and return positions in the stars that mirror what we had on the way out."

"What about other people on board," Kathy persisted, "shouldn't they have a say too?"

"I've already spoken to Aviva," Nikki responded. "She'll go along with the majority. The kids are too young to decide, obviously. Roger's in no condition. My gut tells me we should go with Bo."

"That's been clear since the little insurrection years ago on the way out, hasn't it?" Jack finally spoke up. Everyone looked at him.

Bo could never understand why anyone would care jackshit what Jack thought. He wasn't a scientist, he wasn't a technician, he was at best just an historian . . .

Kathy looked at Jack.

Hiro cleared his throat as if to speak. He has the crucial vote, Bo realized—a gardener, a cook, for crissakes! Nikki was for Bo. Bo was for Bo. Kathy and Jack for anyone else. McLaren and Aaron were out of it. Aviva said she'd go with the majority—

"I think we should make it unanimous for Bo, then," Hiro said.

Jack looked at Hiro a long time. Then again at Kathy.

"Yes, let's make it unanimous," Jack said, and reached out for Kathy's hand.

"OK," she said, quiet as a flower. Bo noticed that she couldn't bring herself to smile.

But that was fine with him, more than fine. Now he'd have access to Aaron's office, all of his records. Maybe they'd be able to return to Earth without a hitch after all. Maybe Bo's sense that Aaron and his roundtable of dreamers were up to something no good was paranoia after all.

These backward wheels of destiny had somehow finally conspired to put him in the driver's seat.

Nikki was asleep next to Bo. The cream of Aaron's files was in a dataglass under Bo's bed. He reached under and patted the screen. It felt good to his hand. It was a great comfort to him. But he had no illusions about the kind of power he now had. It was fleeting, just like anything on a screen.

Nikki stirred. She slid her hand over Bo's chest. "You're still awake," she said. "Let's get some sleep."

"I have a lot to think about."

"There are a million things that can go wrong," she said. "We've just got to concentrate on our game plan. Anyway, I've checked the computers a dozen times—our course back to Earth is steady."

"Computers," Bo said. "I can't put my faith in them. Our computers, all of our equipment, showed us all sorts of nonexistent things on our way out."

"Maybe they were echoes from other trips," Nikki said dreamily. "I overheard Jack and Aaron talking in the corridor about something like that. They think maybe our ship will bounce back from Earth to Alpha Centauri, just like it's bounced back here. And I was thinkin' maybe it'll keep on bouncing, bouncing back and forth, like a Ping-Pong ball in space. . . ." She rolled over. The tip of her backside just touched the soft skin on Bo's thigh.

"What good is being captain on a Ping-Pong ship like that?"

" 's good." Nikki's speech was sleep-slurred. "In couple years we're back in the solar system. Redock Mars Vest, kiss the ship good-bye, just get off, go. Rest is who knows."

Yeah, the rest is who knows, the rest is silence, the rest is sleep, the rest is death. Wasn't that Hamlet? Bo suddenly felt some of the thick pressure that Aaron must have been in.

Bo didn't want speculation, he didn't want rest—he wanted certainty and life. Maybe the two were incompatible. Maybe the only real choice was the heat-death predictability of every planet and star, or an uncertain ride forever through the black hole of space.

He rolled Nikki over.

As long as he was so deep into dark space, he might as well enjoy it.

Seventeen

Kathy

Billy Jay Kramer's "Bad to Me" and the Four Tops' "Bernadette" were playing in an endless, back-to-back loop. The two songs sounded right together. Kathy didn't know why. Maybe because they both began with *B*. Maybe because she had once heard them played back-to-back on some Top 40 radio station in a prior lifetime, or as an egg in an egg in her grandmother's ovary. . . .

Few people understood what she got from music. Aaron did. But he was asleep in the next room.

"Mommy?" Alicia skipped in from the sunroom with a bouquet of buttercups and a question. "Mommy? How many days before we get back to Earth?"

"Oh, I don't know, honey." Kathy touched the flowers and ran her hand through Alicia's soft brown hair. "A lot of days—more than six hundred. These flowers are beautiful—I'm going to put them in the vase right over there."

"Wow!" Alicia's eyes opened wide. "Six hundred! That's more than a million, right? A lot of days." She filled the vase with water and brought it to Kathy. Alicia's eyebrows were knotted now, as if she was wrestling with some sort of complex problem. She was looking more like her father every day.

"Mommy?"

"Yes, sweetheart."

"Mommy, I don't know if I really want to go back to Earth. I'll miss my room here. It's our home," Alicia said.

"Well, you'll have a lot more room back on Earth—you won't have to share your room with your brother."

"But I *like* sharing Noah's room. When he's sleeping, or visiting Uncle Roger or someone, I get to play with his toys."

"Hmm, I see what you mean," Kathy said. "But you'll have plenty of great new toys to play with on Earth."

"Can I get a bicycle?" Alicia asked. "Like the one I saw in the virtel?"

"Sure, we'll definitely get you a bicycle on Earth—lots of great new toys," Kathy assured her.

Alicia still didn't look entirely convinced. "OK," she said. "But I still really like it here and don't care if we never get back to Earth and just keep flying and flying around and—"

"Have you been talking with Uncle Jack about this again?" Kathy asked.

"He made me promise not to tell," Alicia said.

"It's OK, honey," Kathy said. "I'm glad that you have the kind of personality that you'll be happy wherever we are—here on the ship or back on Earth."

"Person Ali means people like me, right?"

"It means you have a soul that sings with the cosmos," her mother replied.

Kathy had realized long ago that Noah and Alicia were impossible to shield on this ship. They couldn't help but know that they were heading back to Earth—because in fact they were—but they also couldn't help overhearing some of the talk about rebounding back to ACA. So the kids had to have mixed feelings about whatever happened.

Kathy sighed. As a researcher, she had found this trip the most exhilarating project of her life—she would gladly live the rest of her life in space. But as a mother, she much preferred this trip ending happily ever after, with everyone back on Earth.

Waves washing toes on a beach somewhere, little Licia pouring water back and forth into a hole, Noah masterminding a sandcastle project, everyone telling each other stories about the time they traveled to another star . . . Aaron living forever to see not only his daughter but her children, their grandchildren, grow up . . . And Roger regaining his power of speech, his mind, for Kathy knew that he still had it, buried deep somewhere. Roger had so much he could give to Noah, to everyone. . . .

Kathy's science told her that DNA had hardwired her brain and bartended her hormones to make her children's happiness and survival important above all else. Back on Earth, even on Mars Vest, such desire found many paths of expression. Some were compatible with larger pursuits of knowledge and the universe. This was appropriate for the human species. Nature, once understood, usually worked to make things easier, not harder, for people. Good doctors grasped that. Homo sapiens could pursue its biological survival at the same time as it fulfilled its cosmic responsibility of understanding and moving out to the stars.

But out here between the stars, where the vistas and light streams and potentials for knowledge were infinite, the paths to her children's survival turned out to be very limited. In fact, there was likely just one.

One path, one path only, to life.

But which one?

Aviva was in Hiro's garden. Kathy hadn't really seen her since she'd finished the beautiful digitraits of Noah and Alicia last month. Of course, they were never really finished. Aviva's talent, a combination of traditional artistic ability and keen programming know-how, was exquisite. The "intelligent portraits" of Noah and Alicia actually changed a little each day. Tiny modules in the screen with algorithms of the kids' DNA kept the portraits always current, always looking like the real faces as they grew. It was still too soon to notice any difference between these and traditional, static portraits—the kids hadn't changed in any discernible way in a month, other than Noah's inane pigtails, and in any case hairstyle was a function of whim, not DNA, so the digitraits couldn't pick that up. But Aviva had also done some stunning d-traits of several shrubs. She'd told no one about them except Hiro and Kathy, at first, and the two had been astonished. The d-traits now displayed the subtle blue-grays of the dwarf firs perfectly, more than six months after Aviva had captured their shiny greens on screen, and embedded the pixels with just the right algorithms for color change and aging. Of course, human DNA was a damn sight more complex than the DNA of little Christmas trees, but the principle of its embodiment in Aviva's pixels was the same.

Its implications for permanent records of their voyage were towering. At last they had an image document that might survive the inexorable backward flow, because it simulated the antientropic, forward flow of DNA—the flow that animated their lives and minds, and likely kept Alicia and Noah in existence on the ship. Portraits that aged, literally. Oscar Wilde gone wild and digital, like so much else in the twenty-first century . . .

Aviva looked up. "Hi. How's Aaron?"

"Holding his own," Kathy said. "You putting the flower gardens to screen? Wonderful idea!"

"Thanks." Aviva smiled. "I want to get everything on this ship into screen mode. My renderings obviously could never be as convincing as the scientific evidence we lost, but at least they'll provide some inkling for the people on Earth of what we saw out there."

"Yes," Kathy said. "Your ACA planet series should be a crucial part of that." Kathy closed her eyes and was there again. Just like that. She shivered to the mixed chords of delicate beauty and buzzed semiconsciousness, soft-breeze tinkling and wind chimes clanging, that this memory of N'urth always aroused.

"Hiro's a very evocative narrator," Aviva said. "His words will be my eyes for the planet series."

"An evocative world . . . ," Kathy breathed.

"Oh," Aviva said suddenly. "Hiro told me you were coming. He had to check some sort of leakage over in aqua—he said you should look for him over there. He tried to call you, but there was no answer."

"Ah, I was noncom in the pool," Kathy said, pulling herself away from the intoxicating contemplation. "But I'm glad I came by here anyway."

A cool breeze snuck up behind her in the garden as she left to find Hiro.

Kathy was late for her meeting with Hiro, which made her late for her next meeting. Once you lose a beat in a day, you can never recover, she thought. Even when the days themselves were going backward.

Jack was already there in her office. He still had the keycode. "You look serious today," he said. "Everything OK?"

"I guess so," Kathy said. "I don't know. For some reason, I've got the ACA planet and traveling backward in time on my brain today. I close my eyes and can almost feel my blood reversing circulation—my red blood cells giving back their oxygen, veins pumping blood from my heart—but when I look, my veins are blue. Sometimes it's harder than usual to make sense of our local lives being in normal time while the place we live in—this ship—goes in reverse time. You ever have days like that?"

Jack looked at her without answering. It had been a while since she'd talked to Jack about feelings, his or hers . . . his and hers.

"Not exactly like that," he finally said. "But other kinds of disorienting stuff. We're in an upside-down situation here. Anything we write or program today without a genetic algorithm is gone tomorrow, so we have to write it again or put it in a program to copy it. We're accustomed to jotting something down on a piece of paper, and it's there the next time we look—that was a great comfort in the early days of computers, which were prone to crash. But both are toast in this time rollback. Only our memories endure on their own. Only living processes and things tied to them—the life field of this ship. It used to be the other way around—usually physical records endured, and specific flesh and memory failed. That's our usual orientation for control. So it's not surprising that we're always out of step with something or other out here. Some days it's worse. All we can do is ride it out."

She walked over and put her arms around him. He leaned back in his chair, so that the top of his head was tucked under her chin. "It's been a long time," Kathy said quietly. "I know you were lonely. I'm sorry."

"It's OK," he said. "You couldn't be in two beds at once. I understood that."

"I still love you," Kathy said. "You know that." There were tears in her eyes. She tried to blink them back—she hadn't planned on this.

"I know," he said. "And I, you—always."

"I'm so worried about the kids. Let's say we *do* go all the way back to Earth and we stay there an instant too long. Let's say the kids *do* disappear. I don't think I could live through that. I sometimes think maybe the answer is that I should go off on a shuttle with both of them—that way their life forces will outweigh mine, and maybe we'll get away. That's anxiety more than science speaking, I know, but—"

"Shhh, it's OK." Jack was up and his arms were around Kathy and his face was so close that his skin absorbed her tears. "Going off in the shuttle isn't the answer," he said softly. "That could lead to death right away. We just have to keep on course to Earth and hope . . ."

And Kathy realized that his mouth had stopped talking and was over hers, and it felt so good to kiss him—

"Ahem," a voice said at the rear door, which opened to the bed-room.

She broke free and turned to the door, embarrassed.

"Aaron!"

Jack poured the customary cup of Darjeeling for his old friend. The relationship between these two still amazed Kathy—each as cool as one of Hiro's cucumbers, seeming not the least bit flustered.

"All right." Aaron sat down and opened his glimmering notebook. "Let's get down to our business for today. First, how are things on the Bo front?"

"Good," Jack said. "I saw him this morning. He's in good shape, the ship's in good shape. He's running the show fine—in some ways better than you." Jack's left eye twinkled.

"I see you're in fine form today too," Aaron said.

"Well, to give credit where credit is due," Jack replied, "I've got to say that putting Bo in command was a masterstroke—one of your best moves on this whole trip. His energies are now absorbed in trivia, yours are free to focus on important things, and should Bo try anything not in our interests, we'll see it coming a mile away. Brilliant, really."

"Thank you." Aaron smiled.

"The emotional price was awful," Kathy said.

"I know," Aaron said, and put his hand on hers.

"I'm still not sure how the kids are really taking this," Kathy said. "I mean, Noah's OK—he's older than we are, in some ways—but Alicia . . . It's hell to tell a six-year-old that a few of her favorite people are going to *pretend* that her daddy's very sick, even though he isn't, really, and you can't let anyone else know about the secret."

"She's not too good with secrets, is she?" Jack said affectionately.

"I know it's been hard," Aaron said. "I'll try to spend some time with her again soon. But we had no other choice—not telling Alicia, letting her think that I really *had* had a heart attack, and was close to death when I wasn't, would've been far worse. You know that."

"Not engaging in this pretense in the first place would've been less worse," Kathy said.

Aaron and Jack both began reciting all the good reasons for the faked heart attack. Kathy wasn't interested.

"Right, I know all that," she said. "But the children aside, I still can't feel good about your turning power over to Bo—power should always be held on to, if at all possible."

"That's just what we're doing," Aaron said. "Holding on to power by letting Ivanoff think he has it. This was the best way."

She shook her head. "Power is essentially unpredictable. You can't foresee with certainty what Ivanoff—what anyone—will do with it." But there was nothing to be gained in pushing this any further—Aaron, after all, just couldn't walk into his old office and resume command. His coronary ploy had gone too far for that. He'd have to go the route of getting gradually better, as they'd planned, so as not to alarm Bo. Good thing she was his doctor—the only doctor on board. "Anyway, we can't go back in time and change what we did." She smiled wanly at the irony, as did Jack and Aaron. "I agree that on balance it was better to tell the kids than not."

"Good," Aaron said. "How are we doing in keeping my fine health secret, then?"

"I think all right," Kathy said. "Certainly Bo and Nikki are acting like they have no idea. I don't think Aviva knows. Maybe Hiro has an inkling; I don't know. I saw him just an hour ago, and I had a feeling he had a feeling—like he knew just who'd be sitting around this table now and what we'd be talking about. But I always have a feeling that Hiro knows more than he lets on."

"Wouldn't be the worst thing in the world if we brought Hiro in with us," Jack said. "Wouldn't surprise me if he knew what we were doing right from the start. The man has a deep intelligence."

"That he does," Aaron said. "Not surprising that he's risen in importance here during our voyage."

"He's risen along with the ascendancy of life processes on our ship. Life is timeproof here; nonliving matter falls behind. The engineer's a janitor; the gardener is king," Jack said.

"Nice," Aaron replied.

The three had become prone, for some reason, to cast their predicament in vivid little sayings. Like the sayings of Chairman Mao, Jack said, no doubt having Mao on some part of his brain because the Chinese leader's philosophy had been riding high again before they'd left, in the one part of Asia where Communism had stubbornly resurfaced.

It was as if their hold on reality here, such as it was, was so tenuous that they had to regularly recite its mantras, volunteer its lessons already known, to convince themselves anew that it was real—that it and they were really going on.

"Inert matter's completely under the thumb of entropy," Kathy said, playing her part. "Matter's a slave to time's arrow—it can't help but go along with it, whichever way it's pointed, even backward. But life and intelligence break the material mold, they go their own way against entropy, at least for a while."

"Amen," Aaron said, taking a sip from his cup of tea.

Tea segued into an early, unplanned supper. Good thing the kids were with Aviva, Kathy thought—it was so rare that she got to spend more than an hour alone with Jack and Aaron at the same time.

Jack pushed away his pie plate and smacked his lips. "Outstanding. So what's left to discuss?"

"Well," Aaron said, and glanced at his notebook, "the usual triumvirate of problems. Bo and the dangers from within. Naomi Senzer and who knows what might happen when we get within shouting proximity of Earth. And then, of course, the biggest problem of all: what the universe or the rule of space and time or whatever the hell we want to call it has in store for us."

"Bo's taken care of," Jack said.

"OK, but not Naomi," Aaron said. "If she knew what was happening, she wouldn't just stand by and let us go back out into deep space. But who knows what will be in her head when she sees us? To her it might well seem like our voyage was just on the verge of beginning. Not again, but for the first time."

"I still can't get a clear image in my mind of what will happen at the point of complete return," Kathy said, "at the point when we're literally back to where we began."

"Thousands of scenarios," Aaron replied. "But I guess we can divide them into two categories. In both cases, the time rollback continues right up to the precise instant of our departure from Mars Vestibule sixteen years ago. In Category One, our voyage ends there—the motion and time flux and everything stops. This is what Bo and Nikki are hoping for. We all disembark—and pray that the kids survive, that they're still with us. I have no idea what Naomi and Percival and the people back home will make of this. But if the kids survive this, who cares? We'll make the best of this whatever it looks like to everyone else on Earth.

"But we can't be sure that will happen—that our trip will end with that reunion. In the alternative, in Category Two, we begin moving back out to ACA the instant after we return. Time begins ticking forward again. Presumably the kids will be OK in this category. We don't know if anyone will be able to get off the ship in this scenario—and we don't know what Naomi will think or do when she sees our ship leaving again, *if* she sees it leaving again. For all we know, the two departures will blend into one for the people back home—maybe like two parallel universes of action, in which only we on board perceive the two, because only we are part of both of them.

"Billions of people saw the *Light Through* embark the first time. A first trip to the stars is a big thing. Now our time rollback may well rob the world of its payoff—the pleasure of seeing the ship return triumphant from Alpha Centauri, the satisfaction of knowing that it made it to the stars and back—if our return reads to them like nothing more than our original departure. Damn shame about that too." Aaron shook his head. "But it's best for the kids, and it's out of our control anyway. And I guess if the people on Earth didn't know that we'd already been out here—if the rollback left no memory of our leaving—then they couldn't miss a payoff to what they didn't know in the first place."

"They won't miss it, but the enthusiasm we wanted to rekindle for the space program will. We'll be back to square one on that," Kathy said. And this twist was painful indeed—to travel all this way, to work for years before and during their voyage to inspire people to reach for the stars, only to be caught in some weird time loop which could turn their return into the beginning, the one, same beginning, and therein deprive their accomplishment of any meaning for anyone other than themselves.

Kathy once would have grieved about such a loss as she would for the loss of a child. But now she *had* real children, and they meant more to her. "But we'll all be sixteen years older," she said. "Eight years forward to ACA at half speed of light, eight years backward to Earth at the same speed equals zero time passed for Earth and Naomi but sixteen years of aging for us. And Naomi will see the kids when she scans us. So she'll know that something is different."

"She'll also see that Sarah's gone," Aaron said.

Sarah's body had never returned to their ship. Jack had thought at first that it might. It was, after all, nonliving matter. But he finally concluded that maybe the universe distinguished between formerly alive and sentient, and never alive and sentient in the first place, and treated the formerly sentient differently. Kathy did not mind that Sarah's body had not returned, if there was no way to revive it. If this rollback respected the sanctity of death that had happened out here, maybe it would also respect the sanctity of two new lives that had been brought into being. Maybe . . .

"Time travel's impossible to understand logically," Jack was saying. "There's no point giving ourselves a headache trying to fathom what Naomi Senzer's state of mind will be."

"I know," Kathy said quietly.

"We have more important problems—mainly the universe itself and its unknown laws," Jack said. "I sometimes get the feeling that it makes these up as we go along. It reacts to our presence and re-creates itself for our amusement."

"Someone please tell it that we could stand being a little less amused," Aaron said.

"Remember Story Musgrave's exhibit at the Museum of Modern Art?" Kathy asked. "Ran there for years."

"How could I ever forget it," Aaron said. "The Hubble he repaired set the stage for all the megatelescopes and the Hubble II, which got this whole trip going when it picked up the shift between ACA/ACB and Proxima Centauri in the first place."

Kathy nodded. "Well, there's one frame in the central repair collage that's always stuck in my mind. Musgrave's perched over a crucial repair. He's five hundred pounds of clumsy, weightless mass in his space suit, and no part of his body can touch any part of the Hubble, except for where he's making the repair, and except for some kind of footrest. His back looks like it has maybe an inch of moving room, and his arms have nowhere to lean. Even the slightest encounter can leave dust in the Hubble structure, which can undo the good of the repair."

"Yes, I remember that," Aaron said.

"And Story's voiceover commentary, and the words on the screen, describe how he felt at that moment. That his body somehow was a repairing needle in the hand of the cosmos, as well as an expression of the specific training he had undergone, the knowledge and initiative that he as an individual had brought to that moment. And how the mix had to be just right—how he had to listen to the underlying cosmic tempo as well as know just when to inject his own thought into the stitch."

"And that's our story, isn't it?" Jack frowned at his own pun.

"Yeah," Kathy said.

"We've got to know just how long to go with the flow of the cosmos, and when to inject our own human moves into this process," Jack said.

"The Hubble was broken," Aaron said. "And Story called upon the universe and fixed it. How can we repair the universe?"

Part 3

Vanished Reunions

Eighteen

Noah looked at the sun on his twelfth birthday. Aaron was beside him. They knew the human solar system would soon come into view.

"Just a matter of days now." Aaron squinted at the sun, now the size of a sweet pea. It warmed his skin, anyway, and even though no heat could possibly pass through the real-view window.

The sun. No, the Sun. "You sort of half expect to see an orange spot beside it, though, don't you," Aaron reflected.

"Looks just great to me," Noah said, his voice far deeper than Aaron remembered his being at twelve. "I've seen pictures of this, di-giprints, for as long as I can remember, but they're nothing compared to what's actually out there. I can feel the presence of the planets, tingling with people."

"They have no idea we're here," Aaron said. "They're living their lives in normal, forward time, so when they look out at the stars they see our ship as it was in this place sixteen years ago, on the way out. We're still in another dimension—the backward-time dimension—which hasn't remerged with the original yet."

"No Alicia on that ship when it first left here, no me," Noah said. "Dad could talk; you and Jack were younger guys."

"All in all I'd say we're better off now." Aaron put his arm around the boy, practically a man already. "Someday we'll get your father to talk again."

"I still wish we could stay on Earth, at least for a while." Noah turned his attention back to the real-view window. "I know that we probably won't even get the chance, but if there were a way . . ."

"You've been a planet person since the day you were born." Aaron smiled. "When we first got to ACA, you drove me crazy about taking you to N'urth. You talked your mother and me into it, but, whew, did I catch hell from some of the others for taking you."

Noah smiled too. Aaron understood his need to be on Earth, to be with more people. But that chance wasn't Aaron's to give him. It was out of Aaron's hands, out of everyone's, as always. "But I'm glad I took you along to N'urth, anyway," Aaron added.

"It's just a fuzzy memory to me now," Noah said, "more a sensation than an image. Aviva's done some pretty good d-traits of N'urth, though. One even has people. Too bad there weren't actually people there, other than us."

"I guess what I'm trying to say is that I'm not sure there are really people out there on Earth and Mars—not for us, not now," Aaron said. He needed Noah to understand this.

"You mean because we're traveling back in time?"

"Right," Aaron said. "Because the people out there can't exist for us in this state in a real way. We can't interact with them, can't possibly affect them in any way. We can't see them yet, but when we do, I think we'll only be sampling them, in reverse, not really seeing them in a normal way. I guess it would be like trying to interact with someone in a recording. People living in different time flows are probably like recordings to each other—played in opposite directions, in our case, if that makes any sense."

Noah considered. "But when we reach Mars Vestibule, when we reunite completely with the past, what about then? Why wouldn't we be able to really interact with everybody then? At that point, we'll all be in the same time frame, right?"

Noah was more tentative than he had been as a child. Gone like the mists of N'urth was the splash-in-your-face assurance he once had had about everything. Children don't know enough to be unsure.

"Maybe," Aaron said. "I don't know if we can just reinsert ourselves into Mars and Earth and the solar system, into its time sequence. We've been out of it now for sixteen years."

"Too bad we're not really like a tape or a recording," Noah said. "They get requeued back to the beginning all the time, with no problem."

"No, in that sense we're not a recording," Aaron replied. "We're beings with free will living *inside* a recording. This ship being sucked back in time—"

Aaron's com beeped. Good—he didn't want to go much further along these lines with Noah. No point increasing Noah's anxiety beyond the high levels that it had already quite understandably reached.

"Bo wants you over in your—his—office." It was Kathy. "He says he has a new message from Naomi."

"What—a replay of an earlier—?"

"No," Kathy said. "Bo says it's a brand-new message, welcoming us back home."

"Isn't that impossible?" Noah asked.

Bo was jumping with delight. "I told you it would work out—I *told* you it would be OK. None of you believed me!"

Nikki objected. "I believed you."

"Never mind," Aaron said. "Our situation has nothing to do with Bo's or anyone's predictions. Reality is the way it is."

Bo glared. "So is that supposed to be a criticism of me? We have a message here from your Naomi Senzer, obviously of current vintage, as you'll see. It's wrong about just one thing: She thinks you're still in charge."

"Impossible," Aaron said.

"What," Bo asked, "that you're no longer in charge? Obviously that's not only possible but true."

"No," Aaron said, "what's impossible is that Naomi suddenly sends us a message now. How could she break through the reverse time flow?"

Nikki put her hand on Bo's shoulder. "Maybe the time rollback is slowing down to the point of normalcy," she said, "and one of the first things we're seeing of this is Naomi's ability to break through and send us this message. This could be good news, Aaron."

"Could be," Aaron said. No point in fanning the flames any further. Keep 'em lit just enough to keep Bo and Nikki off balance, not enough to provoke open warfare. That had been his strategy these past few years. "Can I see it, please?"

"Of course!" Bo clapped Aaron on the back. "That's why I wanted you to be with me now—not to argue, to celebrate!"

He put Naomi's message on the screen.

"You can't imagine how thrilled I was to get a glimpse of your ship," Naomi said. She looked just as Aaron would have expected had they not been in a time rollback—hair somewhat grayer, mousier, maybe a bit more dyed or rinsed or whatever they called it in this century, clothes slightly different in cut and style—an image that announced nearly two decades' passage. This was far more convincing than the Mars Vestibule date stamp, which was easy enough to fake. "If it really was your ship— I mean, we just got the briefest look at you," Naomi continued. "You've been out of touch for so long, we thought . . . maybe the worst. But if our readings are right, you should be back here in a few days. I told the president—she was delighted! You probably don't know her—Jane Oglesby—she was elected four years ago. An unknown from Alaska. I'm secretary of space domains now, serving in my third administration. JFC created the new post, cabinet level, and appointed me at the end of his term, in large part because of the excitement about what you discovered on your voyage. I just got off the phone with him. He's thrilled! We all are, Aaron, all of us. Everything's changed here. Space development's in high gear again, lots of great projects under way, and it's never coming down. I hope you receive this, and you and the crew are well. Your whole trip was an act of faith, you know—it's hard to believe it worked out, and you're all right. I'm so glad. A great big hug for you soon." Her smile seemed to linger on the screen like the Cheshire Cat's after the rest of her image had faded.

"I don't believe a word of it," Aaron said.

"Why not?" Jack asked with acid sarcasm. "One great big hug trumps everything we've been thinking for the past eight years. We're supposed to be traveling back in time, she's supposed to have no idea where we've been, what we've done, yet there she is, big mop of appropriately aged hair, welcoming us back home after our long journey. What's there not to believe? It's all there on the screen. It must be true."

"Be as carping as you like," Nikki said. "But the message *is* right there on the screen. And it's real. I can show you the tracking."

Aaron waved his hand. "Means nothing." He was sure she could, and the fact that she was offering made that suspect as a reliable proof.

"I don't get you people, I really don't." Bo looked at Aaron and Jack with a glance that would've encompassed Kathy too, except she was on the other side of the room. "What the hell are you so afraid of? We're a few days away from home. We receive a message that shatters our preconceptions of what's been happening to us. So, OK— we revise our hypothesis. The fact is, we're here. Our working theory about how we got here was wrong. That's the way of science, right? What's the problem?"

"That's only half of science," Aaron said. "The other half, when you're hit in the face with evidence that contradicts your theory, is you reexamine the source of the evidence to make sure it's valid. Make sure your equipment wasn't faulty or tampered with."

"Here we go again," Nikki said. "Every time our instruments tell you something you don't like, you blame it on the instruments."

"Have we sent a reply to her gray-headed eminence?" Kathy asked.

"Yes," Bo said. "I, uh, I sent a brief one."

"And?" Kathy prodded.

Bo shrugged. "It got eaten up same way as everything else we've tried sending off this ship."

"So whatever's going on," Kathy said, "we still seem subject to the same rollback effects or whatever they are."

Bo shrugged again.

"What *is* your new, revised theory, by the way?" Kathy asked.

"Look," said Bo, his voice rising. "I don't really give a rat's ass about theories anymore, OK? Maybe I wasn't clear about that. I care about getting home, getting all of us home, alive. But you want a theory for this? You want to play your theory games to the bitter end? Fine. Try this one: We haven't been traveling back in time at all. We've been traveling back to Sol and Earth, all right, but in real, forward, normal time. And the strange effects we've experienced—well, they're obviously due to something else that's going on out there."

"Strange effects that include traveling at half-C speed from ACA back to Sol, with no fuel—with constantly increasing fuel—and these effects don't involve a time rollback?" Kathy said. "Hard to believe."

"You asked, I told you," Bo said. "It doesn't matter."

Jack exhaled loudly.

"And what the hell are *you* sighing about?" Bo turned on him.

"You've got a better theory? What—some Apache mumbo jumbo? I'm supposed to pay more serious attention to that than science?"

Jack smiled slightly. "I was commenting on the absurdity of saying it doesn't matter. I think it very much does."

"I'll tell you what I think is bothering you people," Nikki spoke up. "You're afraid that you'll look like fools coming back to Earth empty-handed after sixteen years. We've got no objective records of our journey—no direct images, no sounds, no readings, nothing. You'll have to face Naomi, tell your story, answer her questions, with nothing but your . . . your recollections in your hand."

That can't be right, Aaron thought.

Aaron, Jack, and Kathy took seats around the table in Kathy's office. They were too upset to think about making tea.

"Let's say Naomi's message is really what it seems," Kathy said. "Why can't we live with that?"

"It would mean that anything and everything we think happened to us in the past sixteen years—except that we've actually been away for sixteen years—might not have actually happened," Aaron replied. "The kids are, of course, here and real, and Sarah's clearly *not* here, but everything else . . . well, for all we know, all we did was travel a light-week beyond the Oort, floated around in some hallucinogenic soup that also fooled all the instruments all the time—or at least our perception of the instruments—and just a few days ago we turned around. We can live with that, sure. But do you really believe that's what happened?"

"You can fool all of the instruments some of the time, some of the instruments all of the time, but you can't fool—"

"Stop it," Kathy said sharply to Jack. "The kids would be safer, more secure, in that Oort scenario. No time rollback to flatten them."

Jack shook his head. "I wish it were so. But Aaron's right. That message can't be real."

Kathy looked tired. "For years we've been pulling in every nuance, every scrap of statistic, to convince ourselves that the rollback was actually happening. Now we have Naomi's face to the contrary. And let's face it, her face is far more convincing than most of the other evidence."

"Yeah, on the face of it," Jack said.

"Why, exactly, don't you believe it?" Aaron asked Jack. "I mean, other than our conviction that we *are* in a time rollback, and this makes such a message from Naomi impossible. But what else in the message itself? If it's faked, there should be things wrong with it. Things we should be able to spot."

Jack considered. "It's too perfect. She looks too much like what we'd expect her to look like after sixteen years, and her story about who's now president, her appointment to the cabinet, that reads too well. I don't know . . . her hair is too deftly grayed. I don't buy it. A woman with her vanity would've kept it a darker color."

Aaron nodded. "I didn't like her story, either, but there was at least one thing in her recitation that only she and I could know."

"What?" Kathy asked.

Aaron told them about the message Naomi claimed to have received about their great discovery near ACA. "She mentioned the excitement that word of our discovery—presumably of the hulk—created back home. But the time rollback should have rolled back that message into oblivion."

"It must have," Jack said. "And all that Naomi's reference to it in her current so-called message shows is that whoever faked it had knowledge of the original message."

"Who?" Aaron asked.

"Anyone on the ship," Jack said. "Bo, Nikki, anyone."

"And you think that even before we made the turn around ACA, someone risked trespassing my code and read private messages between Naomi and me? Whoever it was had to be pretty good," Aaron responded.

"Like I said," Jack said. "We've got some good candidates."

"Still inconclusive," Kathy said. "We're trying to decide whether Naomi's new message is real. Aaron says that something she says counts against the time rollback—something that refers to a private communication between them years ago. You say, no problem, any of us could've had unauthorized access to that communication. But we have no hard evidence of that either. So you're using one supposition to support another. Awful lot of *ad hocs* in that chain."

"Well, I still don't care for the color of the lady's hair," Jack said. "Nothing *ad hoc* or suppositional about that."

"How do you know that shade of gray isn't high style in American politics right now?" Kathy asked.

"What? Precisely the shade that we would expect to see after sixteen years of her aging? Not very likely," Jack retorted.

"I wish we had something stronger than her hair," Aaron said. "Hell, for all we know, the woman's been wearing a goddamned hairpiece all of these years."

"They probably say the same thing about you . . . ," Jack said.

"I checked tracking on the message," Kathy said wearily. "It's exactly as Nikki says. The individual words—aside from the overall problem we're grappling with here—seem all right. The transmission specs are what we'd expect of an incoming message from Mars V—"

"Just what we'd expect from a message of Nikki's fabrication," Aaron said.

"So now you think it's a fabrication by Nikki?" Kathy asked.

"Forget about Nikki and her smarts and her motives," Jack said. "Ultimately what we've got here can be decided only on the basis of the message itself. It's still here for our viewing. It presents itself as the first nonliving process that's endured in our time rollback. That's the crucial point—does it measure up to that? We've got to sift every megabyte of it with that in mind. If it holds up, that means either the rollback is over, or it never occurred, though I don't believe—"

"Yes," Aaron said, and thought for a long time. He was concentrating on tiny snowflakes, like those on the edge of a video screen, that danced now at the very edge of his awareness. These things were tricky—you could lose them in an instant if you reached out too quickly to touch them, if the heat of your fingertips made them melt. . . .

Jack and Kathy were staring at him, waiting.

"Let's bring Aviva into this," he said.

Aviva Zerez had been twenty-three when she left Mars Vestibule for the stars, but everyone said she looked fourteen. Now she was nearing forty, but everyone on the ship still thought she looked maybe sixteen or seventeen.

Aaron's sense of her had blended more and more into his sense of Alicia the past few years—partly because her digitraits of Alicia and Noah were centerpieces in his new office, partly because she had been the closest to a friend Alicia's own age that Alicia had had on the ship.

Some people were like that—they looked young almost all of their lives, up to the very brink of decrepit old age. Others looked adult almost from the day they were born. Sarah Chichester had been like that. Aviva's digitrait of her looked not only like Sarah the day before she died, but like photographs of her thirty or more years earlier. "She had the kind of DNA that sprung into adult features very early on, and then kept them pretty well locked in that way," Aviva said, pulling up a series of DNA algorithms—Sarah's—on the digitrait, algorithms that were mostly indecipherable to everyone in the room except Aviva. "Her digitrait looks more like a photograph than a digitrait, because the underlying algorithms are so rigid."

She put another image on the screen—Naomi Senzer smiling like the Cheshire Cat at the end of her message. "You were right about this one," Aviva said. Her eyes connected with Aaron's, then swept around to Jack and Kathy. "This message from Naomi Senzer was neither from Naomi nor Mars Vest—it's a living program based on sixteen-year-old images and recordings of Naomi that, ah, grew into the message you saw. Brilliant piece of work—the algorithms are stunning."

"That's why the message didn't die," Jack mused. "It's a living process—a digital living process—like your d-traits."

Aviva nodded.

"And getting this digigrown message to say currently applicable things—like welcome back home—is trivially easy, I assume," Jack continued.

"Trivially easy. Yes," Aviva said.

"Who has the knowledge to create such a program?" Kathy asked. "Other than you, of course."

"No, this is way beyond my ability to create," Aviva said. "I have all I can do with still images. This is as far beyond me as Hitchcock from Daguerre."

"So, who, then? If you were pressed for your best guess," Kathy asked.

"Obviously, Nikki is the only one with the computer talent to do this—but the aesthetic quality goes way beyond what I would've expected of her. And Hiro has . . . well, he has the sense of image, but I'm not sure of his mathematics, and anyway, I—"

"That's OK," Aaron said. No point in pushing her on Hiro. He had guessed for a while that they had more than a professional relationship. "Nikki's the only one with any reason to do this."

"How so?" Kathy asked.

"Let's assume she believes, as we all did, that we've in fact been traveling in a time rollup back to Earth," Aaron said. "By throwing us a curve like this—by making us doubt whether we've been traveling backward in time—she dilutes our focus on what might actually happen the instant the rollback is complete. She, on the other hand, is able to keep all of her attention on that. So at that crucial moment, she and Bo are able to respond more effectively to whatever happens than we can."

"Seems a lot of trouble to go through for just a leg-up like that," Kathy said. "And I can't quite see Nikki planning all of it—she's sharp, yes, but not that Machiavellian."

"Maybe Nikki's doing someone else's bidding," Jack said.

"Whose? She rides Bo, not vice versa," Kathy said.

Aaron looked at Aviva—they didn't often talk like this in front of her. Still, there was no way they could seal her off from it now. "Aviva, do you think it possible that earlier communications from Naomi could also have been digigrown? In fact, what about all the rest of the data we've received during this trip—the images of N'urth, ACA from afar—"

Aviva shook her head. "No way I can tell now; all of those disappeared long ago in the time rollback."

"Then that suggests they weren't digigrown," Kathy said.

Aviva nodded.

Aaron nodded too, but something slightly different was courting his attention. "Let me make sure I'm understanding something," he said to Aviva. "If any earlier messages from Percival or whomever were living forms—artificial-life algorithms—then they should have survived the time rollback. And the same applies to all the other data: Any datum which we thought was a recording of a real event but which was actually an A-L fabrication should have survived. Right? Because they were sims of living processes, just like your d-traits. But in fact they did not. We've lost all our earlier data—only the reports that we've re-created and locked into autocopying programs have survived—and the same with the messages. So is this proof positive that they weren't digigrown?"

"I'm not completely sure what you're getting at," Aviva said. "But, yes, messages and data that were generated by artificial-life algorithms should have made it through the time rollback—just like Hiro's plants and my digiprints and anything else running on DNA or A-L active codes. Whether the code is natural or artificial, whether it comes from an organism's DNA or was created from scratch by me to capture an event—whether it operates in living tissue or hardware—none of that should make a difference. If it's a living algorithm—either DNA or A-L—then it's antientropic and should have survived the time rollback, at least from what we know about the rollback so far."

"But does their not surviving then mean that they were not the result of A-L?" Aaron persisted.

"Well, why else wouldn't they have survived?" Aviva asked.

"Because maybe someone erased them," Jack said, suddenly on to where Aaron was going. "We think the natural course of A-L programs in our time rollback is that they endure—unlike regular data files, which don't. But that doesn't make the A-L stuff immune to deliberate deletion, does it? For crissakes, you can kill a living organism and dispose of the body, right?"

"Sarah died and she didn't come back," Kathy agreed.

Aviva thought. "Well, if you put it that way, you're right, of course. Someone could erase my digiprints, and then they'd be gone, just like flat data. Though maybe not entirely . . ."

"How would that work?" Aaron urged.

"Well, Nikki's the expert on that," Aviva said, "on the metaphysics of erased data—where it is, what it is, how we can get at it. But let me try. I know the footprints of this morning's message, the traces it would leave in any directory even after it was erased. Let's see if I can find any sign of similar prints. Let's see—"

Aaron swung a screen over to her, and in a single jiggle of his fingers gave Aviva stealth access to the ship's entire net.

"Yeah," she said after a long few minutes. "They're here. The prints are clear. I can see traces of five earlier messages."

"Whose prints?" Kathy asked. "Nikki's?"

"Same prints as today's," Aviva said.

"The message I got from Percival just as we entered the ACA system," Aaron said.

"No. Not that one. The dates don't match."

"What? Which ones, then?" Aaron demanded.

"I can't recover the messages themselves, only the dates," Aviva said and rattled off two dates.

Aaron frowned, shook his head. "Five damn birthday messages from Naomi and my grown children back on Earth."

"Birthday messages?" Kathy asked.

"Doesn't make sense," Aaron said. "Why go through the trouble?"

"To perfect her craft," Jack said. "What better way than birthday greetings to try out a radical new technique that makes forgeries of people talking? Who would pay any real attention to that?"

Aaron's mouth was open. "She was planning this all the way back then?"

"I'll tell you one thing," Aviva said. "Whoever did this obviously has a lot more computer talent than I realized, and has had it for a long time. Nikki's the only one I can think of who even remotely fits that bill."

"We did realize it," Kathy mused, "or at least we should have realized what was right in front of our eyes. Nikki outprogrammed Bo during the mutiny crisis on the way out without batting an eyelash."

"What about the rest of the data?" Jack asked, suddenly agitated. "The N'urth images, all that stuff? Don't tell us they were just electron milkshakes too. Don't tell us all of our work—"

"I'm amazed to see you care so much," Aaron said truthfully.

"No," Aviva said, looking again at her screen. "Nothing else I can see here. No traces of A-L except the five earlier messages."

"You sure?" Aaron asked.

"Yes," Aviva said. "A-L traces are very distinctive once you know what you're looking for."

"Did you reply to any of the birthday greetings?" Kathy asked.

"No," Aaron admitted. "I guess I was too busy."

"If you had, Nikki no doubt would've made sure that they weren't sent," Kathy said.

Jack nodded. "So assuming this track we're on is right, we've had three messages created, likely by Nikki, to appear like they were from Naomi—two old happy birthdays to Aaron and today's bombshell. Plus the three other birthday cards from Aaron's children on Earth. But the rest of our telecom data was real. Which is why it disappeared in the time rollback. Which I guess offers some evidence that we have indeed been time back-pedaling, though the web is getting tangled indeed."

"I'm sure I'm right about the print tracings," Aviva said.

"I'm glad," Aaron said.

"Aaron?" Aviva asked. "Can I say something to you—to all of you?"

"Of course."

"Well, we've talked about this before, but I just wanted to say to you again that I—and Hiro too—we appreciate everything you've done for us, all three of you. I know we didn't support you on everything, but that's because we were frightened. I think it's much easier for humanity as a concept, a group, to go out to the stars than any one person. Humanity gets the glory on the backs of individuals who feel the pressure, the anxiety, the little paper cuts on their fingers. I know you've suffered a lot—I think everyone on this ship has. But now the trip is almost over, and, well, I just wanted you to know, and Hiro feels this way too, that—"

"I know," Aaron said, and reached out and squeezed her hand.

"We appreciate you and Hiro too," Jack said.

Kathy walked over to Aviva and kissed her on the forehead. She sat down next to her.

"So what do we do now?" Kathy said.

"Well, we have three, maybe four more days until we arrive at Mars Vestibule and our rollback is complete," Aaron replied. "And then we still don't know what's actually going to happen."

Kathy was in the shower.

Aaron was in bed.

He did have some notions about what might happen at the point of reunion, but none was appealing.

None included a welcome home from a humanity appreciative of what they'd tried to do on its behalf—the sacrifices that Aviva had been talking about. That possibility had evaporated with Naomi's fabricated message.

If this time reversal was really happening, maybe hundreds, even thousands of ships had made the trip to Alpha Centauri in some human past, to other stars too, only to return in a time swing that left the Earth utterly ignorant of their voyages.

If that was the truth of the stars and travel between them, maybe that's why so many people back home seemed so uninterested in any serious pursuit of space as a human future—seemed even put off by it. Maybe all of their talk about let's get our house in order on Earth before we reach for the stars was just an unconscious defense mechanism, a dodge on behalf of a deep, self-protective, genetically instilled need to avoid the futility of travel to another star, the absurdity of the time loop that the *Light Through* was going through right now. Just one of an infinity of ships bouncing back and forth forever . . .

Or, for all Aaron knew, perhaps they were all the same ship. Maybe the *Light Through* itself had somehow been this way before—maybe that's why their initial launch had succeeded in happening against all odds, on the strength of an Indian legend and an unproven theory, as Bo had not been wrong in pointing out all of these years. Maybe their ship *had* to be launched because it was already in motion.

Whatever was truly happening, none of Aaron's scenarios for their return included much peace or sanity, the sip of contentment that he would have wanted everyone on board to have had as they looked back and contemplated a voyage on the whole extraordinarily well done.

And none of the scenarios even included lives that continued unbroken.

Had Naomi's message been real, had the time reversal not been real, had they been approaching Mars Vestibule on her terms, then the kids' lives would have been secure, almost without a doubt. Kathy wasn't wrong to have yearned for that.

But as it was, they were still in the lap of paradox and their frail best guesses as to how to get around it. . . .

Kathy came out of the shower. Her terry-cloth bathrobe was open at the waist. Her sleek, wet body always looked good to Aaron.

She slipped under their covers.

"No songs tonight?" he asked. Kathy almost always put on a loop of music when they went to bed.

"No," she said. "We're beyond the music of the spheres now."

Aaron didn't say anything more. Not about the music, not about the tears he felt on his shoulder.

Aviva had really said it all.

Humanity goes to the stars.

People feel the pain.

Nineteen

Sunny-side-up egg on the plate. Seemed that everywhere Aaron looked this week he was staring into the sun. He tore into this one with his fork.

"Third egg you've had this week, Daddy," Alicia said. "Mommy says—"

"Yeah, I know what Mommy says, sweetheart," Aaron said. "But this is one of those weeks when I need a lot of protein."

Kathy walked over and put a cup of Darjeeling in front of him and gave him a look that said, What are you trying to do, get a heart attack for real now to top off our trip?

No point in telling her that the latest studies said that egg cholesterol contributed to clean arteries in some cases—because the latest studies were actually more than sixteen years old, had likely been contradicted, confirmed, and contradicted again in the eight years in forward time in which the *Light Through* had made its journey to ACA—eight years that no longer existed, hadn't even happened yet for the people back here. So he just smiled at Kathy and sipped his tea.

Unlike the egg on his plate, the sun outside was getting bigger. Another few days at most, and their implosion, their trip backward to the beginning, would be over.

What then?

"Aviva should be here any minute," Kathy said.

"Oh, good," Alicia said, "she can help me with my salamander print."

"Not today, honey," Kathy said. "Aviva has some work to do with Daddy."

"Maybe she'll still have some time for your salamander," Aaron said. "I know the people on Earth would love to see your salamander on the screen."

"OK." Alicia bounded off her chair and gave him a kiss. "I'm going over to Hiro's garden to get another look at her—the spots on her skin are just beginning to come out."

Aaron hugged his daughter and she left.

"Aviva's digitraits are great," Kathy said, "but they won't be proof of anything."

"I know," Aaron said. "Naomi'll want snapshots of real events, images untainted by subjectivity, immaculate conceptions of reality, not paintings and programs. But who knows, the d-traits may jar some interest on Earth anyway."

"A snapshot can be digitally manipulated too," Kathy said. "Nothing's sacred in the digital age."

"I know."

"How are we going to get the d-traits off the ship?" Kathy asked.

"I guess whoever gets off the ship will take them. Electrons on wafers don't weigh much. A larger problem is that we still have no idea if they'll survive beyond the point of reunion with forward time." No sense in repeating the obvious, more important question that cleared its throat constantly now in everyone's head, even in Bo's, Aaron knew, for all his swaggering—would *they* survive that shift? Would staying on the ship or leaving be more conducive to survival? "Still, I can't see any harm in having Aviva prepare as many d-traits as she can," Aaron continued. "We've certainly got nothing better to do at this stage."

Kathy came over and put her arms around his back and neck. He soaked in every bit of it.

Aviva's digital portraits were nonpareil. She'd been working on some of these for years now, but, like many artists, had waited until the last minute to put in some of her best program touches. The results, like all digital concoctions, were ultimately based on numeric relations, but her images were as far away from painting by the numbers as Impressionism was from its raw elements of water and light. Monet and Aviva had much in common, Aaron thought, though Aviva had done more than capture the pure light of reality that had splashed through Monet's eyes a century and a half earlier. She had captured the light in motion, in imperceptibly developing reality, and without the slight-of-eye of motion photography. She had distilled the contents of everyone's perceptions, recollections, garnered from years of conversations, into A-L algorithms that captured, reanimated, literally brought each of the major discoveries of their voyage into brief sequences of life.

There was N'urth from twelve different perspectives, ranging from the soft green invitation it issued the hour Aaron's party arrived to the cloying clutch it had on them as they left. And here was that hulk again, maddeningly unclear, an ultimately ineffable form that Aviva had somehow impossibly captured with perfect precision. But Alpha Centauri A was the real star of this exhibition—as indeed it should have been—glistening, glowing, beaming at its orange sister, beckoning from a dozen angles of approach, nearly burning their faces, spitting them back in the direction from which they came in a way no one except maybe Wise Oak had envisioned beforehand. But Aviva had rendered it all with a crystal-clear vision of hindsight.

Aaron lingered over the last image on his screen. "These in themselves make our voyage worthwhile," he said.

"Thank you," Aviva said, and she might have blushed. "But I think what you've been saying about them is right—they'll be looked at as lovely fantasies, if they get through to Earth, unless some of us can be there to convince people that these scenes were real. A picture is worth a thousand words, but most of them still come with titles and captions. And a programmed painting is always more suspect than a photograph—always taken as more expressive of the creator's hand than the object depicted—even though it may show the exact same piece of reality."

"And these can be shown on any screen, in any order, linked in any way the viewer wants?" Aaron asked, preferring the comforting detail rather than the underlying question Aviva was raising again. He had no good answer to that question. Sometimes he felt like the bandleader on the *Titanic,* heroically focusing on the music as the ship went down.

"Yes," Aviva said. "They're self-contained and self-implementing, but should also be operational on all known equipment. Of course, that means all equipment known to me sixteen years ago. I can't be sure that something new didn't come along—no, of course not, nothing new *could* have come along if no time has actually passed back here."

"That's right," Aaron said. He was thinking again about the sun— Sol—and the plate where his egg had been. Nothing but a few stains of yellow and white had been left. "Difficult things, those little algorithms, aren't they?" he said. "Lots of guesswork. If you'd done a digiprint a few days ago of the egg I ate for breakfast this morning, it no doubt would have masterfully hatched into a chicken eventually. As it is," he laughed hoarsely, "it's now chomped to smithereens and undergoing total chemical deconstruction in my stomach."

"DNA isn't everything," Aviva said. "The most genetically predetermined trait in existence means nothing if the environment gobbles up the organism the DNA is in."

"You've done an incredible job," Aaron said. "We'll figure out some way to make sure our trip endures as more than just a beautiful fantasy. And your work will play a crucial role in this, I'm sure."

There was a slender tear in her eye. Aaron pictured it dropping on her keyboard as she labored, hitting just one key, with just enough pressure to depress the key halfway. Would it make a mark on the screen? He wondered what that single half-mark, that mark with a 50 percent probability of being made, would do to the overall picture....

Likely much the same as a ship returning from a trip to Alpha Centauri in a way that played as if it had never been there.

"It's time we had a talk," he said, surprising Nikki at lunch.

"Well, sure, Aaron—come in, sit down."

"Thanks." He cleared the least cluttered chair—one thing he'd always liked about Nikki was that her office was almost as messy as his—and sat down. "Look, we've got a day or two at most left, the new readings—"

"I know," Nikki said.

"—and I think the time for pretense between us is over. We owe it to ourselves, and the chances for everyone's survival here, to be as honest as possible now. We should at least be sure that we're all reporting everything correctly as we make reunion. We should at least be able to rely on what we're getting from each other. God knows we'll have no idea if we can rely on what we get from beyond this ship."

"OK," Nikki said. "Go on."

"Well, we've tagged your little message from Naomi as an A-L concoction," Aaron said. "I can't say I know exactly why you did it. It doesn't matter at this point. What counts now is that everyone on this ship has to be clear that to the best of our knowledge we've in fact been traveling back eight years in time."

Nikki stared at him. "You know, you started the deceit with your little heart attack charade, and who knows what else before."

"Nikki, I—"

"Oh, I know you had your good reasons," she said. "I know you needed to get Bo off your back. But by not including me on the inside, you put me on the outside. There's no in between."

"Nikki, I needed someone who was close to Bo to be thoroughly convincing, otherwise—"

"And you couldn't count on me to give a good performance, so you had to lie to me. Kathy, of course, knew the truth—how convenient she's the ship's doctor. And Jack, I'm sure, was in on everything."

Aaron reached out and took her hand. "You've been absolutely essential to this trip—to our survival so far. You've come through at every crisis. You know that. You know that I know that."

"Thank you," she said. "Can I put that on my résumé when we get back?"

"Can't we forget about this?" Aaron asked. "You forget about the heart attack and I'll forget about the message from Naomi? And then we can rely on each other today or tomorrow or whenever it happens."

Nikki nodded. "I want this to be over already. You want the truth? I faked the message from Naomi because I can't trust you. I wouldn't put it past you to pull the *Light Through* right back out into space at the last minute if you thought that would serve some kind of higher purpose. I figured that if you thought we weren't in a time rollback after all, and Naomi was in contact with us, that might stay your hand. You want the truth? I'm sick of this ship. I'm sick of Bo and his bad breath. Sick of the pissant drizzle that passes for rain in Hiro's magical garden. I wanna get caught in a real goddamn downpour again. I wanna pass out drunk on a park bench somewhere and get soaked to the bones if I feel like it. Sixteen years in a flying petri dish is too long, Aaron."

"We'll be there very soon," Aaron said.

"And what's gonna happen then?" Nikki asked.

"I don't know," Aaron said, his favorite response of late, though probably it had been on top of the list throughout the trip. "I think it all depends on how long our ship can maintain its internal state."

"You mean how long we—our people on board—can keep our current sense of time?"

"Right," Aaron said. "Clearly we have an internal environment in this ship that has allowed us to live and think normally in forward time even though the ship has been traveling backward. We don't know what will happen to that once we reunite with normal time—Mars Vest at the instant we left sixteen years ago."

"But why should anything happen?" Nikki asked. "I mean, we'll be reuniting with people who are in normal time, so why won't we be able to just . . . fit in, and then live normal lives?"

"Because their normal time is sixteen years earlier than ours. We have knowledge of sixteen years of events on our voyage which haven't happened in their universe. How can we just fit in?"

"But we have next to no knowledge of what happened on *Earth* in that time," Nikki said. "On Earth, only eight years passed—as we were traveling out to ACA—and now those eight years should be rolled back up in our return. But we know nearly nothing even of those first eight years on Earth. It's as if they didn't happen for us either. We've had so little contact from Earth since we left."

"I know," Aaron said. He wanted to say, *even less than it would seem.*

"I—I'm sorry, Aaron. You know about the earlier messages too, then."

"It's OK," Aaron said. She'd always been good at reading him.

Nikki shook her head. "Naomi didn't trust you completely, either. She warned me about you. She said I should keep some kind of card up my sleeve, because I might need it on the voyage. She was a real player, that woman. So I fiddled around with those birthday greetings. I knew those algorithms, if I could perfect them, would give me some kind of edge. After that scene on the way out with Bo, when you pressured me into overriding him, I knew I'd need any edge over you I could get."

Aaron nodded. "I understand. It's water under the bridge—of this ship or whatever. I'm sorry for what I contributed to it. But the bigger point you were making, about us having had little contact from Earth, is still a very big problem. Can we just come back and coexist in an earlier time when, true, we've had no real interactive connection with them in the interim, but we've nonetheless been living and experiencing the future out here anyway?"

"You think we can't?" Nikki asked.

"I don't know," Aaron said. "The universe has a way of finding a way—*something's* going to happen in the next few days. I guess the real question is, will we like it? Will we even know it when it happens?"

Aaron stopped by Roger's room on his way over to Jack's.

He was sitting there, expressionless, the way he'd looked just about all of these past eight years.

A heartrending, terrible waste.

Yet Aaron knew Roger was aware of what was going on. Alicia said she talked to him once in a while. A lot of that had to be make-believe, but, still, it had a ring of truth to it. He wished Roger could have more time with Alicia. He sometimes thought that Alicia more than anyone else held the key to understanding what had gone wrong all those years ago inside Roger's head.

"I think there's a good chance you'll be talking again if we get through the next few days, old buddy."

No response from Roger.

"In fact, I've got a feeling the reunion will be kinder to you than anyone else on board."

For Roger, at least, there'd be a tradeoff. If he snapped back to the way he'd been sixteen years earlier, he'd lose all recollection of this trip, of people who truly loved him here, the knowledge that he had a son. And that would be awful.

But he'd also regain his speech and communicative abilities, and lose whatever it was that had taken all of that away from him.

For the rest who might snap back sixteen years—they would just lose sixteen years of life experience. Just a loss, with no such compensation.

For the kids . . . Aaron shuddered. He still couldn't see them surviving the reunion; they had no prior life of sixteen years earlier to click into. Their only chance was maybe, somehow, on this ship—

"Typo," Roger said. "Tyop."

"I know," Aaron said. When the adults returned from their temporary disarrangement of being four light-years from the star around which they were born, each in one way or another would still be in a profound state of disinformation. Maybe Roger was talking about their exquisitely disarranged lives.

Aaron long had thought that the most likely explanation of Roger's inability to communicate was that he'd somehow seen an infinitely recursive future that he and everyone on the ship were part of—their ship caught in a river that flowed both ways between the two stars eternally, a fate so enormously inexplicable that it had defeated forever Roger's capacity to talk about it, or anything else.

Maybe that's why Alicia seemed to have the most luck with him. She never asked Roger to talk, she never requested any information from him, explicitly or implicitly. All she wanted was his love. And that he seemed quite able to give her.

But if glimpsing some endless loop that he was a part of was the cause of Roger's aphasia of the soul, then returning to Earth wasn't in the cards for Roger. Or, if he did return, that should break the infinite loop, at least for him, and thereby invalidate the animus of his silence. So why, then, was he silent? Was his current silence somehow irrevocable evidence that he would never return to Earth?

Aaron pondered: If I exercise my free will to insist that Roger did return, if I so chose, could my free will be *that* circumscribed? Would something prevent me from liberating Roger from this loop?

Maybe so—their return from ACA had nothing to do with free will.

He wished he could ask Roger. Ask him if he'd prefer to return to Earth and likely lose all knowledge of his son, or stay aboard with that knowledge but with no way to communicate. He wished he could ask that. But what would it accomplish? Roger couldn't answer. And Roger had no more free will in this than anyone.

Aaron stood up. As he'd been telling everyone the past few days, whatever was going to happen would happen. There was no point exhausting himself any further in pursuit of an answer that was utterly unattainable today, but would be in their hands tomorrow without their even trying.

Aaron was tired of generating ever more food for thought for this rapacious engine of paradox that raged inside himself. He was tired of feeding what could not be fed.

He sometimes thought that his inability to stop this feeding frenzy in his head was his biggest paradox of all.

Better stop thinking about that too now.

"It'll all be over soon," he said.

He put his hand on his loyal friend's shoulder. This friend who now felt like a son to him, but whose own son was older than Aaron's daughter by the same remarkable woman. The stars, our better halves, make for complicated families.

Jack's room, and Jack, smelled of Kathy's fragrance.

"I've got most of Aviva's prints packed away," Jack said. "They're really something."

"Equally per customer?" Aaron asked.

Jack nodded.

By distributing the prints among the returning people, they had heightened the likelihood that at least some of the screens would somehow get through. Each screen was hard-moduled to display a complete set of the d-traits. And Aviva had put enough redundancy into these prints that as much as 90 percent of them could be lost without unreconstructable damage to the story of their voyage. Each d-trait series was like a holographic hypermedia colony: It could usually be totally reconstructed from any fragment of the hologram, any one member of the colony.

"I'm still concerned that if those who return to Earth lose their memories, then no one will be around to point out the significance of the d-traits," Jack said.

"I know," Aaron said, "but what more can we do? Surely the d-traits will attract some interest somewhere."

"I guess Roger's our best chance." Jack rubbed his chin. "Maybe somehow in those crossed wires of his a memory will resurface after they reboot on Earth."

"Hell of a situation we've gotten ourselves into, haven't we," Aaron said. "We either live without memories on Earth, or travel back to Alpha Centauri with plenty of memories but no real way of sharing them with our species. Assuming, of course, that our analysis is right."

"If our analysis is right, the kids have even less choice than that," Jack said. "They're lucky, though, to have parents like you and Kathy."

"Well, you're in every way that really counts their father too," Aaron said.

Jack smiled. "They're good kids. I'd miss them if for some reason I couldn't be with them."

"The only way you won't be with them is if we all wink out of existence at the reunion, so there's no point in your worrying about it."

Aaron was glad they were approaching that omega point, one way or another.

No, he wasn't—for everything he cared about hinged on this ending just one, very specific way.

Twenty

And now the years that recently had shrunk into days and then hours were down to minutes.

Nikki was next to Aaron at the main viewscreen.

Naomi and the small group that had seen them off were there on the screen, sixteen years earlier. Except it was happening now. Happening again, for Aaron and Nikki.

Percival and Primakov were there too. A bit off to the side, sixteen years earlier.

The greatest moment of their lives.

Aaron saw the radiance of expectation on their faces, over varying deeper degrees of relief and resentment for not being on the mission. He had missed some of that, the first time, when he had last seen his team.

Not surprising. He had seen the future in between.

"Not a bad homecoming picture," Nikki said.

"True, but don't forget we're looking at the departure aftermath, not a welcoming party," Aaron said. "That's the gang about fifty-five minutes after we left, sixteen years ago."

"I know," Nikki said. "So you're sure you're not coming with us?"

"Nothing for me back there," Aaron said. "Everything here for me in the stars. You won't see my children—my grown children—in that crowd. Naomi had invited them. But they hadn't approved. Even their birthday cards were faked. And how much longer will I live, anyway?

Another ten, fifteen, twenty years? I'd rather spend that time in the stars—with my new family, my real family."

"I understand," Nikki said. "I said good-bye to Hiro and Aviva and the kids in the garden. You're wise to keep them away from the actual exit-access point—no telling what kind of crazy physical fluctuations will be going on there at the instant of total reunion." She looked at him. "You're doing the right thing. All of you. I hope you feel the same about me—and Bo. And Roger."

"We have to give Roger his chance on Earth," Aaron said. "We can't do any more for him here. You and Bo too. You're entitled to breathe fresh air and walk among people—just anonymous people— any time you please. As for the rest of us, well, the kids are our people now—Kathy's and Jack's and mine. And now that Hiro and Aviva are expecting a child, their lives are tied to the ship too. We can't risk the children in a space-time existence they were never a part of." Aaron didn't know for sure whether Hiro and Aviva would have stayed had Aviva not been pregnant. Maybe their decision to have a baby was in some way designed to fix their minds in favor of staying. Whatever their reasons, he was glad, both about their staying and the baby.

Funny how pregnancy, which had seemed so outrageous at first with Kathy, now seemed appropriate, almost to be expected, with Aviva. It was as if the vacuum of interstellar space required filling by humans who found themselves in its precincts and recognized its need.

"I'll miss you," Nikki said. "Hard to believe that I'm saying it, that I'm feeling it, but it's true. I'll miss you."

No, you won't, Aaron thought. In less than an hour, you'll barely know me.

"I just pray I'll have the *memory* to miss you, to miss all this," Nikki said and gestured around the view room.

Aaron put his arm on her shoulder. She hugged him.

"We'll try to come through for you, Aaron, for the human species," Nikki said, and he felt her tears on his cheek. Tears were flowing faster than water these past few hours. "All the fighting, all the tension, seems so trivial now, doesn't it? We'll somehow get through to them back here. It won't all have been a waste. We'll get our story out, somehow."

"I know you will," Aaron said, and thought, Well, what's one more last little lie between us now? It couldn't do any harm. At least this one derived from the best of intentions. Well, maybe they all had, all along.

"I've always admired your decency," Aaron said. "And we couldn't have made it this far without your brains." And that was no lie, not in the slightest.

She hugged him again and pulled away. "Watch for my signal, after we dock and disembark," she said. "That way you'll know that my memory made it through Point Reunion."

Two groups entered at opposite ends of a long corridor.

Aaron rubbed his eyes and stared at them on the screen.

One group, numbering seven, saw only an empty corridor ahead, leading to a portal to the ship that would take them to Alpha Centauri. They walked with the eyes of humanity on their backs, overhead, and on their faces—humanity's witness to the boarding of the first human trip to the stars. And Aaron's eyes were upon them too. Twice now. One from where he'd seen them depart sixteen years earlier. One from the view room of the *Light Through,* just back from that trip to the stars.

The other group numbered three, and they could clearly see the group of seven—three of whom were their younger selves—approaching in the corridor. Or, at least two of them could see the approaching seven. For no one other than Roger McLaren in his current condition could know what, if anything, he was seeing.

It was clear to everyone on the *Light Through* that, on the starship at least, all memories were intact and all minds were functioning as they had been. That was good news. But it said nothing about what would happen to the people who had left the ship, how long the ship's stasis field would continue, how long before the galactic current began carrying them back out to Alpha Centauri, if that's what it did.

Jack and I—our earlier selves—will be walking through the public portal in about twenty minutes, Aaron thought. Naomi will be waving us away for what she thought was the first time, but what we on the ship will know was the second. Or maybe somehow there would be two ships leaving, two *Light Through*s at the same time, one which was new, and one which was sixteen years old and had already traveled out to ACA and back. Two ships, slightly different crews, the second superimposed on the first, or maybe in some kind of tandem, parallel universes . . .

"Getting to the point of no return," Nikki said, *sotto voce,* into the tiny microphone she had pasted under her chin. Bo and even Roger— even Roger, just in case he suddenly began talking and expressed a desire not to leave the ship—had one too. "I guess it's go now or forever hold our whatevers," Nikki said.

Nikki looked just like what her younger self looked like, approaching in the corridor. Same with Bo and Roger. Same clothes, same hairstyles, nearly exactly the same faces—the quick reconstructive DNA facials Kathy had given them had worked wonders. All too common back on Earth, if Aaron recalled correctly. They were intended now to help the three returnees blend in as seamlessly as possible with the past they were about to reenter.

Aaron looked back at the group of seven. God, there was Sarah.

She was walking to her death. He should run out, scream out, warn her— He couldn't do that. Too much else depended on everything happening just as it had the first time.

"Go," Aaron said to Nikki and Bo and Roger. "And Godspeed."

But Nikki stopped.

The approaching group of seven walked blithely forward, still a good two city blocks away from the group of three.

"Won't the *Light Through* look like it has a smaller crew?" Nikki asked.

"You mean our current ship? Well, with Aviva's baby, our ship could scan as eight lives as it departs—I don't know how precise the scan is at that distance for the newly conceived. That is one less than our original nine. But I'm not even sure our current ship will be the one that is scanned and not the earlier version, so—"

"Come on." Bo put his arm around Nikki. "Aaron has the right of this. We can't figure all of it out now. Who knows, maybe our return will have an effect yet farther back in time, and change everyone's understanding of the voyage in the first place, so they think it's just a crew of eight. We have no way of knowing that now. We have no time to debate it—but we'll find out for sure in a few minutes."

Bo raised his clenched fist in the old gesture of solidarity, of brothers in arms, that he knew Aaron could see. Brothers in arms against the universe. Aaron and Bo. Did Bo know now that he'd never been in charge, not even for a moment? Aaron got no satisfaction from that. Even now, Bo was likely still not completely clear about what was going on—that Nikki and he would likely know nothing for sure after the next few minutes, except what they knew sixteen years earlier, before their voyage began. They'd lose sixteen years of their lives—be in the same place they were sixteen years before—except they'd be sixteen years older. Maybe Bo did understand but didn't care. Either way, Bo and Nikki would have no perspective, no fulfilling closure, on any of this.

Aaron took no satisfaction in that either. In fact, it made him sick to think about it.

The group of three—Nikki and Bo and Roger—walked on.

Aaron had lived with these three like a family for sixteen years. A dysfunctional one most of the time, but a family. And Roger meant much more to him than that.

What would they feel as they walked by their earlier selves and therein entered the time-space of sixteen years before? What would an instant blanking of sixteen years of memories and life feel like? What would the rest of the world see? What would happen to it?

"We've got the prints here," Bo whispered, just a handshake away now from his earlier self. "Even if our memories get eaten up, this will somehow jog our recollections. We'll mount a new expedition, we'll come meet you in the stars. Remember that! Always remember! Don't despair!"

And Aaron knew that was the last thing he'd ever hear from Bo.

The three were now past their earlier selves.

Physically, everything seemed as it was—no sudden explosions or implosions or whatever the hell might have happened in time-space bangs and singularities. Just sameness. A quiet, apparently unexceptional continuity. Good at least for that. Everyone was still alive.

Aaron turned and looked around the view room. Kathy and Jack and Hiro were glued to the screens, straining to see even the slightest signal, the smallest gesture that could be taken to mean Bo and Nikki's memories had survived intact.

Aaron looked too.

He looked at Roger, walking farther and farther away from their ship. Roger had already said good-bye to him, to everyone, years before, really. In that message he'd left them on N'urth. Jack had shaken his hand an hour ago, then broken down and cried. First time Aaron had ever seen that.

Let Roger find some peace on Earth. He's paid his dues in heaven and hell.

And Roger walked on, mute as always, as the Vestibule corridor on the far end began closing in around him and Bo and Nikki.

Kathy squeezed Aaron's hand and said, "He seems no different there than here."

Hiro punched up extreme close-ups of each of the three from five different angles—a last chance to see any sign of remembrance.

Aaron focused on Nikki's face, on her posture, the way her arms moved, the way her legs walked step by step by step. . . . He looked with every ounce of his eyesight, every last drop of optical neural energy he could muster. Come on, Nikki. Give us a sign—some small movement out of the ordinary, some tiny gesture, some facial expression, so we'll know that the past sixteen years haven't gone from you entirely. . . .

He saw nothing.

No signal, no sign. Nothing.

He stopped looking at her face. He couldn't bear seeing such total absence in her face.

"Nada," Jack said quietly. "She's sixteen years back in the past. Bo's sixteen years in the past. So's Roger, just like everyone else there. We don't exist here for them."

"At least they're alive," Kathy voiced what Aaron had been thinking. "How will the rest of the world react to them, seeing three of the original crew walk back?"

"I don't know," Aaron said. "All we know is that the first time out, there was no report of three not going on board, because of course the first time that didn't happen. Maybe we'll find out in a few minutes."

"At least they were walking and breathing," Kathy said in reassurance.

Aaron nodded. "But not talking. . . . Where are the seven—you and Roger and Sarah and Nikki and Bo and Aviva and Hiro—who were approaching our ship?" he asked hoarsely.

"Already on board, sixteen years ago, in the first version of the *Light Through,*" Jack said, not sounding very certain.

"So where are *we*?" Kathy asked. "I mean us, here, in this room, right now?"

"I don't know," Aaron said. "Hovering right over the original, shimmering within and outside and around it, in one sense—but separate from it, parallel—"

The com chime sounded. Aviva's face appeared on the screen. She looked disoriented. Groggy.

"What's the matter?" Hiro and Aaron said at the same time.

"Where are the kids?" Kathy asked.

Aviva looked confused. "I don't know."

"It's OK," Aaron said. "We've been looking at nothing but who's been leaving the ship. We'd have seen Noah and Alicia if they tried to leave. They're still on board. They have to be." He paced around and looked again at the small room on the screen, as if the children were somehow still there.

"Noah said he wanted me to look at some new virtel he'd produced," Aviva said, still rubbing her eyes. She had joined the others in the view room. "I remember looking at it, the swirling colors, and . . . I don't know, I guess I fell asleep—I don't know how that happened—and they were gone. I'm sorry," she said and started crying.

"It's all right," Aaron said. "They couldn't have gone anywhere. And this wasn't your fault—something must have put you to sleep. Maybe the impact of approaching Point Reunion on someone in your condition . . . We should have thought of that."

"No, something more," Hiro grunted, turning away from a digital programmic printout of the virtel Aviva had been watching. "This is some kind of hypnotherapy virtel, designed to coax the brain waves into sleep. See those gamma-wave algorithms over there?"

Kathy nodded, still too frantic for speech.

"OK, let's do a full ship scan for the children," Aaron said.

Hiro quickly jabbed some commands into the console.

"Won't tell us much," Jack said, before the scan indeed turned up empty. "Since we've been in stasis, most of the ship's instruments have been frozen."

Kathy made a strangled sound.

"It's all right," Aaron said again. "There's no way they could've left without our seeing it."

"We don't *know* that," she finally sobbed. "They could've vanished the instant they *tried* to leave. We have no idea how this reunion shift actually works—for all we know, their very *intention* to leave could've provoked some sort of time-cleansing response. Maybe they just disappeared, whatever they were thinking." She could barely talk. "We still don't really know how all that QM stuff worked. We don't know *anything*!" Now she was screaming.

"OK," Aaron said, trying to calm her, as well as himself. "We'll search the ship, hands on, room by room, closet by bathroom. We'll find them. I *promise* you. Aviva—do you feel well enough to stay here and let us know if you see anything more on the screen?"

She nodded. "I'm sorry . . . ," she said again to Kathy.

Kathy put her arms around her, crying. "It wasn't your fault. Noah's very headstrong, just like everyone else on this damn ship."

"I don't know how much longer the ship will stay in stasis," Jack said.

Aaron glared at him. "So? You've got any better ideas?"

Jack just shook his head.

He and Hiro searched separately. Aaron searched with Kathy—he didn't want to leave her on her own.

They found Alicia, huddled and whimpering in Hiro's garden, a few minutes later.

"Honey!" Kathy ran when she saw her and scooped her up.

"Mommy, Mommy!" Alicia said through heaves and tears. "I tried to stop him—I told him he could *die!*—but he wouldn't listen."

Aaron stroked her head. "It's OK, sweetheart. Noah told you he was leaving?"

She shook her head yes.

"Did he say how?"

Alicia shook her head no, bit her lip, and resumed crying.

"It's OK," Aaron repeated. But damnit—they hadn't seen him leave. How could he have gotten around the cameras? Around lenses that never blink? The boy was good with technical stuff on the ship, but not that good—not good enough to reprogram the cameras to show a false image, an image that disguised his departure, without leaving a trace of the reprogramming in the system. . . .

Not good enough for that—at least, Aaron hoped not. This whole trip had been laced with false programming. He called Hiro, Jack, and Aviva, and told them about finding Alicia.

"Hiro, are any of the diagnostic systems working yet?" Aaron asked.

"Yes, the main diagnostic system was always working. It runs on a self-sustaining power source that can't go off."

"Good." Aaron asked Hiro to run a quick diagnostic on the camera system.

That took about ninety seconds. "No sign of reprogramming," Hiro said.

Aaron sighed with relief. He'd been right—Noah wasn't that good. Then he thought: Could Noah have been not only that good, but better, at programming, so that he not only reprogrammed the cameras to disguise his leaving but also to disguise the reprogramming?

No, even Nikki hadn't been able to do that.

But where, then, was Noah?

He had to be somewhere on the ship.

"Aviva," Aaron asked on the com, "anything new?"

"No—no sign of Noah. Any sight of him on your end?"

"No."

Same lack of news from Hiro and Jack.

They continued searching.

Aviva called again, about ten minutes later, just as Kathy and Aaron and Alicia completed a futile search of engineering. "Come right away," Aviva said, in a tone that sliced Aaron's insides to shreds.

"Noah?" Aaron asked.

Kathy held on to Alicia and looked as if she were dying.

"Jack," Aviva replied.

"I'm going to look for him—on the outside," Jack said, a footstep and a heartbeat away from the center of the public corridor to the past— the one with Naomi and Percival and the handful of others—a corridor that would blank out sixteen years of life.

"Why?" Aaron said. "There's nothing you can do there. Even if

Noah went through the exit, and he's OK, you likely won't know what he looks like once you go through."

Aaron could see his younger self, sixteen years earlier, hugging Percival. He looked away, and concentrated on Jack, the older Jack, turned now toward his younger self, who looked like he was looking right at the older Jack, right damn at him. . . .

"And we don't know for sure that Noah went through," Kathy was saying, expressing what even Aaron was beginning to feel was more a desperate hope than a likelihood at this point. They'd searched the ship and turned up nothing.

"Right," Jack said. "We don't know any damn thing for sure here. Never did. But you're on the ship in case Noah is there, and I'll be here for him in case he made it through. That way we've got all the bases covered for the boy."

That same damn stubbornness the man had shown all his life, even as a kid in the goddamn lot Aaron had moved into. "But you won't remember—"

"Bullshit," Jack said. "Who knows that for sure? I've got connections with ancient people, remember? Who knows what I'll be able to recall or not? Wise Oak remembered lots of things no one else could. And I carry within me the wisdom of many generations—I've always known that. One little cosmic anomaly's not gonna stop me."

"Jack, listen to me," Kathy pleaded. "Come back with us."

"No," Jack said. "*You* listen to *me*. I love you—all of you. Even you, Professor, even though you always were a chronocentric, logocentric, every other damn *centric* for whatever-the-hell-it-is bastard who loves philosophy too much for his own damn good. I'm going to go after Noah—and if he isn't here, well, maybe I'll figure out a way to give Roger a little help explaining all of Aviva's beautiful pictures."

"Please, Jack," Kathy began again, "you've got a life to live with us."

"What? A long life like Russell and Shaw? I never believed in that anyway. I only went through the gene therapy to satisfy Aaron. Whatever genes I have in me, they didn't make me a philosopher *or* a dramatist."

"I love what your genes made you; I always will," Kathy said, hugging Alicia and Aaron close to her.

Aaron tried to say something, but his voice broke. He said nothing more. No point. He knew it was too late. He knew his friend. He knew them both—the younger Jack and the older Jack, who now crossed each other in the middle of the corridor.

The older Jack walked on, gave no sign, his face no different from what it had been just a second before.

"You look like you've just seen a ghost, Jack," Aaron's younger self said to the younger Jack, as they walked together down the corridor toward the *Light Through,* sixteen years earlier.

But Aaron's older self barely heard that—his eyes and and his brain were burning with too many tears about too many things.

"The ship's beginning to pull back—to pull out," Hiro said. "I can feel it, and the ship's peripheral instruments are beginning to come back on-line."

The viewscreen showed Naomi and the group waving good-bye, one more time, exactly as they had sixteen years before. Aaron was goddamn sick of this replay.

Kathy, shaking, clutching Alicia, gave Aaron a look that said she'd go through the door too if it weren't for Alicia. Aaron felt the same.

"Anything we should do now?" Hiro prompted.

Aaron shook his head. How could Noah be out there?

Aaron kept returning to the same thing: They would have seen him on the screen.

"All crew-supported systems are now on automatic," Aviva reported from the other side of the room. "The algorithm relays we put in over the past few weeks have all kicked in now, and they're working."

"Good," Aaron mumbled. He couldn't take his mind off Noah.

He felt Hiro's hand on his shoulder. "We're alive, Aaron. That's what you've got to think of now. Alicia's here, and we've got to take care of her. Whatever it is that happened out there, they survived and we survived—we both made it through. Let's keep searching here for Noah."

Aaron nodded.

"Should we try sending a message to Naomi now?" Aviva asked. "All the com systems seem back on-line."

"Yeah," Aaron replied, still thinking mostly about Noah. They had created several messages that would briefly explain what had happened—that they survived the rendezvous and were on their way back out into space, as they now apparently were. They could eventually tell their whole story to Naomi and Earth this way, if communication could be established. They could also ask Naomi to look for Noah.

"It's not working," Aviva said. "It looks from here like the message is reaching her com port, but it's not registering."

Aaron nodded again.

"We must be out of synch with her in some way," Hiro said. "She and the original *Light Through* with its crew are on one plane, we are on another. Even though we're in the same time . . ."

"Should I try again?" Aviva asked.

"Yeah," Aaron answered.

They got the same signal: transmission unreceived.

"Let's keep looking for Noah," Aaron said.

They searched the rest of the day and into the night, keeping one eye on the viewscreen for any sign of Noah back on Mars Vestibule. They searched the same places, over and over again, like squirrels scratching the ground for acorns they had buried. They found no sign of Noah. Just like the acorns buried under the concrete poured over Jack's lot in the Bronx so many years ago . . .

The ship began picking up speed near the asteroid belt. Just like the first time. But it felt a little faster. Maybe like the way driving to a place the second time always seemed to take less time than the first.

The sun was beginning to recede again.

The fuel had diminished slightly, just as it should have for time-forward travel in space.

"Let's try to get some sleep," Aaron said to Kathy. Alicia was in bed, already sleeping, between them.

"OK," Kathy said.

Maybe Hiro and Aviva could see this accursed ship through this next trip.

Aaron wasn't sure he had the soul to do it anymore.

A soft, cool hand on his forehead woke him.

He opened his eyes. Kathy came into focus.

"I had an idea," she said. "There's one more place where he might be—Alicia just told me about something. I don't want to go there myself. Please come?"

"Sure." Aaron pulled on his pants and a soiled shirt. "Where?"

The lights on the ship indicated early morning. Alicia led Kathy by the hand. She told them about the time, years earlier, when she had just been a little girl, and Noah had tried to steal a shuttle ship. She'd woken Kathy up to tell her that a few minutes earlier. That's what had given Kathy the idea.

They walked their way slowly down the hall, three blind mice, to the shuttle bay.

Of course, the shuttle. The one place they hadn't thought to look inside of. Aaron had confirmed with his own eyes that the small craft was still ensconced in its moorings. It hadn't gone anywhere, with or without Noah. But could the boy have gone inside, rigged the programming to conceal his presence? To what end?

Aaron jumped up to the shuttle door and finger-danced the open-sesame jig on the keypad.

The door stayed shut.

Aaron tried again.

Same result.

He pounded his fist on the keypad in frustration.

A good way to break it.

"What's going on?" Kathy asked from below.

"The door won't open," Aaron said.

"What's that mean?"

"It might mean the door is stuck, it might mean Noah locked himself in with manual override. . . . Noah," Aaron said as sternly as he could, "open this door. Now!" He pounded again on the pad.

No response.

"Is he there?" Kathy asked.

"Is he *there*?" Kathy asked again.

"I don't know," Aaron finally said.

That's all he'd been telling people he loved, people he cared about, for sixteen years.

He pounded on the pad again, on the door, again and again. He pounded. His wrist felt on the verge of shattering. "Noah, open up!"

Eventually, he slid off the platform back to the floor. Kathy and Alicia were crying. When the hell would he ever learn his lesson—

when would he learn what he was so fond of telling everyone else: To want something, to desire it so much that your very soul was tearing, that still wasn't enough to make it so.

When would he learn?

When he was a hundred?

He put his arm, a limp, beaten dishrag, around Kathy and Alicia and they walked toward the door.

Alicia turned around, then broke away.

"Mommy, Daddy," she shouted. "Look!"

And Aaron turned around. The shuttle door was open.

And Noah stood inside, eyes red and lips trembling.

Aaron ran with Kathy and pulled Noah down from the shuttle and into his arms. "It's OK, son, I know why you did this, we're not mad, we love you," Aaron said over and over again.

"I wanted to see where you came from—where *I* came from," Noah said. "I thought if I went there with the shuttle, away from this ship, I could avoid the time flip, and then come back here with you and Jack and Mom."

"It's OK," Kathy said. "We love you."

Aaron felt a stab in his heart about Jack. Nothing could be complete joy—even holding Noah like this. But it would do. They could tell Noah about Jack later. Tell Noah that Uncle Jack had fulfilled Wise Oak's vision by returning. How Jack had perhaps really *become* Wise Oak by returning . . .

"But the shuttle wouldn't move," Noah was saying. "It was stuck in the stasis. And then when our ship started moving away again, I didn't know what to do."

Stasis had prevented Noah from moving the shuttle. Ten years earlier this boy might have moved a starship and remade a planet.

"It's OK," Kathy and Aaron said.

They walked to the view room. Hiro and Aviva joined them. They were jubilant.

The shuttle had been stuck in stasis—thank the cosmos or the universe or whatever it was that saw to such things for that.

But their ship, the *Light Through,* was moving. Again.

Ahead lay Jupiter and the outer planets and the sparkling Oort and who knew what else back on Alpha Centauri this time around.

Epilogue

The chime jolted Naomi Senzer out of her memo.

"Damn you, I thought I told you no interruptions unless it was urgent."

"Well, does extremely peculiar to the point of inexplicability touch any part of the urgent fringe?"

"All right," she said. "What is it, then?"

"Good to see you, Naomi." A man entered and extended a flaccid hand.

"Jack." Naomi stood up, genuinely surprised. "I thought someone was using your name when my assistant said you wanted to see me."

"No, it's me," Jack said. "One of the few things I'm sure of these days."

"You were supposed to be on the ship with Aaron—I saw the both of you off. What the hell did you do, sneak off at the last minute?" The readings indeed had reported numbers of people on board that didn't add up. The readings had sometimes reported two ships under way, not one. And a phantom message or two. Chalk it up to the ship's unprecedented speed at that distance—it was probably throwing off the Hubble's tracking. She'd messaged Aaron about it several times, but so far had received no reply.

"I don't know," Jack said.

"What do you mean? Are you OK?" He looked awful—she'd never really noticed before the deep, intensely grooved lines in his face. They reminded her of the cracks she'd seen on the surface plates of Mercury.

She didn't know what she could possibly expect to find out from him. Getting a straight answer from him right here in her office was less likely than from Aaron on his way to the stars.

She couldn't believe, even now, that she'd let herself be persuaded into letting this expedition proceed.

"I don't know," Jack said again. "I mean, I guess I sneaked off. Yeah. But that's not really why I came to see you."

"Well, don't be shy. You maybe had another vision you wanted to share?"

"In a way, yes. It's not as clear as a vision. It's more a—a feeling—but one that I'm more and more sure of as the days go by. I think this may not be the first time our ship went to Alpha Centauri."

"Look." Naomi pointed to her desk screen, the universal gesture of executives too busy to talk. "I really don't have time for this now. You had your chance. You left the ship. Now I think you'd do best to just forget about this whole project—you already did your damage in talking Aaron and me into letting it happen. I'm sorry I took you seriously in the first place." She swore to God, she'd put this nutcase in a hospital right now if she wasn't concerned that that would call attention to her own lack of sanity in this project. She'd been having a full-time job as it was keeping reporters from the fact that half the science for this half-C trip came from some maharishi on the Hudson.

Jack put up a placating hand. "I'm sorry—I know you don't like me—but I wouldn't have come to you if I wasn't desperate. I'm telling you that I think Aaron and the ship may be stuck in some sort of, I don't know, merry-go-round. And I was on it. And unless we do something, it'll keep traveling back and forth, over and over again."

"Unless I do something like what?"

"I don't know."

"Over and over again," Naomi said. "You mean like your Iroquois river?"

"Yeah, sort of," Jack said. "I guess so."

"And you feel like you've been there—in this river—already?"

"Yeah," Jack said.

"So you've been to the star and back, and maybe you're really Wise Oak?" Naomi prodded.

"Yes—no. I mean, no, I don't really think I'm Wise Oak," Jack said.

"You don't really think you're Wise Oak. Good. Progress. Now, is there anyone else around who shares your, ah, feelings about this trip?" And please don't parade a bunch of butt-naked Indians in here to see me, she thought. I take my pleasures elsewhere.

"Yes, I think so," Jack said. "But I can't remember who they are. . . ."

"Ah-ha. OK. Anything else?"

"Well, I had a dream that there may be some pictures around that could prove this. I saw the same pictures in a vision—"

"But don't tell me," Naomi interrupted, "you don't actually have any of those in your possession either, right?"

"No."

This man was too pathetic to even put in a hospital. It looked to Naomi like Jack Lumet, never completely together in the first place, had suffered some sort of further mental breakdown when he'd high-tailed it off the ship. Or maybe that's why he left the ship. Jesus H., the pathology in this world!

"All right, Jack. Here's my card with a more direct number if you think of anything more." She had to keep reminding herself that, as distasteful as she found this, it was far better than him babbling his visions to the media.

"Please, I know I'm not making much sense," Jack said. "I haven't been myself the past few weeks. I'm confused. I know that. But I really think I'm in touch with something here that—"

"Right, just call the number on the card."

She thought she saw a shadow of anger in his eyes. Just for a second he looked like the Jack she had said good-bye to just last month by the ship. He started to say something—something that sounded like a threat if she didn't take him seriously—but then he gained shaky control of himself and left with a mumbled thank-you.

The man was dangerous.

Something would have to be done.

Just not now.

"Roger, if that bugjob ever drops by here again unannounced and you foist him on me, I'll dump both you and that urgent tongue of yours right back behind a desk on the Potomac. Got that?" She was glad that Roger had had second thoughts at the last minute about going. Smart move for him—he had a successful life ahead here—and smart move for her. She could use him here on her team, where the real action was.

Of course, with Nikki Dee off the ship as well, that left her only one other person on board who could keep an eye on Aaron. Her most secret of secret resources. Redundancy. Thank God for that. Aaron had been right that you couldn't have too much of it on a project like this. It was really the only defense against the unexpected.

"Understood, Madam," McLaren answered smartly. "And meanwhile, the president's office called to remind you about the press conference next Monday in New York."

She sighed. She was getting to like semipermanent residence in Mars Vest. The low-g tea was great. Aaron was right about that too. And the view . . .

"All right, book me a seat on tomorrow's shuttle. Call Nikki Dee at research and tell her I'll want her to come with me."

Back to Earth, back up here, back to Earth—with an election coming up, and the second fully digital one in the U.S. at that, the Demo Party was jerking her and her space expertise around like a goddamn yo-yo.

Politics.

Now there was a creek that really did flow both ways.

McLaren placed the calls, all the while looking at a digital portrait of what seemed to be a featureless dark ship, reminiscent in a way of the *Light Through* to Alpha Centauri he had almost embarked on. . . .

Naomi had been honest with Nikki and him and the others at that special private briefing before the mission—she'd told them how uncertain the chances were for the starship's safe return—and she'd been genuinely glad when in the very last minutes before the launch the two had decided not to go. He gave her credit for that—not like Alexei Primakov, who'd gone apoplectic when Bo Ivanoff had done the same.

He couldn't recall an actual conversation with Ivanoff about leaving the ship—nor, for that matter, with Nikki. But he was unclear about a lot of things having to do with that almost-trip. He recalled walking down the long corridor with the six others toward the ship. He'd had his doubts about going, sure, just like everyone, except maybe Aaron and Jack. But he'd come to terms with himself about the trip and the risk. At least he *thought* he had. Then he found himself trudging along with Nikki and Bo *away* from the ship. What were they doing walking the wrong way, walking away? None of them could say exactly why. It was as if the three had somehow suddenly made a decision not to go, and had suffered some brief crisis of pain so intense about the decision that their minds had mercifully fogged it over.

At least, that's how it seemed to Roger and, from his many talks with Nikki and Bo, to them as well. The three now shared some sort of deep, unarticulated bond. Part of it was guilt about not going. How would the ship function without them? Extraordinary redundancy had been built into the crew's abilities, he knew that, but still . . . He could see Aaron's face at night, he could see Kathy Lotari's face. He liked those faces. He felt guilty.

But guilt wasn't the only thing. There was something else, something even deeper that he could not identify.

He thought about Jack. When had *he* left the ship? Jack had been so sure of himself, so profoundly at peace with himself about the voyage. Why would he leave?

Who the hell else had left the ship?

Roger wondered if the ship were maybe on some kind of automatic pilot—a robot ship after all—with no one on board. That's what Naomi had really wanted all along.

Maybe the crew was just pretense . . . but pretense for who?

Jack's just showing up here like this must have had something to do with what was really going on. Where had he been these past few weeks? Mars Vest had many off-line nooks and crannies, places with delights that no computer scan could locate. But Jack hadn't looked like he'd been having too good a time.

They'd exchanged contact info before Roger had let Jack in to see Naomi. Roger made a note to definitely look Jack up. . . .

The truth was, a very strong part of Roger still felt like going. It wasn't like him to change his mind about something that important

238 / Paul Levinson

after months of grueling preparation. Where had that last-minute impulse come from?

Roger focused again on the digital portrait of the featureless ship. He shuddered.

Strange, he had no idea where that picture had come from either.

It had turned up in his belongings a few days after the ship had left—probably slipped into one of his vest pockets years earlier by one of his friends in the rain forests, a memento he either couldn't recall or never had seen in the first place.

He stroked the keys. The image fed off some kind of program, probably the work of one of the high-tech witch doctors along the Amazon. He'd never seen anything quite like it before.

So far the program had produced two images.

One was of a small boy. Oddly compelling, beautiful, really, with eyes that somehow looked just like Roger's maternal grandfather's. He wondered how long ago the image had been programmed—how old the boy was now. It reminded him of a tintype he had picked up at a flea market in London when he was a kid, of a woman who looked at him across 125 years with longing eyes. Had she any idea, when she'd posed for that picture, that someday he would be drinking it in on the other side of time? He'd felt that somehow, somewhere, that woman was still alive.

He felt the same way about the boy in the digital portrait. More so, like the boy was somehow connected to him. . . .

And then the portrait of the cypher ship. Just a ship, with no clear form. It frightened him in some dank, empty way, like a tin can rattling around in some corner of his history that he couldn't put his finger on.

But its appeal, like eyes behind sunglasses, was irresistible. . . .